Cloaked in Deception

A SPENCER & REID MYSTERY
BOOK FOUR

CARA DEVLIN

First Cup Press

Copyright © 2025 by Cara Devlin

All rights reserved.

No part of this book may be reproduced in any form or by any electronic or mechanical means, including information storage and retrieval systems, without written permission from the author, except for the use of brief quotations in a book review.

Any references to historical events, real people, or real places are used fictitiously. Names and characters are products of the author's imagination.

Edited by Jennifer Wargula

ISBN paperback: 979-8-992305739

Chapter One

June 1884

A knot in the pit of Jasper Reid's stomach tightened as he entered the room. He should have listened to instinct and stayed away.

Sir Eamon Giles's front parlor wasn't nearly large enough to hold the thirty men and women packed into it. The guests stood shoulder to shoulder while sipping drinks and making insipid conversation, all of them waiting for the gong of the dinner bell. To avoid being drawn into any of the close throngs of discussion, Jasper quickly claimed a spot in the far corner of the room, next to a window. The raised sash let in gusts of rain-scented evening air, and he breathed it in as he took a snifter of whisky from a passing server's tray. He hadn't the patience for idle chatter. His father was the only reason he'd come here this evening.

Before falling ill, the late Gregory Reid, Detective Chief Superintendent of Scotland Yard, had sat on the

Board of Governors for the Metropolitan and City Police Orphanage. The orphanage was a charity for the families of police officers killed in the line of duty or whose injuries sustained on the job prevented them from working again. Jasper's father had championed the orphanage, once even traveling southwest of London to Twickenham for a day's visit. So, when an invitation to its annual benefit dinner was extended to Jasper two weeks before, in honor of his late father's dedication to the charity, he'd accepted without hesitation.

Since then, however, he'd come to regret his decision.

Frenetic laughter erupted near a wall of bookshelves. In the close quarters, it felt like knives flaying Jasper's eardrums. A woman adorned in an outrageous display of diamonds and sapphires—the value of which could have easily funded the orphanage for at least a year—was fawning over the City of London Police Commissioner, Sir James Fraser, and the Metropolitan Police Commissioner, Sir Frederick Danvers. The Metropolitan Police Force and that of the City of London were two separate organizations, the latter holding jurisdiction over just one square mile in the city center, from the area around Temple to the Tower of London and up to the ward of Cripplegate. The Met policed the much larger London metropolitan area, with a much larger force. However, when it came to the orphanage fund, the two came together in its support.

The working men of both forces only had so much to give to charity, so into the mix of benefactors came the wealthy, titled men and women of London—like the lady flirting with Commissioner Fraser as she touched the sapphire pendant resting on the mounds of her generous décolletage. They'd turned out in their finest, all poised to give generously to the less fortunate. The merging of class and status had stuffed the room to the cornices, and with it came an inevitable friction.

Jasper drained his snifter of whisky and caught the attention of a uniformed server. If he had to be here, he might as well take advantage of the good liquor. The server parted through a few circles of guests to make his way over to him. As the crowd shifted, the other side of the room opened into view. There, in the opposite corner of the parlor, a young woman stood alone with her back to the room. She was statue still as she gazed out a window into the falling dusk and the coming rainstorm.

The server entered Jasper's line of sight. "Another drink, sir?"

He nodded and set the empty glass on the tray, then canted his head to observe the woman again.

Jasper knew her by her dark, sable hair and the lithe lines of her neck and shoulders, which were modestly covered by the high, ruffled neck of a spruce green gown. The trim tuck of her waist drew his eyes next. A month ago, Jasper had settled his hand there. He still recalled how it felt under his palm.

Even more familiar to him, however, was her posture. It radiated cool detachment. She didn't want to be here either. He couldn't think of why she would be in the first place.

Although he knew the young woman was Leonora Spencer, when she turned to face the crowded room, Jasper still lost his breath. It had been two weeks since he'd last seen Leo—they had both testified in court against Emma Bates, the woman who'd been found guilty of conspiracy to commit murder and the planning of a bombing outside Scotland Yard. It had been a busy afternoon, and the proceedings at court hadn't allowed them much time to exchange anything but pleasantries. Especially nothing having to do with the kiss they'd shared at the end of May, after Leo and Jasper had caught and arrested Mrs. Bates for her crimes.

They'd been in his study, alone in his home. After a heated exchange, they'd been standing close. The temptation to kiss her had been all-consuming, and when he'd given in to it, she'd welcomed him—briefly, at least. She'd left, unnerved and yet also flushed with pleasure. Leo had enjoyed the kiss; that much, he knew. What he wasn't as certain of, however, was if she could forgive him for the secrets he'd kept for as long as he'd known her: his true identity and the role he'd played the night of her family's murders.

Leo had claimed she needed time to think, and although she'd promised she would not stay away for months, as she had when she first learned the truth of his past, it had now been four long weeks. Each one had passed with glacial speed.

Across the parlor, the soft, full lips Jasper hadn't been able to stop thinking about curved into a benign grin. Leo wasn't directing her smile at him though.

A well-dressed man appeared at her side, extending a small glass of red wine to her. She accepted it, her hands encased in matching long, green silk gloves, and murmured her thanks. Jasper recognized the man as the Spring Street Morgue's new assistant coroner, Mr. Connor Quinn. The sudden buoyancy of Jasper's stomach and chest upon seeing Leo faltered.

The waiter returned, again blocking Jasper's view. He took his drink from the proffered tray, and when the waiter moved along, a pair of intense hazel eyes collided with his. Across the room, Leo went still, the glass of wine paused at her mouth as she stared over the rim at him. He dragged in a breath and, in that moment, knew he'd been wrong to have waited weeks for her to come to him.

Though he hadn't a clue what he would say to her, especially now that a month had passed, he started across the overcrowded room to where she and Quinn were standing. Leo seemed to brace herself, lowering her glass and hitching her chin as though preparing to meet an adversary.

Christ. He'd given Leo too much time to think, to remember how he'd deceived her all those years. He should have gone to her straight after their kiss. But he'd hesitated, honoring his promise to give her the space and time she'd requested of him. Now, it seemed he had given her too much time, had hesitated too long, and, as his father had often said, *hesitation is just a long route to regret.* It seemed Jasper had plenty of regret when it came to Leonora Spencer.

He joined them, and when neither he nor Leo did more than nod awkwardly in greeting, Connor Quinn cleared his throat.

"Detective Inspector Reid, I didn't realize you would be here tonight, though I suppose I should have. Your father sat on the Board, correct?"

"He did." Jasper was curious as to how the assistant coroner would have known that.

He must have asked the question with his expression

because Leo provided the answer. "Mr. Quinn's grandfather is also a governor on the Board."

She kept her voice soft, even, and, like her posture while staring out the window just a minute ago, distant. He noticed she wouldn't meet his eyes for more than a second before averting them.

"I've been forced to attend my grandfather's charity galas since I started medical school," Quinn said with a good-natured grin, but when Jasper and Leo both remained straight-faced, he turned serious again. "This year, I thought it would be an opportune time to introduce Miss Spencer to him."

Gregory Reid's warning about hesitation resounded between Jasper's ears again. Connor Quinn's grandfather, he belatedly recalled, was Sir Eamon Giles, a knighted barrister and the city's chief coroner.

Leo sipped her wine, still avoiding his eyes.

"I think it went rather well, don't you?" Quinn asked her, a touch too jovially. He was either oblivious to the tension around him or desperate to ignore it.

"Time will tell," Leo murmured.

The three of them fell into another drop of quiet. *Where in hell was that dinner gong?* Jasper sipped his whisky and seriously contemplated begging off for the evening. His appetite had soured, and he wasn't sure the whisky was worth staying for.

Besides, staying might only encourage the Board of Governors to extend an official offer to join their ranks. Commissioner Danvers had already pulled Jasper aside a few days ago to suggest he take his father's seat.

"If you've an eye toward remaining at the Met, these are connections you'd do well to cultivate, Reid," the commissioner had suggested, adding, "Especially after the last few tumultuous months you've had on the force."

The trouble had started six months ago, in January, when Jasper and Leo exposed the former Met police commissioner, Sir Nathaniel Vickers, as a murderer. It continued in March, when Jasper had been forced to relinquish a man he'd just arrested, Terrence Nelson, into the hands of another criminal, his cousin, Andrew Carter. Part of the ruthless gang known as the East Rips, Andrew had held Leo at knifepoint, demanding Jasper's prisoner be turned over so that he could mete out his own justice for the murder of his bride, Gabriela. There had been no choice for Jasper; he hadn't doubted Andrew's bloodthirsty threat to pluck out Leo's eye. But Detective Chief Inspector Dermot Coughlan, Superintendent Clive Monroe, and Commissioner Danvers, had only berated him for having a woman at his side to begin with. The fact that it had been primarily Leo who could be credited with the capture of Terrence Nelson and with the exposure of Sir Nathaniel's heinous crimes hadn't mattered. The two incidents had left a stain upon Scotland Yard's Criminal Investigation Department.

Commissioner Danvers's suggestion for Jasper to rub elbows with the higher-ups at the Metropolitan and City Police Orphanage benefit dinner had been a barely disguised order—if he wanted to keep his job, Jasper would need to make nice and toe the line.

After several more moments of uncomfortable silence, Quinn craned his neck to peer through the masses in the small parlor. "Ah, there's Grandfather." He addressed Leo, saying, "Excuse me a moment, won't you?" then dashed off.

Jasper frowned as the assistant coroner parted the crowd, moving toward their host. "What are you doing here with him?" he whispered loudly to Leo.

Granted, *'How have you been?'* would have been more polite, but he'd never had a knack for safe, courteous chatter.

"Mr. Quinn has already explained," she replied, an edge of irritation in her tone now, rather than its prior coolness.

"He's introducing you to his grandfather, yes, but why?"

Leo shot him a sidelong glance before facing forward again, giving him her profile. Jasper followed her cross glare. It landed on Quinn, who had reached Sir Eamon. The chief coroner looked relieved for the interruption; he'd been in close conference with an older woman, whose plain, somewhat dowdy gown and rough bearing conveyed that she was not one of the privileged patrons in the room. The woman was clearly upset, her scowl fixed into the lines of age on her face, which was well-worn with that particular expression.

Sir Eamon, however, grinned placatingly and patted his grandson on the shoulder before seeming to make introductions. The woman did not reciprocate. She moved off with the sharp strides of someone unhappy with her lot.

Jasper understood the feeling.

The chill between him and Leo wasn't something he'd anticipated, especially given the perpetual warmth he'd felt whenever he thought of her. She'd asked for time. He'd given it. And yet, here she was with Connor Quinn, meeting the man's grandfather.

Hell. Was there something between them?

Perhaps by kissing her, he'd interrupted whatever fledgling trust she'd started to put back into him. After she'd found out he'd been born into the notorious Carter family, that it had been his family who'd slaughtered hers, and that he had been the one to hide her in the steamer trunk in her family's attic to save her life, Leo hadn't spoken to him for two full months. If the bombing at Scotland Yard that killed Police Constable John Lloyd and implicated one of her acquaintances, Mrs. Geraldine Stewart, a women's suffrage leader, had not come about, Jasper wasn't certain she would have broken her vow to never speak to him again. But Leo had involved herself in proving Mrs. Stewart's innocence and, in doing so, reluctantly allowed a fragile peace to grow between them. It hadn't absolved Jasper from the truth: He'd lied to her, and to Gregory Reid, for sixteen years. But he'd started to hope that Leo might eventually be able to forgive him.

With no word from her these past four weeks, he'd begun to worry he'd mucked it all up with that kiss—an unforgettable kiss that had been in no way chaste.

Finally, Leo turned to him and lowered her voice to conceal it from those standing around them. "I am here because Connor has seen my uncle's tremors."

Jasper pushed aside a prickle of annoyance at the familiar use of the assistant coroner's given name and focused on what Leo had revealed. Claude Feldman, a city coroner at Spring Street Morgue, had been suffering from a palsy of his hands for several months. The affliction had been worsening, so much so that Leo had started to step in and help her uncle with any tasks that required steady hands, such as precise closing sutures. It was completely unauthorized, of course. With the appointment of Connor Quinn to the morgue, they'd known concealing Claude's shaking hands would be impossible.

"Quinn has told his grandfather?" Jasper presumed.

She balked, appearing offended. "Mr. Quinn is a good man, and he likes my uncle. It wasn't he who told the chief coroner about Claude's palsy. It was Mr. Higgins."

Jasper recalled the first medical student who had worked at the morgue—or more accurately, stood around uselessly. He'd had connections to the chief coroner too.

"Has Claude lost his position, then?"

Jasper hadn't heard news of it, but he had been concentrating on a string of arsons along the waterfront and a counterfeiting operation in Wapping. The two cases had kept him busy and away from the Spring Street Morgue.

"He's been finished for a week now," she answered, her voice catching with emotion.

Jasper sighed. "I'm sorry, Leo."

Claude had to be nearly seventy years old. Shaking hands or no, it was probably high time for him to retire anyway. Not that Jasper would say so; Leo would only perceive the comment as unfeeling rather than logical.

She accepted his condolences with a skeptical nod, then shrugged. "Connor has been promoted, and he wants me to stay on, as his official morgue clerk. He thought an introduction to the chief coroner would be beneficial to my remaining on staff there."

At that revelation, Jasper wasn't sure which he felt more keenly: skepticism that she would be given a paid position at the morgue, relief that she would keep the job she clearly enjoyed, or suspicion over why Connor Quinn would go to such trouble on her behalf.

He was still grappling with how to respond without upsetting her when the dinner gong sounded. *Finally.* The noise in the room grew exponentially as people started for the door. Jasper indicated they should go in too, and they fell into step at the back of the crowd.

"I thought you would apply at Hogarth and Tipson once Claude was gone from the morgue," he said, referring to the funeral service on Cambridge Circus.

"I will if I must, but I'd much rather stay on at Spring Street. It turns out that Connor and I work well together."

Jasper clenched his teeth and made no reply, though as they followed the crowd through the parlor's connecting door to a large dining room, he could not ignore the invisible spear lancing the center of his chest. *Damn it all.* Though it was rare for him, he knew jealousy when he felt it.

A long table glittered with china, silver, crystal, and flickering tapered candles. Overhead, a gasolier threw off gilded light on the place settings, each assigned a name placard. Uniformed servers were helping the guests find their seats, and Jasper and Leo were separated as they were each shown to their seats. He was placed between a woman and an older gentleman—Mrs. Buckley and Sir Walter Conrad, according to their name placards—and Leo was settled across the table, diagonal to him. Connor Quinn was to her left, and to her right was the sour-faced older woman who had been conversing with Sir Eamon earlier.

Leo met Jasper's eyes before Quinn said something to her, drawing her attention away again. Next to him, Mrs.

Buckley murmured a polite hello and asked which police force he worked for.

"Scotland Yard, madam," he replied, to which Sir Walter snorted. Derisively, no doubt. Jasper ignored the man as the hum of conversation began to quiet. Sir Eamon stood at the head of the table, his wife, at the opposite end, and he waited until all eyes were on him before addressing them.

"Welcome, friends, welcome. On behalf of myself and the Metropolitan and City Police Orphanage Fund, I thank you for your unwavering support of our truly important work. As you all know, our public servants are the lifeblood of this city, upholding law and order, and—"

The doors at both ends of the dining room flew open with startling violence, cutting off the chief coroner mid-sentence. Several men, their faces draped with black cloth, stormed inside. Each held a revolver. Jasper stood, his pulse streaming out in alarm. Several more officers around the table pushed back their chairs too, and cries of distress from both men and women resounded.

"Stay in your seats!" a tall man in the group shouted to be heard above the clamor. He leveled his weapon at Sir Eamon. "*Sit down*. Everyone! Back into your seats."

The chief coroner sank into his chair as the other masked men—five in all—fanned out around the table. Stymied, Jasper, and the others who'd stood with him, returned to their seats as ordered. Though many of the men were in uniform, they did not have weapons. As a detective, Jasper had been issued a revolver, but he hadn't had any reason to carry it with him that evening.

Across the table, Leo twisted in her chair to see the intruders, and in that moment, Jasper wished like hell that he'd been seated next to her. Had he been, he would have put his hand over hers to stop her from slipping the knife next to her plate into her lap, as he watched her do right then.

"Quiet!" the masked group leader shouted. His deep voice silenced the murmurings of confusion and panic almost immediately. "Hands on the table. All of you. Do it now."

"What is the meaning of this?" Sir Eamon asked from his chair, placing his hands flat onto the table as directed. "How dare you come in here—"

"Enough," the same masked man said. "Do as I tell you, and we will be gone within moments. Disobey, and there will be consequences. Am I understood?"

Nervous murmurings ran up and down the length of the table. A few muted wails of fear came from the chief coroner's wife and the woman next to her as one of the intruders placed himself behind them. Another stood behind Jasper's shoulder, and a third had positioned himself near Sir Eamon at the head of the table. The tall intruder who'd spoken remained at the backs of those seated on the opposite side of the table, a handful of places down from Leo. Her hands were now on the table, though the silver knife was missing. She had to have pocketed it.

The fifth masked man had gone to the door leading to the kitchen. He'd locked it and made the two servers in the dining room lower themselves to a prone position on the floor.

The black cloth draping the intruders' heads had slits cut out for their eyes. Long beards extended from the bottom of each head covering, and each man wore a brown, pin-striped suit, though a few were ill-fitting. Their matching appearances distracted Jasper for a moment before the leader spoke again, calmly and clearly.

"Good. Now, ladies, remove your jewels and place them on the table in front of you."

A robbery. *That's what this was?* The women in attendance were certainly wearing their best jewels. Leo as well. Jasper had noted the string of pearls adorning her neck and the matching pearl earrings. His father had left them to her in his will, and now, her eyebrows pulled taut as she realized that she was to lose them to these thieves.

He would have wrung all five of their necks if he could, but with weapons aimed at the dinner guests, Jasper could only sit, bristling with fury.

Ladies began to adhere to the command, including Leo, who blinked rapidly as she lifted her gloved hands to remove the earrings.

"This is preposterous," Sir Walter, to Jasper's left, said loudly. "Who do you think you are, coming in here and staging this robbery? You have no right!"

The man punctuated his complaint with the slamming of his fists on the table, and then he stood up, kicking his chair back behind him.

Instead of ordering the man to sit down and be quiet, the masked leader paused. Then, he strode swiftly down the table toward Leo. Jasper's heart thudded to a painful stop as the man, without a shred of hesitation, put the barrel of his revolver to the back of the head of the older woman seated to Leo's right—and pulled the trigger.

Chapter Two

She'd known the benefit dinner would be awful. Earlier, while dressing for the evening, Leo nearly sent word to Connor that she was bowing out. The anticipation of mingling with dozens of people whom she did not know, and who would eye her with disapproval and curiosity should they learn that she worked in a morgue, had given her indigestion for days in advance. But Connor had insisted his grandfather's generosity always abounded at the Orphanage Fund's benefit dinner and that they should put it to good use. There would be no better time, he'd claimed, to convince the chief coroner that Leo was a credit to the smooth operation of the Spring Street Morgue.

But now, as the report of the gun blasted through Leo's ears, she lamented letting Connor have his way.

She screamed, clapping her hand over her ear as something warm and wet misted the right side of her face. Shock blinded her for a moment, and when her vision cleared, she stared with abject horror at the woman who'd been seated next to her. Mrs. Seabright, according to her name placard, was face down on the table. She'd been thrown forward, her body now limp, her skull a ruined mess. And the blood…it pooled swiftly onto the white linen tablecloth. Loud, frantic screams—no longer Leo's own—chorused along the table, causing the sharp ringing in her right ear to throb even more painfully.

"Silence! Do as I say and stay in your seats, or another one of you will die!" the tall man shouted to be heard above the chaos.

The smell of gunpowder, the metallic tang of blood, and the rosewater scent the dead woman had been wearing, mixed in Leo's nose until she thought she would be sick.

A heavy hand came down on her right shoulder and tugged her back in her chair. The black-gloved fingertips of the murderer's hand entered her peripheral vision, and she went rigid.

"Shut your mouths, all of you!"

It wasn't the masked man who'd ordered this. It was Jasper. Stunned, Leo's unblinking eyes collided with his. His hands were locked into fists on the table, and when he shifted his ferocious glare to the man holding her shoulder, never had she seen such wrath. Or such fear.

Leo suddenly had the asinine desire to crawl across the table to him. Earlier, when she'd seen Jasper in the parlor, brooding into his glass of whisky, her heart and stomach had all but plummeted to her kneecaps.

She'd been avoiding him for weeks, for precisely the reason that ensued when he'd come to stand with her and Connor in uncomfortable silence. She didn't know what to say to him. Didn't know what was supposed to happened now that they had kissed. Leo hadn't expected it, and she certainly hadn't expected him to confess afterward that he cared for her. She'd hadn't known what to say or how to feel beyond tingly and unsteady on her feet. Weeks had passed, and she was still caught between knowing that she cared for Jasper in return and yet hesitant to tell him. Because then…what next?

She supposed, right now, none of that mattered.

Her attention strayed to the dead woman, Mrs. Seabright, whose arms were winged out on the table. She had done nothing. Nothing at all, and yet this man had killed her in cold blood. *Consequences*, he had warned, for not staying seated.

The older man next to Jasper, who'd risen in complaint, had already collapsed back into his seat, his face taking on a greenish cast.

Jasper's bellowed command worked. The room fell silent.

"I hope you take me seriously now," the man said. "Jewels. All of them, on the table. Quickly."

Whimpers and stifled sobs accompanied the women as they removed rings, earrings, bracelets, necklaces, and brooches. The valuables were scooped up into a cloth sack by another one of the intruders as quickly as the women dropped them onto the table.

"You as well," the man said, shoving Leo's shoulder.

Her hands trembling, and with a heavy lump of frustration in the pit of her stomach, she unhooked the string of pearls the Inspector had left her in his will. They, and the pearl earrings she had removed previously, disappeared as soon as she placed the matching set on the table. Her heart dropped, though the loss of the jewelry seemed a small price to pay so long as no one else died.

"You are in a room full of police officers, you fool," a man in his crisp, dark blue police uniform said. "You cannot imagine you will get away with this."

The locked door to the kitchen corridor rattled, the knob twisting unsuccessfully. The gunshot and screams had surely been heard in the kitchen.

"I do not have to imagine it. I know it," the masked man said calmly. He was well-spoken, his enunciation crisp. Almost aristocratic.

That confusing thought dissolved as the still-hot metal of the revolver's muzzle touched the side of Leo's head above her ear. It warmed her scalp through her hair, and a bubble of air escaped her mouth as a gasp. The quiver of panic in her chest threatened to choke her.

"You've gotten what you came for," Jasper said, his voice rough and raspy. "Leave her be and lower your weapon."

The muzzle pressed harder against her skull. "Follow us from this house, and she dies."

Leo's eyes skipped to the poor lady next to her, the pool of blood on the tablecloth having expanded to soak the linen under Leo's wine glass. This man was not to be trifled with. The dead woman was evidence of that.

"Stand," he ordered Leo.

For a moment, she wasn't certain she could trust her legs to obey. But Leo refused to appear frightened—it would only embolden Jasper to do something impulsive. She stood from her chair, forcing her legs to hold her. Connor Quinn had frozen in his seat, just as everyone else had. Worry and disbelief turned his brown eyes glassy as he watched her rise. The four other masked men rushed for the door through which they'd streamed no more than a few minutes previously.

The man holding her shoulder shifted his bruising grip to her elbow and yanked. Her feet tripped over themselves, but he didn't slow. Though she couldn't see Jasper, Leo heard him utter a hoarse expletive as the man dragged her from the dining room, into the front hall of the chief coroner's home, and toward the open front entrance. There, a servant lay upon the polished floor, unconscious.

"No one will follow you," Leo promised. Jasper would thrash anyone who attempted it. "You don't have to take me."

They rushed outside into the rain. The storm that had been brewing all afternoon had finally unleashed its whipping winds.

The grip on her arm did not ease. At the end of the short walk leading to the road, a black coach waited. The windows were draped, and a driver sat ready at the reins. His beaver hat was pulled low, and he wore an unseasonable plaid scarf, wound around his jaw up to his nose to obscure his face. Still, Leo tried to focus, tried to see as much as she could. Her memory was such that later, she would be able to recall everything in minute detail. If she could resist panicking, she might be able to help Jasper and the Criminal Investigation Department at Scotland Yard track down these criminals and arrest them.

That was, so long as the masked men allowed her to live.

The door to the coach was already open, and Leo was ushered onto the step and shoved inside. A musty odor assaulted her nostrils. She was flung to the bench, and a cloud of dust erupted from the lumpy cushions. As the other men piled inside, the coachman called to the horses to be away. The wheels were moving even before the fifth and final thief had closed the door behind him. As this last man threw himself onto the opposite bench, he reached for his head covering and began to pull it up.

"Keep that on, you imbecile," the leader snapped.

The man quickly released the black draped mask, but the cloth had caught on his long beard. Leo frowned. The beard appeared to have shifted to the side. Was it false? Peering at the others, visible by a single lantern that swung from a bracket on the wall, she noticed that all the beards had a uniformly artificial appearance.

"What was that back there?" the man with the crooked beard asked. He was breathing heavily, and his hand clenched the bag of stolen jewels tightly. "You never said anything about kill—"

"Shut your mouth," their leader said harshly. "We don't want our guest to hear too much, do we?"

The order gave Leo a glimmer of hope: Should any of them reveal their face or address someone in their party by name, they would have no choice but to be rid of her. But if they did not, did that mean he planned to let her go?

Though involuntary shivers tracked through her body, she paid attention to her surroundings: The coach was shabby, the green velvet cushions faded and threadbare. The black drapes were bordered by gold piping and tassels, and a small brass plate was affixed to the wall behind the bench opposite hers. The swinging lantern light revealed the word *Best* still visible on the engraved plate, but the black paint filling the rest of the words had been chipped, rendering it illegible.

The man holding the bag of jewels had a long scar on the back of his left hand, she noted. The marking curved from the knuckle of his ring finger to the flesh between his thumb and forefinger. Except for the leader, none of them had worn gloves, and none of them uttered a word. However, they were not covert in the uneasy glances they exchanged. It was clear something unplanned had taken place. Leo had a good idea what that thing was.

"You could have shot into the air, in warning," she said to the leader, even though a swell of nausea nearly stoppered her throat. "You didn't have to kill an innocent woman."

She was seated in the center of the bench, between him and one of the other men. The leader was close enough that his hip pressed against hers. He looked down at her. The cutouts in his mask were large enough for Leo to make out dark lashes and dusky blue irises. The unlined skin around his eyes hinted that he wasn't yet out of his twenties or early thirties.

"Who was that man at the table?" he asked rather than reply to her comment. "The one who looked like he wanted to tear out my throat?"

He had to be referring to Jasper and the blistering glare he'd thrown at the masked men's leader; it had seared into Leo's memory.

"I don't know whom you mean," she answered.

The cloth over his mouth billowed when he laughed. He didn't believe her, but Leo did not care. She wouldn't give up Jasper's name even if he put his revolver to her head again.

"If he attempts to chase after us, he'll be sorry," the man said. He still held the gun, though he'd let it come to rest in his lap.

The coach rattled onward at an expeditious clip. With the curtains drawn, she had no idea where they were or in which direction they'd gone after leaving the chief coroner's home on Kennington Circle.

She grew impatient, not knowing when they would stop and release her. Or if they would at all. In the uneasy quiet, another potential danger occurred to her. They were five men in all. She was one woman. They'd already proved to be thieves, and at least one of them, a killer. What other dastardly things might they do?

She tried to breathe evenly. If she was forced to, she would attempt to employ the dinner knife she'd put into her dress pocket when the men had first burst into the dining room. She hadn't stopped to think when she did it; it had been reflexive. And thankfully, her dress had been just unfashionable enough to have pockets.

Not that a dinner knife would be much of a defense against five men with guns. But having it, feeling the weight of it against her thigh, was an ounce of comfort she wouldn't otherwise have.

Minutes spooled out. The silent tension in the coach grew corrosive. Leo shifted on the lumpy bench cushion, her right ear still ringing from the gunshot fired so close to her. It hadn't ruptured her eardrum, however, unlike the blast of the bomb outside Scotland Yard in May had done.

The leader of the thieves suddenly raised his voice and called to the coachman, "Is there anyone after us?"

After a pause, an answering "Clear" sounded from the driver's bench.

The leader whistled, and the coach wheels began to slow. Leo's heart leaped. She touched her skirt pocket, felt the sharp dinner knife hidden there, ready. But when the coach rocked to a stop, the leader only opened the door. Rain and wind whipped inside. Leo peered out into the darkness.

"You're truly going to let me go?" she asked, skeptical.

"Didn't I say I would?" He gestured for the exit.

"You speak as if your word should mean something," Leo said before she could curb her tongue.

"Brassy," the man said with a light laugh. "I would invite you to stay, but we are rather in a hurry."

She maneuvered around the men's boots and legs to the exit, refusing the killer's hand when he extended it. As a result, she nearly tumbled to the ground as she cleared the coach.

Immediately, the door slammed shut, and the horses tore away, quickly leaving her in the dust. Or rather, mud. Rain pelted her shoulders as she stared at the coach disappearing down the road. She exhaled long and hard and, with a cramp in her throat, realized a sob was threatening to erupt. Leo swallowed it, refusing to cry. She was safe. *Alive*. They'd let her go. Though she could not fathom why. The man had killed Mrs. Seabright without so much as a blink—and yet, excepting that he'd dropped her off in the middle of nowhere, he'd shown Leo something close to civility.

As the clattering of the coach subsided into the distance, the drumming of the downpour took over. Leo shivered. Her dress was already soaked through, and her shoes squelched in an inch of mud along the darkened road. There were no buildings or lampposts near her, no familiar markers to clue her in as to where she was. But as her eyes adjusted to the dim light, she thought she might be near a field.

Turning around, she spotted light on the horizon. The glow of civilization, perhaps a quarter mile away. Jasper would be frantic with worry, and her uncle, when he learned what had happened, would be too. The sooner she got home, the sooner she could put their minds at ease. And then she could help Scotland Yard figure out who the masked men were. For now, there was nothing she could do except walk.

She tucked her head down against the rain and started forward.

Chapter Three

Leo shoved open the door to the police station and staggered inside. The small constabulary had been her destination as soon as she realized where the criminals had let her out: within the vast cricket lawns and woods of Battersea Park.

The storm winds had brought pockets of briny air, so Leo had known she was close to the Thames. Walking past a boating lake and well-manicured cricket and croquet grounds, she'd come to guess her location. Then, upon clearing the wooded perimeter of the park and coming out onto Albert Road, her guess was confirmed.

Battersea was part of Division V, something she knew thanks to the Metropolitan Police divisions map she'd seen on countless occasions in the Inspector's office at Scotland Yard—and something she recalled easily due to her peculiar memory.

As with nearly everything Leo viewed, the framed map that had hung upon Gregory Reid's office wall had been stored in her mind as an exact image. Once she realized she was in Battersea, she pulled up the image of the map and looked at it once again, the details as clear and precise as if she were standing before the real thing. There were times when her photographic memory could be overwhelming, and times when it made her feel somewhat of an oddity. But as she used the map's guidance to point her in the direction of the closest constabulary station, that on Battersea Bridge Road, Leo was grateful for her brain's uncommon quirk.

It didn't solve the problem of her empty pockets though. She hadn't even a halfpenny to hire a cab to get her to the constabulary station. Nothing but a dinner knife in her pocket, which she kept her fingers wrapped around as she walked through the ceaseless rain and wind toward the busier streets of Battersea. It was mostly middle-class there, so Leo didn't feel particularly threatened, but the few times she hailed a passing cab, the drivers had either passed her by or demanded she show them the fare upfront. Her sodden appearance had surely left them in doubt that she would be able to afford it. When she tried to explain her situation, they drove on.

Now, as the station door shut behind her, Leo felt like collapsing in exhaustion into one of the vacant chairs pushed against the wall. However, given the gaping looks she received from the two officers on duty, she stayed on her feet.

"Good evening," she said. They continued to stare, agog.

She did appear rather alarming. The hem of her gown sent rivulets of water onto the tiled floor; her shoes were encased in mud and utterly ruined; her hair, which had been pinned up into a fashionable twist, now hung in dark, sopping hanks around her shoulders. At least the blood that had sprayed her face when Mrs. Seabright was shot, had likely been cleansed away in the rain.

"What's happened to you then, miss?" one of the officers asked as he stood. He'd been lounging in his chair, boots up on the desk.

"It's a long and complicated story, but I need you to wire Scotland Yard," she said, jaw chattering. Despite it being late June, the temperature had fallen since sunset. Drenched as she was, the night air left her cold.

The two police officers—a constable and a sergeant by their uniform insignias—exchanged a look of amusement. The sergeant crossed his arms over his chest. "Scotland Yard, is it? Are you sure you don't need me to wire Buckingham Palace, too, while I'm at it?"

The two men shared a chuckle. She'd expected she might face some questioning and remained calm.

"I understand it's an unusual request, but I assure you, the police are looking for me." At the new arching of their brows, she explained, "I was taken from a benefit dinner where a woman was killed. There were Met officers in attendance and city police, too, and they will be out searching for me right now. Please, if you'd wire Scotland Yard—"

"I think you've tipped back a few too many glasses of sherry tonight, miss. Why don't you take a seat over there and calm yourself," the sergeant said, gesturing to one of the chairs against the wall.

Leo glared, insulted. "I am not intoxicated, Sergeant. If you wire the Yard, you will find that what I'm saying is true."

As the constable, still lounging at his desk, snorted a

laugh, and the sergeant rolled his eyes, a surge of helplessness descended over her. At Scotland Yard, there were plenty of officers who did not like her or approve of her presence. However, at least there, she never would have been dismissed so cavalierly. It made her feel utterly powerless. And that was unacceptable.

Leo clenched her hands into fists and squared her shivering shoulders. "You must wire Detective Inspector Jasper Reid at the Yard. Tell him Miss Leonora Spencer is here at your station."

The sergeant gave a weary sigh. "Oh, I must? And why is that?"

If the truth wasn't going to sway him, perhaps a lie would. A bold one. She set her chin. "Because I've killed someone, and I'd like to confess to the murder."

The musty blanket was thin and riddled with holes, but it was at least dry and would help ward off the chill. Leo pulled it tighter around her shoulders as she sat on the wooden bench in her cell. All in all, the Battersea station prison wasn't the worst place Leo could have spent the night. It was vastly preferable to being outdoors in the wind and rain, for instance. After the police sergeant locked her inside a small cell, the rain had intensified, pelting the roof relentlessly. Rolling thunder shook the skies, and lightning flashed, illuminating the slim corridor outside the cell. There were only two holding cells in this small constabulary, and thankfully, there was a solid stone wall between hers and the one next door. Unfortunately, it wasn't vacant.

"Who we got there, eh?" a man had slurred as the sergeant escorted Leo toward her cell.

"Mind your tongue, Ralph," the sergeant replied.

But as the officer was under the impression that Leo was a murderess, he didn't admonish Ralph, who appeared to be soused, for the whistles and love ballads he commenced singing.

Hours passed. Leo sat restless, in mounting doubt that the sergeant had telegraphed Scotland Yard as she'd requested. He'd asked whom she'd killed, but she replied that she would not speak to anyone but Detective Inspector Jasper Reid of Scotland Yard. It hadn't made him happy.

She whiled away the time by thinking of the letters she'd been writing. One was to her good friend, Nivedita Brooks, who'd left London for the summer to stay with an aunt in Birmingham. Leo missed her terribly but understood Dita's need to grieve the loss of her beau, Police Constable John Lloyd, in solitude. He'd been killed in the bombing outside Scotland Yard in May. The second letter had been to Mrs. Geraldine Stewart, who had also left London for a while, though Leo suspected she would not return. Her women's suffrage group, the Women's Equality Alliance, had dissolved after she'd been wrongfully accused of murder, and it had not recovered even with her release from police custody. The scandal had cost her husband, Porter Stewart, his reputation too, though Leo reckoned his bribing a member of Parliament into supporting his bid to run for MP had been the real reason for his ruin. Geraldine's choice to stay with her husband had baffled Leo; he'd deceived her in more ways than one. But she had kept up correspondence over the last few weeks from their country home in Kent, and Leo supposed her choices were her own to make.

Leo's clothing had started to dry, as had her hair, but she was still freezing. After fighting the urge for a while, she was forced to relieve herself in the crude bucket placed in the corner of the cell, the blanket held up in front of her for some semblance of privacy.

Ralph's muttered songs and loud belches had softened to drunken snores, and the thunder and rain had tapered significantly, when a commotion resounded from the front of the station. Leo sat taller, listening. A man's familiar deep tenor fired up her spine, and she shot from the bench toward the bars of her cell door. Two months ago, when she'd been held overnight at Scotland Yard by a truculent Special Irish Branch detective inspector, Jasper had been the one to free her then; as the voices and footfalls approached the back corridor of the Battersea station, she was both humiliated and relieved that he had come for her now too.

The sergeant appeared in the corridor, jostling a lantern and a ring of keys. Jasper was close on his heels, his suit from that evening rumpled, his tie loose, and his expression tight with fury. When he saw her, he exhaled visibly and closed his eyes.

"Thank God," he breathed out. "Sergeant, open that door."

"But, sir, she's confessed to a murder."

"I haven't killed anyone," Leo told the officer, shivering again. "It was the only way I could get you to contact the Yard."

"*Sergeant*," Jasper barked. He didn't need to say

anything more. The sergeant found the key and unlocked the cell door, its hinges groaning as he swung it wide.

Leo hadn't taken two steps out before Jasper gripped her arms. "Are you hurt?"

She shook her head, but again, her teeth had started to chatter.

"You're freezing." He spun to glare at the sergeant. "Is this how you treat your prisoners? By throwing them into a cold cell and leaving them to catch their death?"

Leo touched Jasper's elbow. "As much as I'd enjoy listening to you scold the sergeant, I'd much rather go home."

Jasper kept his arm around her as he pushed past the stunned policeman, now appropriately cowed, and swiftly led her from the station.

"I'll have him sacked," he growled as he punted the front door open. A hansom cab waited at the curb in the street, and Jasper hastened them toward it.

Leo let out a laugh, though it shook in her throat. "I'm not sure he deserves that. In retrospect, a drenched woman hurrying into his station, demanding Scotland Yard be contacted had to be the most outlandish thing he'd seen in a long time."

Once settled in the cab, Jasper removed his suit jacket and draped it over her shoulders. "I don't care; I'm still having him sacked."

"You're not angry with him," Leo pointed out, the warmth of his jacket penetrating her skin and seeping into her muscles. She nearly groaned from the comfort of it. "You're angry with the masked men from the benefit dinner."

The cabbie, seated high on the driver's bench behind

the enclosed cab, had started his horses forward toward the river. The blue light of dawn was just barely beginning to push out the night.

Seated on the single bench beside her, his arm still around her shoulders to provide another source of heat, Jasper grimaced. "Tell me what happened."

"They let me off in Battersea Park. They kept their masks on the whole time, but there are some things I observed that might help you in your search for them. For instance, the man who took me, the tall one, he's left-handed—"

Jasper swore under his breath, startling her into silence. "None of that matters right now. Christ, Leo. They could have killed you. I thought…these last few hours…" He shook his head, frustration brimming. And something else: fear. "I thought for certain your body would be found in a ditch somewhere."

Hunkered under his jacket, growing warmer by the second, she laid her palm on his chest. "I'm all right, Jasper."

He looked at her again, the tension along his jaw still jumping. "You weren't…" He hesitated. "Interfered with?"

His voice was a rasp, as if he could barely bring himself to say it. Leo understood his question and the reason he'd asked it. Five men had abducted her. While alone with them in the coach, the notion had streamed through her mind too.

She shook her head. "I'm unharmed, I promise."

He exhaled again, the sound a bit shaky, and nodded. Leo had known that he'd be worried, and from his perspective, it made sense for him to have feared the worst had happened to her.

He scrubbed his cheek, appearing exhausted. "I'll bring you home. We don't have to discuss anything more until tomorrow after you've rested."

"Kid gloves aren't necessary." Her shivering had subsided, and she felt safe, nestled as she was under Jasper's coat and his arm. It was an intimate position, and it brought forward the memory of their kiss. As well as the distance they'd each kept since.

"I'd rather speak of it now," she said, wanting to focus on the crime at hand.

He assented with a nod.

"What I don't understand," she began, "is why that man would so callously murder Mrs. Seabright but then keep his word to let me go when no one followed them."

"Mrs. Seabright," Jasper said, as if the name was unknown to him.

"I saw her name placard," Leo explained, then wondered, "What happened after I left?"

He grunted. "You mean after you were abducted."

"All right, yes, abducted," she said, though she didn't want him to dwell on it. She didn't wish to either. "What happened?"

Their cab had crossed Battersea Bridge and now drove along the Chelsea Embankment, the horizon over the Thames bluing rapidly.

"I don't know. I left straightaway for the Kennington station to contact Scotland Yard and to organize a search party," he answered. "But this man, the one who did all the talking—I saw that he was left-handed too. Was anything else revealed when they had you in the coach?"

His arm flexed and relaxed around her shoulders as he visibly worked to hold in his ire.

"Killing Mrs. Seabright wasn't part of the original plan," Leo said, recalling the shorter masked man who'd started to remove his head covering. "The other men were upset that someone was killed."

She thought of the other things she'd noticed, such as the long scar on the shorter man's hand and the paint-chipped brass plate on the interior wall of the coach with the word *Best* still visible. But with the rattle and sway of the cab, the heat burrowing into her bones and driving out the cold, and Jasper's solid arm around her, her eyelids began to droop. Perhaps it would be better to wait until tomorrow to give her statement after all.

Her eyes had been closed for several moments when Jasper's warm palm grazed her cheek. Parting her lashes, Leo acknowledged that they were huddled close. Close enough so that if he lowered his head a few scant inches, he could bring his mouth to hers again.

Countless times over the last many weeks, Leo had pored over the memory of that kiss, mining it for every detail, no matter how small. Now, she allowed her eyes to drift over his lips. If he were to lean forward and kiss her in the cab, she would let him.

But he didn't.

"Tell me the rest tomorrow," he said, still cupping her cheek gently.

He turned away, facing forward to watch the road ahead.

The cab wended through the empty streets quickly, and within a half hour, they arrived on Duke Street. The windows of her home were dark. It was a startling thought that she could have been through so much overnight while Claude and Flora slept peacefully, totally unaware.

"I don't have my key," she said. Her handbag and wrap had been taken at the door of the chief coroner's home.

Jasper helped her to the pavement, and together, they walked to the front door. Leo brought down the knocker. Although it was nearing dawn, she still felt guilty waking her uncle from his slumber.

As they waited, Jasper said, "I'll send a messenger to Quinn. He was worried about what would become of you when I last saw him at Sir Eamon's home."

"Oh." Leo blinked, surprised at herself. She hadn't thought of Connor once during her ordeal. "That's thoughtful of you."

The unbolting of the locks on the door sounded, and then her uncle was peering out at them in utter confusion. "What in the—Leonora, what has happened? Inspector?"

"I'm perfectly fine, Uncle," she preempted. "I'll tell you everything once I get into some dry clothes."

She slid out from under Jasper's suit jacket and handed it back to him. He folded it over his arm, then, with a departing nod, returned to the waiting cab.

"My dear?" Claude said, as she went inside, and closed the front door. He rarely frowned, as he was doing right then. "I am not going to like this tale, am I?"

"I'll meet you in the kitchen. You'd best make some tea," she replied as she climbed the stairs, dreaming of a warm nightdress, robe, and slippers. "And Uncle? Make sure you add a splash of whisky."

Chapter Four

Jasper hadn't bothered with sleep after delivering Leo home at the brush of dawn. The hellish night had left his mind racing, and as he'd arrived at 23 Charles Street, where Mrs. Zhao had already risen to prepare breakfast, he'd abandoned any hope of rest.

His eyes burned as he left his house just before eight o'clock. Though his head ached from the plaguing memory of Leo being hastened away at the point of a gun—and the older woman who'd been brutally shot in her seat—Jasper was not distracted enough to overlook the fact that he was being followed.

The man had been waiting at the corner of Charles Street and St. James's Square. Jasper gave no indication that he'd seen him. From the corner of his eye, he saw the man fall into step behind him. Three days ago, the same man had been lingering outside Scotland Yard, smoking a pipe and reading a newspaper. The burnt-orange color of his bowler hat was just uncommon enough to stick out in a crowd. Several other times over the last handful of weeks, a prickling sense of being watched had crawled along Jasper's shoulders and up the back of his neck as he went about his day. Easy to brush off once, maybe twice, but not more than that.

Jasper turned onto Haymarket and swung a casual glance over his shoulder. The orange-hatted man was there, though far behind. As he continued, hands in his pockets, Jasper contemplated a response. The man was clearly keeping tabs, perhaps reporting back to someone about his movements.

Was he someone Jasper had arrested in the past? Some ex-convict seeking retribution? Or perhaps the man was a private detective. Though who would have hired him to tail Jasper, and why?

He reached Whitehall Place, where a costermonger was set up, hawking sausage rolls as he did every morning. Pausing at the cart, Jasper took another look back the way he'd come. The orange-hatted man wasn't anywhere to be seen. His jaw ticking in annoyance, Jasper paid the costermonger and took the sausage roll into Scotland Yard. Tension coiled through him as he made his way to the detective department. He would figure out what to do about his unwanted shadow later, but right now, the events of last night were more important.

"Reid," Detective Chief Inspector Dermot Coughlan barked from the entrance to his office. He signaled for Jasper to join him. The chief inspector's office, along with Jasper's had been destroyed in the May bombing, but reconstruction had been swift. Jasper shut the door behind him.

"I'm glad to hear Miss Spencer was found unharmed," Coughlan began. Though he wasn't fond of Leo or her involvement in some of Jasper's past cases, he wasn't malicious and would never wish harm on her. That probably couldn't be said for a few of the other officers in the Criminal Investigation Department.

"She made some observations about the suspects last night that might prove useful," Jasper replied. "I'll get her statement today."

Coughlan cocked a brow. "Keep her involvement limited, Reid. You are on thin ice here as it is. I don't dispute your success last month in solving that parliamentary aide's murder and the Lloyd bombing. It was good police work. But it won you no favors among some of your colleagues."

"Those colleagues being Tomlin," Jasper replied, referring to the Special Irish Branch detective inspector who'd arrested Geraldine Stewart based on negligible evidence. Under scrutiny and challenged by Jasper's own investigation, Tomlin's case against the suffragist had fallen apart. "It is my job to solve crime, sir, not dance around the egos of other detectives."

"Careful not to get too self-righteous," Coughlan warned. "This department functions best when my detectives work well together. Put plainly, Reid, if no one likes you, what makes you think they're going to do their best work for you?"

Jasper clenched his jaw and took the hit on the chin. It was no secret, especially not to him, that he wasn't overly popular with some of the men there. Many believed he'd risen to the rank of detective inspector by riding upon his father's coattails. In all honesty, he'd often wondered if they might be correct. Maybe that was why Jasper tended to work longer hours and delegate fewer tasks to the team of detective constables than his colleagues, and why he was apt to bring work home with him on his days off. He'd made his life revolve around Scotland Yard, and yet...it didn't seem to have changed how others there perceived him.

"Understood," Jasper answered the chief, if only to move the conversation along. He had work to do. "I'd like the case. As I was present at the time of the robbery and shooting, I have an advantage."

Coughlan assented with a nod. "Price and Drake were sent to Sir Eamon's home last night to take witness statements and collect any evidence. Speak to them and get their reports. The victim, Martha Seabright, was brought to Spring Street Morgue." Here, he cocked his brow again, relaying yet another warning to Jasper, albeit silent, about Leonora Spencer.

"It goes without saying," Coughlan went on, "that we need this case solved and the murderer arrested fast. This was a strike against some of our own. Don't get distracted, Reid."

He dismissed Jasper with a jerk of his chin, and Jasper suppressed a scowl as he turned to leave. *Distracted*? He did not become distracted while investigating any case, especially a murder. Most murders were simple to solve, as most killers were not diligent enough in covering their tracks. But there were some cases, as with a few of Jasper's more recent investigations, that diverged from the straight and narrow path the chief inspector would have preferred.

Detective Sergeant Roy Lewis, seated at the desk he no longer had to share now that Jasper had an office again, bounced to his feet as soon as Jasper cleared Coughlan's door. He followed the detective inspector into his new, though still small, office.

"You'll need this," Lewis said, dropping a manila folder onto the desk blotter. "Price and Drake spoke to the guests still there when they arrived, though Sir Eamon said quite a few had already left."

Jasper flipped open the folder and started to read. He had rushed off to search for Leo without stopping to order anyone from the Met or City Police to contain the guests until they could be questioned. Apparently, no one else had thought to do so either.

"Miss Spencer had quite a fright, I hear," Lewis said. Jasper drew in a long, slow breath; it helped to fight the knot of tension cramping his chest whenever he thought of Leo's abduction.

"Thankfully, she is unharmed." The succinct statement felt piteously insufficient for what Leo had endured. And Jasper hadn't been able to do a damn thing to stop it. He'd been powerless during the intrusion as well as afterward, when launching a search for her. That futile state had left him charged, ready to explode. When the telegram had come in that she was at Battersea station, a sob of relief had lodged in his throat.

Leo had assured him that she hadn't been interfered with, but it maddened him that she'd been subjected to the possibility. Five men. One of them, a murderer. Though, from what she said on the cab ride home last night, the other four had not expected anyone to die during their bold break-in.

"That's a relief," Lewis said. "Did I hear right that she got herself locked up in Battersea station by confessing to a murder?"

A grin broke out on Jasper's lips. He shook his head in awe of her ingenuity. "Thank you for reminding me; I need to arrange an upbraiding for the station sergeant there."

"Do I want to know why?" Lewis asked.

"Let's concentrate on what happened at Sir Eamon's dinner," Jasper replied, trying to divert his sergeant's attention away from Leo and back to the case.

He read the reports on the victim quickly. Martha Seabright had been a widow some thirteen years. Her husband, Sergeant Daniel Seabright, a former corporal in the Queen's army who later became a policeman, had been killed while on patrol. He'd been stabbed while foiling a mugging in Clerkenwell. It had taken two days for him to die. Jasper winced, thinking of the suffering the man likely had endured. Mrs. Seabright had been left with three children, and as the Metropolitan and City Police Orphanage had just opened its doors the previous year, in 1870, the Seabright children were among the first the orphanage had taken in.

"Mrs. Seabright was invited to the benefit dinner to stand as an example of the orphanage's goodwill," Jasper read aloud, then lowered the file. "She didn't look happy about something just before dinner was announced. I saw her in a terse discussion with Sir Eamon."

"I didn't read anything about that in the report," Lewis said.

"I'll need to talk to Sir Eamon to find out why their conversation left her in a fit of pique."

The older woman had still been wearing her scowl when taking her seat next to Leo at the table. Briefly, the image of the blood spatter on Leo's face after Martha

Seabright had been shot rose to the front of his mind. At least, the woman had not seen it coming. A blessing maybe, but it did nothing to soothe the curl of loathing he felt for the nameless, faceless man who'd so callously shot Mrs. Seabright in the head. Jasper pushed the memory aside and returned to reading the file on his desk.

The witness statements that Police Constables Price and Drake had collected weren't overly illuminating. Everyone had seen and heard the same things. Except for Marcus Gibson, the footman who'd been positioned at the front door. His statement, taken by Stephen Warnock, newly promoted to the rank of detective sergeant, was brief: At the light rap of the knocker, he'd opened the front door. The five masked men pushed their way inside, the first of whom struck the footman on the head before he could sound the alarm. He claimed not to remember anything after that until he woke, which was after the men escaped with the stolen jewels and their hostage.

"Were the kitchen staff questioned?" Jasper asked, flipping through the pages, searching for their statements.

"Drake said they were barred from the dining room," Lewis replied. "After they heard the gunshot, one of them left through the back door to summon the police. A constable came, but only after the intruders had left."

"Go to the Giles house and speak to the footman, Gibson," Jasper said. "These men targeted the dinner, and they knew when to strike, too as soon as we were all seated at the table. It's possible someone on the chief coroner's staff knows something." Perhaps even gave important information to the masked men to help them plan the robbery.

Lewis nodded. "Sir Eamon's housekeeper hired extra

servers through a catering service. I'll talk to them as well."

It was a good thought. However, it would be short-sighted of them to only look at the staff. Jasper shuffled the papers again until he found the guest list that he'd glanced over a moment ago. At least thirty names filled the sheet. Jasper's eyes paused on a few in particular: Gavin Seabright, a relation no doubt to the victim, though Martha had appeared to be there alone; and two more, Mr. and Mrs. Stanley Hayes. Constance's parents. Jasper had never met them, as he'd ended his courtship with their daughter before having the chance. It was possible they had been in attendance, and he simply hadn't recognized them, nor they him. But they hadn't been interviewed by either Price or Drake.

"They took a risk in letting Miss Spencer go, don't you think?" Lewis observed, drawing Jasper's attention from the guest list. "Why not just shoot her, like the one did the old woman?" Belatedly realizing the crassness of his question, he muttered, "Sorry, guv."

Jasper shook his head. What the detective sergeant asked had merit. Why spare Leo but not Mrs. Seabright?

"Let's find him, so we can ask." Jasper closed the folder. "I'll stop by the Law Courts and see if I can speak to Sir Eamon."

They left his office—Lewis for Giles's home in Kennington and Jasper for the Royal Courts of Justice. But at the department's entrance, they came upon Constable Horace Wiley, who stood, blocking Leo's way inside. Her distaste for the man was etched upon her face, and Jasper's own annoyance boiled up fast.

"Step aside, Wiley," he barked. "I'm expecting Miss Spencer."

The constable did as ordered though his churlish scowl followed Leo as she passed. There was a rumor going around that Wiley had put in for a secondment to the Liverpool City Police, and Jasper hoped it would go through. The man guarded the front desk to the detective department like a bully.

As Leo moved further into the department, Jasper noted that her pace wasn't as brisk as usual, and her eyes looked heavy. Like him, she'd probably dispensed with the idea of sleep.

"Miss Spencer," Lewis greeted her with a friendlier-than-usual nod. She noticed and eyed him with a skeptical glance. The detective sergeant then turned and carried on his way, exiting the room.

Jasper gestured for Leo to enter his office.

"If only Constable Wiley was as happy as Sergeant Lewis is that I'm not dead," she said as he closed the door behind them.

"Wiley is miserable, but he wouldn't wish you dead," Jasper replied.

Leo opened her handbag and sent him a dubious look. "You give him too much credit. Here." She retrieved a sheet of paper and extended it to him.

"Your statement?"

"I thought there would be more," she said with a sigh of disappointment. "Last night, there seemed to be so many things I wanted to tell you."

Jasper took the sheet. Leo was getting used to typing witness statements, and like the others, this one was filled to the margins of the page with details. "It looks like plenty to me."

"Yes, but nothing there provides much for leads. The beards were false. Horsehair, if I had to guess," she said. "So perhaps they were purchased at a costume shop? And the plaque in the coach...I keep trying to see it better in my memory, but the black paint in the engraved lettering was all chipped away except for the word *Best*."

Jasper read through her statement even as she spoke. "You think it was a hired hack?"

"If there are any carriage companies with the word *Best* in their names, we might be able to track it down through the carriages department."

He lowered the typed sheet, thinking of Coughlan's warning. "Leo, your involvement in this case is to be limited to this statement. I will direct Sergeant Brooks to search the registries for any hansom companies with *Best* as part of their names."

"I was using the word 'we' figuratively," Leo said with a shrug of her shoulder.

Jasper didn't quite believe her but returned to her statement without comment. As he read on, the only identifying description she could give for any of the men was a bit about a scar on one man's left hand. It was good information though, especially if they could take in a suspect that had such a marking.

"I assume you already have constables visiting pawnbrokers, searching for the jewels that were stolen?" Leo asked.

There had been a page in the constables' report allocated to the descriptions of the jewels taken, and Price had taken it upon himself to send men to several pawnshops. Jasper recalled the pearl necklace and earrings that Leo had lost.

"I hope we can find them," he said. "And not just to track down these men. I know my father's gifts were important to you."

She shook her head. "I'm sorry to have lost them, but in the end, it is just jewelry."

There was a dejected quality to her voice, and Jasper suspected she'd been more affected by her ordeal than she was letting on. However, he knew better than to pry. She would only close herself off completely if he did.

"Where are you going first?" she asked, changing the topic.

"I'll speak to Sir Eamon."

Interest flickered over her face. "He and Mrs. Seabright seemed to be arguing before dinner last night."

"Yes. I'd like to know what it was about."

"Why would she have been at the dinner?" Leo asked, the dejection clearing as her innate curiosity took over. "She didn't appear to be a wealthy donor."

The information on the victim in the constables' report was classified, though not private. Had the benefit dinner gone on as planned, uninterrupted, Sir Eamon would have likely spoken to the guests of Mrs. Seabright's history with the Orphanage Fund as a grateful recipient of its charitable work. However, giving Leo any more information on the victim would only further kindle her interest in the case. He wanted her far from this investigation, out of harm's way.

"We're still gathering information," Jasper replied, circumventing an answer. Then, after a pause, he reminded her, "I should be going."

She shifted her footing as if realizing that she was being dismissed. And hell, if he didn't feel like a donkey's arse for it. But it was for the best.

"Right. I'm needed at the morgue," she said, starting for the door. As he'd already learned from the chief, Mrs. Seabright's body would be there, waiting.

"Perhaps you should take the day off," he suggested blandly.

When Leo jolted to a halt and speared him with a glare over her shoulder, Jasper knew he'd overstepped.

"You have your job to do, Inspector, and I have mine." With that, she opened the door to his office and left.

Chapter Five

Morning sunlight brightened the gray Portland stone edifice of the Royal Courts of Justice. Positioned on a busy intersection along the Strand, the massive building, with its imposing Gothic style arches and turrets, had only recently been opened by the Queen. The new home of England's High Court and Court of Appeals had been designed to exude integrity and power, but as Jasper entered, he only had the vague sense of pomposity.

He believed in law and justice, of taking criminals off the street and doling out fair punishment. But he could not stomach the politics that went on in the higher echelons of the police and justice systems. The conversation with Chief Inspector Coughlan earlier had left a burr under his skin. Treating mediocre police officers and detectives with kid gloves was no way to improve the outcomes of investigations by the Met. There were plenty of men joining the police force every year, and clearing the department of inept detectives would give opportunity to newer officers once they'd come up through the ranks.

But then, Jasper wasn't in charge at Scotland Yard, and he never would be if he got sacked.

He obtained directions to Sir Eamon's chambers from a clerk in the reception hall and then made his way there. The previous evening, he'd only spoken to the chief coroner briefly before installing himself in the corner of the parlor. He seemed a pleasant enough man, but the interaction hadn't been sufficient for Jasper to form any real opinion of him.

The secretary in the anteroom looked at Jasper's warrant card with grim understanding, then knocked on the closed door to the office. After stepping inside and murmuring in low tones, the secretary emerged again.

"Sir Eamon will see you now."

The chief coroner wasn't alone. Jasper entered the office, a large space dominated by mahogany and leather, and found another man seated in a club chair. This man, whom he'd never seen before, impaled Jasper with a cold glare. With smoke wreathing the air from their cigars, the two appeared to have been having an easy conversation.

"I'm sorry to interrupt your meeting," Jasper said, but Sir Eamon stood and waved the apology off.

"Not at all. I expected someone from the Yard this morning. Do come in. Cigar?"

"No, thank you." He didn't care for them, and he also didn't want to get too snug with the chief coroner.

"Allow me to introduce you," Sir Eamon said, then turned toward his guest, who was still seated and glaring daggers at Jasper. "Detective Inspector Reid, this is Mr.

Stanley Hayes. Stanley was once on the Board of Governors for the orphanage."

A frisson of surprise went through Jasper, followed by one of understanding. The man's hateful look made sense now. Although Jasper had ended his relationship with Constance Hayes before ever meeting her parents, Stanley had surely heard about the working-class man his daughter had been carrying on with. To save face, Constance would have told her parents that she'd been the one to call things off between them, and Jasper would not dispute it. He owed her that much, if only for having drawn out their courtship for too long. Nevertheless, it appeared Stanley Hayes despised him. With the questions Jasper needed to ask, he braced himself for a disagreeable exchange.

"Mr. Hayes," he said with a bob of his head.

Stanley blew out a cloud of cigar smoke. He stayed in his seat and gave no greeting.

"How is Miss Spencer?" Sir Eamon asked, overlooking Stanley's cold demeanor. "I heard the good news that she was released by her abductors without harm."

"She's well, thank you," Jasper said, one eye on Stanley Hayes as he kept the cigar between his molars.

"A relief," Sir Eamon said. "My grandson introduced me to her briefly last evening. Connor thinks very highly of her."

The mention of the new city coroner was a point of irritation, but Jasper was barely given the chance to feel it before Stanley Hayes gave a snort of derisive laughter. Both Jasper and Sir Eamon turned to him, baffled by the man's outburst.

"Ah, yes, I've heard about Miss Spencer," he said, his

low opinion of her not to be missed. "A young woman, working in a morgue? Eamon, your grandson should have more sense than to encourage such indecency."

Constance, too, had disparaged Leo for working in a morgue. It was no surprise Mr. Hayes concurred with his daughter.

The chief coroner raised a brow at his cantankerous guest but did not comment.

"I'm glad you're here, Mr. Hayes," Jasper said, surprising him. He frowned and lowered his cigar. "I've some questions for you as well as for Sir Eamon."

Mr. Hayes brought his crossed leg down to the floor and sat forward. "What questions could you possibly have for me? I was not in attendance last evening."

"Precisely. However, your name, along with that of Mrs. Hayes, were on the guest list my constables were given. Why did you choose not to attend?"

"How is that your concern?"

"I need to speak to all guests on the list, regardless of whether they attended or not," Jasper explained.

"The guests are victims of this band of ruffians. A woman was murdered." Mr. Hayes got to his feet. "I do not see the rationale in questioning the guests as if *they* are suspects. In fact, it is damn insulting."

Jasper did not flinch. He'd had plenty of experience questioning belligerent people. As with them all, Stanley Hayes's complaints would not cause Jasper to rescind his questions.

"I mean no offense, Mr. Hayes, but the rationale for questioning guests is for me to determine, as I am the one investigating the crimes committed," he said as evenly as he could. "Now, you can explain while I'm here why you did not attend the dinner last night, or we can meet at Scotland Yard to discuss it."

Mr. Hayes appealed to the chief coroner with an imploring look. But like Jasper, Sir Eamon only waited for the man's answer.

With a huff, he finally said, "My wife was feeling ill last evening. That is why we did not attend. Is that an adequate response for you, Inspector Reid?"

"It is," Jasper answered with a false grin. "Thank you. I can turn my questions now to the chief coroner."

He scoured Jasper with another look of loathing, then said a terse "Good day" to Sir Eamon, shutting the door forcefully behind him.

"Well, Reid, I would say you've made yourself an enemy," Sir Eamon commented as he walked back toward his desk. He sounded amused rather than upset.

"A daily occurrence, I'm afraid," Jasper replied, and it earned him a chuckle. He wouldn't share why Stanley Hayes had been predisposed to disliking him. "When was Mr. Hayes involved with the orphanage?"

"I'm rather new to the Board. Been on it five years now. But I believe Stanley was one of the original governors when the orphanage opened. At first, it was just a fund, with charity being divvied out to officers' widows, but the governors soon realized an orphanage would alleviate the widows' financial worries more effectively."

By taking on the day-to-day care and expense of keeping the children fed and healthy, Jasper presumed.

"What questions do you have for me?" he asked as he snuffed out his cigar. He seemed direct and efficient, and Jasper was glad for it.

"I observed you in a tense discussion with the victim, Martha Seabright, before dinner," he replied.

The chief coroner sighed, as though he'd known the question would come up. "Yes. I rather think several people witnessed that conversation."

"About what were the two of you speaking?"

Sir Eamon pulled out the wheeled leather chair at his desk and sat. He leaned back and raised his hands in a gesture of puzzlement. "Honestly? I'm not sure. Mrs. Seabright tried to take me aside a few times during the gathering before dinner, but as you can understand, as host, I needed to welcome guests to our home and circulate."

Jasper could understand it, though not by experience. He couldn't think of anything more repellant than hosting a dinner for thirty or more people in his home. His address on Charles Street would have accommodated the numbers, but the place wasn't nearly fashionable enough inside to host the sort of people the chief coroner had invited.

Jasper's father had bequeathed him the home, which was far too large and in too well-heeled a neighborhood to keep up easily on a detective inspector's wages. He'd come to a hard decision recently: He would have to sell his father's house. How Gregory Reid had managed it all these years still baffled him. It wasn't something he and Jasper had ever discussed, and though Jasper had questioned it, he'd never asked his father directly. When his father had fallen terminally ill, the upkeep of the house was the last thing on Jasper's mind.

"How did Mrs. Seabright seem to you?" he asked after

pushing away the drop of his stomach; it happened whenever he thought of leaving 23 Charles Street.

"Distressed," Sir Eamon answered. Then, more thoughtfully, he said, "Panicked, I would say. When she finally did waylay me, she asked the oddest question. She wanted to know if a certain nurse was still employed at the orphanage."

"Which nurse was she curious about?"

Sir Eamon, still frowning at the memory, replied, "A Nurse Radcliff. I answered that yes, she still worked at the orphanage, but Mrs. Seabright didn't say why she wished to know. She simply…stormed off."

There was no obvious reason why Mrs. Seabright's question should have lifted the small hairs on Jasper's arms, however, they stood on end. It was instinct, and it was how he knew this detail was important to the case.

"Do you know of any problem Mrs. Seabright had with this nurse back when her children were placed at the orphanage?" Jasper asked. That had been thirteen years ago. The Seabright children were grown now, presumably.

Sir Eamon sat forward in his chair and propped his forearms on the desk. He clasped his hands in a tight grip. "I read Mrs. Seabright's file the last time I was in Twickenham, after the Board decided to highlight some of the first beneficiaries of the fund." He squeezed his grip, the tension whitening his knuckles. "There were a few things that stood out to me. The youngest child, a little boy about four months of age, died of a fever shortly after arriving. I wouldn't have brought that up in my speech, of course, but…these things happened on occasion."

"She had three children placed at the orphanage,"

Jasper said, recalling the constables' report. "Tell me about the other two."

Sir Eamon loosened his clasped hands now. "A boy, Gavin, aged eleven, and a girl, Paula, the eldest at age fourteen."

"Isn't fourteen a little old to be admitted to an orphanage?" Jasper asked. There were plenty of girls and boys that age working in factories or in service, helping their families to make a living.

"It isn't usual, no. But back then, the orphanage cared for fewer children, and the space was available. Not so anymore. Even after expanding the orphanage to another building nearby, there are more eligible children than there is space."

"What happens to the children you can't take in?" It wasn't necessarily tied to the investigation, but Jasper was curious.

"The fund pays an annuity to the mother every year to assist her in caring for the children at home. It isn't ideal," he said with a shake of his head. "But it is better than nothing."

Gavin Seabright had been invited to the dinner, but when Jasper asked the chief coroner if he'd been in attendance, the answer was no.

"Mrs. Seabright arrived alone. She said her son was indisposed for the evening." The wry twitch of Sir Eamon's eyebrow caught Jasper's interest.

"Do you know Gavin Seabright?" he asked.

"Only what I read of him in the file. A runaway case. Numerous times over the five years he was there, he would disappear. He'd always be brought back by some farmer or shopkeeper after they caught him stealing something." His mouth turned down at the corners as he recalled additional details of the boy's file. "Notes about his behavior were troubling, especially one story about the groundskeeper's dog."

That sounded ominous. "What happened?"

"He killed it. A lethal dose of chloral hydrate, a sleeping sedative. Gavin claimed it was an accident, that he had mixed too much of the powder into the dog's food. He was trying to slip past the dog, so he could run away again."

Jasper took that in with another prickle of interest. So, Gavin had not wanted to be at the orphanage. He might have held some contempt for his mother over it. And last night, he had decided not to attend the dinner.

"And the daughter, Paula?" Jasper asked. "How did she fare?"

"Oh, I think she did rather well. She was only there for two years, then left, went to live with an aunt, and is now married to a successful businessman. Mr. Archibald Blickson, of Blickson Estate Insurance."

Jasper hadn't ever heard of it or him but was curious. "She went to live with an aunt? Not her mother?"

"That is what her file said. And from what I heard, Mrs. Seabright and her sister were not on speaking terms."

Curious. Jasper turned away from the chief coroner toward the window. Outside, a haze of humidity hung in the air, though the stone walls of the Law Courts kept it cool inside the office.

"I would like all the addresses you have on file for the Seabrights, including the aunt," Jasper said.

Sir Eamon assented and, after calling in his secretary, asked that the addresses to be collected for the inspector.

"Where are you going with this, Inspector Reid?" he asked after his secretary left to see to the task. "The men who invaded my home last night can't have had anything to do with Martha Seabright. They were there to steal valuables. The man leading them lost control and shot her. Surely that is all there was to it?"

"Nothing about the leader's actions seemed out of control to me," Jasper replied.

On the contrary, he'd been collected. Focused. And Leo had observed that the other men seemed taken aback by their leader's unscripted use of violence.

Abruptly, more of the fog plaguing him since Leo's abduction cleared. With belated clarity, Jasper realized something he should have already noted: The leader could have just as easily selected Leo to shoot in the head. He'd gone straight to Martha Seabright instead. Because she was old? Less valuable than a younger woman, perhaps, if one wanted to be callous about it. Or had he had another reason for choosing Martha?

The chief coroner's secretary returned with the list of addresses and handed it to Jasper.

"Thank you for your time, Sir Eamon. I'll be in touch," he said, then started away. There were four addresses on the list. The one closest to the Law Courts was also the one he most wanted to visit. It was time to meet Gavin Seabright.

Chapter Six

Leo stormed out of the detective department at Scotland Yard, and an instant tug of regret beleaguered her. It added weight to her heels, slowing her. She'd overreacted to Jasper's suggestion that she take the day off, and though she wanted to blame her snap of temper on exhaustion, that wasn't it entirely.

It was embarrassment.

Leo had already spent an hour that morning at the morgue, typing her witness statement, her eyes drifting to the postmortem room door time and again. The body of Martha Seabright had been delivered overnight, admitted by the night attendant, Mr. Sampson. Leo had never avoided a corpse before. And yet, earlier that morning upon her arrival, she hadn't been able to bring herself to enter the darkened postmortem room.

The presence of dead bodies didn't affect Leo; they didn't turn her stomach, and she wasn't afraid of them as so many others were. Her friend, Dita Brooks, could not even bear to set foot in the Spring Street Morgue. Yet, picturing Martha Seabright on an autopsy table had put a new, strange chill in Leo's bones.

She shouldn't have snapped at Jasper. He hadn't meant to suggest she was unfit for work; he just knew that Mrs. Seabright's body would be a visual reminder of what very well could have happened to *her*.

The night had shaken her. And Leo did not like feeling shaken, but she took small comfort in knowing that Connor soon would be arriving at the morgue.

She took several deep breaths as she approached the packed-dirt lane to the old vestry, where the door to the back office was located. During the summer, she would keep the door propped open to help clear the unpleasant odors that built up as the heat of the day intensified. However, she'd done no such thing earlier that morning when she'd been working in the office, and she had certainly closed the door and locked it on her way out, before going to Scotland Yard.

Now, she saw that the back door was open a scant inch.

She approached slowly, a prickle of awareness darting along her arms and up her neck. It was possible Connor had arrived a few minutes early and had not fully closed the door behind him, though he generally entered the morgue through the front lobby. As Leo opened the door more fully and listened from the threshold, she heard no sounds of movement.

"Hello?" she called, finally stepping inside the building. No reply came. Instinctively, she knew that other than the corpses, she was alone.

Her eyes went to the postmortem room door. It was wide open. Leo hesitated. This wasn't the first time she'd entered the morgue after finding that the lock to the back door had been picked. In January, she'd come in late at night while a man, Mr. Samuel Barrett, had been hiding a box of photographs being used in a blackmailing scheme in the crypt below the morgue. She hadn't known who it was at the time but had glimpsed the figure of a man running off into the burial ground behind the church.

There was still a chill in the air in the back office. It would be gone within the hour, once the morning sun slid through the stained glass windows in the postmortem room. The fetid odor of rot and waste would then begin to mount. Right now, though, Leo only inhaled perfume. Sharp, pungent traces of grassy neroli and sweet bergamot, enough to make her eyes nearly water. Someone had been doused in the stuff, and for the scent to still be so strong, they had not left the morgue long ago.

The scent lingered in the postmortem room too, and when she entered, her eyes went straight to Mrs. Seabright's body. She was still fully clothed and, as such, did not need a sheet to cover her. Mr. Sampson had never broken protocol before to touch a body, so the fact that the woman's right arm had been raised and draped over her chest was startling. Leo's eyes hitched on the positioning as she neared the body, her footsteps echoing off the arched beamed ceiling. The placement of the arm reminded Leo of the way she'd rested the Inspector's hand on his chest the morning he'd died. Leo had sat beside his bed, lacing her fingers through his for a few minutes while saying her goodbyes. Then, she'd placed it on his chest, just like how Mrs. Seabright's hand was positioned now.

She had only seen the woman briefly in life, and Mrs.

Seabright had not wished to exchange pleasantries when they were seated next to each other. However, Leo recalled her chapped hands as they unfolded the fine linen napkin and placed it on her lap—over the handbag she had kept with her rather than stored in the coatroom as other ladies had done with theirs. Her hand now placed palm-down on her chest, appeared work-worn, the nails short and rough.

Someone had come into the morgue, lifted her right hand, and arranged it in this reverent, almost prayerful position.

No longer hesitant, Leo turned on the gasoliers overhead. Part of her job was to catalogue a corpse's possessions, and if she hadn't been a fearful goose earlier that morning, she would have done it—*before* the body had been tampered with. What if the intruder had taken something of importance from Mrs. Seabright?

The body was still adorned in the outdated black, beaded gown she'd had on the previous evening. Looking more closely now, the seams along the shoulders were frayed—evidence that it was either a secondhand gown or that she had worn it many times over the years. Walking around the table, Leo noted the soles of the woman's shoes were scuffed, and she'd taken care to daub blacking on the worn uppers. The handbag she'd kept with her, even at the dinner table, was also present, tucked between her torso and her left arm. It was made of blue silk, and when Leo opened it, she found inside two shillings, a key on a length of ribbon, and a yellowed envelope, which had been split open by a penknife. The person drenched in perfume had not been a thief. Had they been, they would not have left without the handbag, or at least the money inside.

From the envelope, which was addressed to Mrs. Seabright at 19 Well Street, St. Giles, she retrieved a piece of folded notepaper. The crease was well established, and like the envelope, the paper had yellowed with age. Unfolding it, Leo read a few lines of handwriting:

May 14, 1871

Dear Mrs. Seabright,

Enclosed is the agreed upon sum. This concludes our business.

You have done the right thing.

- N. C. R.

The lack of a postmark on the envelope hinted that it had been delivered by private messenger. Though there was nothing to indicate who N. C. R. was, the handwriting was slanted and practiced, a sign that the sender had been well-educated.

So, Mrs. Seabright had accepted an amount of money for a decision she'd made thirteen years ago. A business decision? There was nothing else in the envelope to provide more clues, certainly no money. Why would she have brought this missive to the benefit dinner? And might it have to do with the terse words she'd exchanged with Sir Eamon?

The familiar sounds of the lobby's front doors being unlocked interrupted her musing. Connor came in through the postmortem room door a moment later and pulled up short when he saw her.

"Thank heaven, Miss Spencer." He exhaled a gust of air. "A constable knocked on my door at six o'clock this morning with a message that you'd been found, but he wouldn't say anything more." He came toward her, shrugging out of his light summer jacket. "Are you injured? How did you escape?"

He stopped when he saw Mrs. Seabright's body on the table and gave a forlorn shake of his head.

"I'll tell you everything while we work," Leo said. A sense of normalcy returned to her as she put the letter back into the handbag and went to fetch paper and pencil.

Together, they prepared the body for the postmortem examination. It had taken Connor some time to adjust to undressing bodies with a woman standing at his side. He'd flushed fiercely at first and still did if they made eye contact during the process, but he was coming around to the truth of the matter: Leo's professionalism was unflinching when it came to this sort of thing.

It was one of the reasons why he wanted her to be hired as the official morgue clerk. According to Connor, too many of his fellow medical students at university had been indolent or pompous or only there because they were following a well-trodden path that their fathers and grandfathers had taken before them. Connor could have become a physician and opened a practice, but after watching a surgeon perform an autopsy, he claimed to have become fascinated with the secrets a body could whisper after death.

As Leo had come to know him better over the last handful of weeks, she'd faced the fact that he would be replacing her uncle at the morgue. So had Claude. And they both agreed that the chief coroner's pick could have been much worse.

"How did Mr. Feldman handle the news about last

night?" Connor asked once the naked corpse was covered by a sheet. "He must have been worried."

"I'm grateful he was unaware of everything until after I'd been found," she answered. Her uncle would be turning seventy next month, and though his health seemed otherwise top rate, the tremors that plagued his hands worried her.

After arriving home near dawn and changing into dry, warm clothes, Leo had sat near the kitchen stove with a pot of tea while telling her uncle everything. He'd been horrified, to say the least, but in his usual patient manner, he'd let her tell the whole story before asking questions. One of those questions had flummoxed Leo completely: "Why that woman?"

She hadn't known how to answer that. Initially, she'd assumed the man had randomly chosen someone to sacrifice so that his orders would be taken seriously. But seated at the kitchen table with her uncle, safe and warm, Leo was able to look back on the moment with more clarity. The killer had taken three or four strides to stand directly behind Mrs. Seabright's chair. Why hadn't he selected the middle-aged man with muttonchops and a pair of gold spectacles who'd been seated at the table right in front of him?

Perhaps he had wanted to persuade them all by showing his willingness to kill an unarmed, helpless woman.

So then, why had he overlooked the woman with a peacock plume spearing her upswept hair who was seated next to the man with the gold spectacles? Leo could see them all in her mind; each guest seated at the table, their neighbors, their clothing. And that woman would have made a closer target. So would have Leo.

"My grandfather was speaking to the poor woman before dinner," Connor commented as he pulled on his surgical coat.

"I noticed," Leo replied. "Did you happen to overhear any of their conversation?"

It was a prying question and perhaps a little strange. A twist of Connor's mouth seemed to say as much. But he then shook his head. "No, I'm sorry. Why do you ask?"

She shrugged off his inquiry. "No reason. Just curious."

Connor stepped into a pair of tall, vulcanized rubber boots. "It was the detective inspector who found you?"

"In a manner of speaking." She didn't want to get into too much detail about how she'd spent the night in the Battersea police station. Or that she'd confessed to a non-existent murder.

"He was in high dudgeon after you were taken," Connor said, going next to his tool kit. A full postmortem was required, even though the woman's cause of death was apparent—and had been witnessed by them both. "He wasn't in a much better mood before that, however, when we first saw him in the front parlor."

Jasper had appeared strained, Leo recalled. But likely so had she. She'd waited too long to speak to him about their kiss and her decision to either forgive him and move forward…or not to. She hadn't yet made her decision, even a month later.

"I could be wrong, but I think Inspector Reid is under the impression that I took you to last night's benefit dinner with romantic aspirations," Connor said, an amused grin cinching the corner of his mouth. "And he didn't like it one bit."

Leo met his mischievous look and tried not to grin. She'd perceived that too. It had irritated her as much as it had given her a little thrill to see Jasper wrestle with unexpected jealousy. She had no right to indulge in such a feeling though, when she was guilty of indecision.

"I think that might just be his usual demeanor," Leo said lightly, brushing off the comment. She didn't wish to discuss Jasper with the coroner, even if she was starting to consider Connor a friend. But then, she considered something. "You *don't* have romantic aspirations toward me, do you?"

She'd certainly never sensed them, if so.

Connor laughed as he opened his kit and selected a scalpel. "Miss Spencer, I like you very much, but no, my feelings toward you are strictly professional."

It was what she'd thought, and it was a relief. "As are mine toward you," she replied. "Now that we've cleared that up, I think you should know something."

Connor drew back the sheet, exposing the corpse beneath. "Yes?"

"Someone broke into the morgue this morning."

He released the sheet and lowered the scalpel. "What? Are you sure? Has anything been taken?"

"I don't think it was a thief." She told him about the back door being ajar, the strong scent of perfume left behind, and the positioning of Martha Seabright's hand upon her chest.

"I noticed that before we undressed her," Connor said.

"Her handbag still has two shillings inside, so whoever

it was took her hand, placed it on her chest, but did not rummage through her things," Leo explained.

"A loved one, maybe?" he suggested. "Though, breaking into the morgue makes little sense. Why not wait for someone to arrive here this morning and ask to see her body?"

Leo didn't have an answer. As they quietly began the postmortem examination, they stayed in their own thoughts about the break-in. However, their focus soon became directed toward the corpse. With her pencil and paper, Leo documented his findings, though she did stand further away from the table than usual. Not once in the five years of assisting her uncle had she grown queasy during a postmortem. However now, her exhaustion, coupled with an empty stomach, worked against her.

Connor cited the obvious cause of death—a single bullet discharged into the brain, entering through the left parietal bone. He also found evidence of heart disease and cancer of the lung, both of which, given time to progress, would have eventually killed her. More interesting, however, were some markings on Martha Seabright's bare skin: circular scars scattered across her chest and arms, and even on her thighs.

A suspicion sank through Leo. "The shape of these scars... Are you thinking what I am?"

Connor sighed. "Unfortunately, I believe so. The burning tip of a cigar, left against the skin for any length of time, would certainly leave such marks."

This wasn't the first time Leo had seen burn marks upon a corpse's skin. Scores of women and children had lain on the morgue's tables with similar scars. Their abusers often kept the evidence of their cruelty hidden from sight: on the torsos, arms, and legs of their victims.

"They all look to be pale and smooth," she said. "So, they're old scars."

"By a decade, at least," Connor confirmed.

The parallel lines of scarring on the palm of Leo's right hand were also white with age, and though they were still raised, the two weals had started to smooth over, as most scars did over time. Her memory brought forward the scar on Jasper's left pectoral chest wall, inflicted by the same shard of porcelain that had cut Leo's palm. His scar hadn't healed as well as hers probably because he hadn't tended to it as carefully as the Inspector and Mrs. Zhao had done for Leo's. He'd hidden it under his shirt, knowing that it marked him as the boy whom Leo had stabbed in the attic.

Although she'd come to terms with the truth of his identity, and it no longer felt as massive a betrayal as it had at first, pangs of sadness still stroked through her chest when she thought of Jasper's deepest secret. One question that continued to nag at her was if he would have ever come forward with the truth if she had not discovered it on her own. Would he have drawn her close and kissed her, if she'd still been living in ignorance about the boy who had saved her from certain death that night?

The question was one of many that had held her back from seeking out Jasper since the night in his study.

Leo jotted down the number of burn scars, their placement on the corpse's body, and their exact measurements as once again, her mind returned to the few moments she had been in Jasper's arms four weeks ago. Even though Jasper had escaped the Carters, had renounced them, it didn't change the fact that his blood relations had murdered her family. Kissing Jasper had felt incontestably right, and yet, the smallest sliver of betrayal had lodged under her skin afterward. A sliver that had continued to grow since that night.

What would her parents think of her? Her brother and little sister?

Right then, the bell in the morgue lobby pealed, distracting Leo from her dismal, guilty thoughts.

"I'll see who it is," she said, hoping it would be someone to do with Mrs. Seabright. Her body would need to be formally identified and claimed, and perhaps her family would have some idea about who had come to pay her body an early morning visit.

As Leo approached the door to the lobby, it opened. Stephen Warnock of Scotland Yard peered into the post-mortem room, then pulled to a stop, hesitant to enter any further. She looked past him, expecting Jasper to enter next. But the officer was alone.

"Constable," she said, unable to mask her surprise. "How can we help you?"

Belatedly, he doffed his hat. "It's detective sergeant now, miss. I've passed my examinations and had a promotion," he corrected, his pride shining through.

"Congratulations, Sergeant Warnock. It's well deserved, I'm sure."

She wasn't truly certain, but it seemed an encouraging thing to say. Besides, Warnock had never been rude toward her, as some of the others at the Yard had been.

"I've had a message from Inspector Reid. He's asked me to meet him in St. Bride, and I'm to bring you with me."

That sounded serious. She crossed a look with Connor, who had started to place closing sutures, before turning back to the sergeant. "Why? What has happened?"

"He's found a body," he answered. "And he wants you to have a look at it."

Chapter Seven

All Jasper knew so far was that the man lying dead inside Gavin Seabright's rented room was not the tenant himself.

He had arrived at the address on Dorset Street shortly after leaving the Law Courts. It was a Friday morning, close to noon, and if Gavin Seabright held down a job, he was more likely to be found at work than at home. However, after scrutinizing the Metropolitan Police warrant card Jasper displayed while introducing himself, the landlady, Mrs. Beardsley, reported that Mr. Seabright had returned home from work a few hours before.

"Is that unusual?" Jasper asked once he'd been allowed across the threshold to stand in the narrow foyer. "Or does he often return in the middle of a workday?"

With a huff of contempt, Mrs. Beardsley replied, "What do you think I do, Inspector? Prop a chair here and watch the door all day long, then? I got myself ten lodgers to see to and plenty to do without keepin' tabs on who comes and goes."

With a weary groan, muttering that these were respectable lodgings and the police showing up wasn't good for business, she'd gone upstairs to alert Mr. Seabright to his guest. From the bottom step, Jasper heard several knocks, and Mrs. Beardsley's raised voice, telling her lodger twice that he was to come downstairs to talk to a Scotland Yard inspector. A few seconds of silence followed her last summons. Then came her shout: "Inspector!"

Jasper took the stairs two at a time to find the landlady staring into the room. "I tried the knob," she told him. "It weren't locked."

By her awestruck expression, he wasn't surprised to find a body lying upon the floor inside the room.

Mrs. Beardsley propped her work-chapped hands on her hips and, with a crinkle of her brow, announced, "Haven't the faintest who he is. It ain't Mr. Seabright, that's fer certain. But this bloke were here, callin' on me lodger just before breakfast. I don't like mornin' callers. It ain't polite."

The dead man was roughly twenty-five years of age and appeared to have suffered a head wound; his temple had an acute depression, and a fair amount of blood had pooled around his head on the underlying carpet. He'd come to lie next to a small coal stove, which would have heated the room during the colder months. The finial on top of the stove was a short iron spike, and there were traces of blood on it.

With evidence of a struggle—the shaving stand had been knocked over as well as a chair—Jasper thought the most likely scenario was that the victim, whoever he was, had fallen during a fight and struck his temple on the sharp finial, receiving a killing blow.

Now, nearly an hour later, Jasper stood by the window, impatient for Warnock and Leo to arrive. He'd finished interviewing the landlady and had searched the small room, leaving him time to second-guess his decision to summon Leo. Doing so went against Chief Inspector Coughlan's express order to limit her involvement and Jasper's own desire to shield her from any more distress. But in this investigation, there was no time to lose. There was no question, especially after Jasper had taken a closer look at the victim, that Leo could provide insight about the body.

At the sound of their arrival downstairs, Jasper went to meet them. Mrs. Beardsley led them up to the room and took the opportunity to complain.

"You'll need to be takin' him out the back door, Inspector. I can't have a dead body carted through the front, right, where everybody and their cousin'll see it."

"Yes, of course, Mrs. Beardsley," he replied. "I might have more questions for you, if you can remain close by."

The request was met with another aggravated moan, but she didn't object. Jasper suspected a part of her was enjoying the unusual calamity, as it would give her plenty to carp about for some time to come.

Leo quizzed him with a look as he moved aside to allow her and Warnock to pass into the room.

"Sergeant Warnock tells me you believe I know this man," she said, going directly to the body and squatting at his feet.

Her dark green dress was the somber, serviceable kind she wore to work, and as she assessed the body on the floor, she did so with the same concentration she would have shown any corpse at the morgue.

"Maybe not his name," Jasper replied, crouching beside her. He lifted the man's left hand. "But what about this?"

Leo inhaled sharply when her eyes landed on the long, curved scar on the man's hand. As he'd hoped, she recognized it. Jasper had noticed the scar while going through the man's pockets, searching for any identifying documents. He'd had none. But the scar had captured his attention.

"What is it?" Warnock asked, craning his neck. He stood further away, near the window, and wore the queasy look of someone unaccustomed to dead bodies. He would get used to it in time.

"This man," Leo replied, moving to the side of the body opposite Jasper. "He was one of the intruders from last night. I recognize the scar on his hand."

She'd included a description of it in her statement. The scar, shaped like a C, ran from the knuckle on the man's ring finger to the thumb.

"Are you sure?" Warnock asked. "Lots of men have scars on their hands, especially if they're laborers."

"She is sure," Jasper replied, unwilling to explain to the newly promoted detective sergeant about Leo's flawless memory. She, too, didn't like to draw attention to it. "This room is rented by Gavin Seabright," he went on, straightening to his feet. "But this isn't Gavin. The body has no identification, and the landlady doesn't know who he is either. She says he called on Gavin this morning around seven o'clock."

Leo canted her head as she inspected the wound at the man's temple, then peeled off her glove to touch his neck.

"His body temperature is cool but not dramatically so." Using her fingertips, she opened one of the man's eyes wider. "Clouding of the cornea and rigor just setting in around the facial muscles. I'd estimate he's been dead three or four hours."

That would mean he died around eight or nine o'clock that morning.

Jasper called for Mrs. Beardsley. She whirled into the room as though she'd been waiting just outside the door, listening.

"Were you at home this morning?"

She crossed her arms and gave him a look of blamelessness. "I were here some. But I didn't hear this racket, and I surely would've." She gestured toward the upended shaving stand, the smashed pitcher and basin on the floor, and the overturned chair.

"When did you leave the house?" he asked.

Her eyes narrowed in thought. "'Round half seven I set out for the Farringdon Market. I got me six lodgers who pay extra for chop with their tea, and Mondays are the best days for mutton. Must get there early for it. I were back by nine."

"And when did Mr. Seabright return?" Jasper asked.

"Quarter past ten, I'd say."

"You actually saw him? Didn't just hear him come in?"

She sighed and nodded.

Leo moved toward the mess on the floor, crouching down to sift through some of the detritus. "Did you see either Mr. Seabright or this man leave the house before you set out for the market stalls?"

The landlady gave her a curious once-over, as if wondering who Leo was and why she was there. But rather than question her or give some longwinded answer, Mrs. Beardsley gave a pleasantly succinct one: "No."

"Mr. Seabright must've left at some point though, if you saw him come back in just after ten," Warnock said to Mrs. Beardsley. "Where does he work?"

"Last I knew, he were a caretaker at St. Bartholomew's."

Jasper nodded to the detective sergeant. "Go to the hospital and see if he was there at all this morning."

"He wasn't," Leo said, stopping Warnock before he could take a stride toward the door. She was still near the floor and had picked up a brown cologne bottle made of thick glass. She had pulled out the stopper and put her nose to the opening.

"Why do you say that?" Jasper asked.

"Because I believe he broke into the morgue this morning to visit his mother."

The revelation sent a charge down his spine. "*What?*"

Leo stood and extended the bottle. With the stopper free, the strong odor was detectable from an arm's length away. "When I returned from seeing you at Scotland Yard this morning, this same scent saturated the air inside the morgue. The lock on the back door had been picked, and Mrs. Seabright's hand had been placed on her chest."

Jasper grumbled under his breath. That was the second time since January someone had picked the morgue's lock. He was beginning to think he should add the dirt path behind the church vestry to a constable's regular circuit.

Standing at the entrance to the room, Mrs. Beardsley

waved a hand in front of her face. "Oh, aye, that's his scent. Pours the stuff on."

Those who didn't bathe regularly tended to daub perfume on themselves to cover up the odors from not washing. At lodging houses like this one, laundry services cost extra, as did bath water. When Jasper lived in bachelor's rooms on Glasshouse Street prior to moving back to Charles Street, a few of his more frugal fellow lodgers had done the same.

"Thank you, Mrs. Beardsley," Jasper said, then ushered her back into the hallway and closed the door to the room.

"Gavin Seabright would have been at the morgue right around eight o'clock," Leo said.

Jasper took the bottle from her and corked it, his nose crinkling in distaste. "All right, then. This morning, one of the men responsible for Martha Seabright's murder shows up here at her son's lodgings."

"In the carriage, this man," Leo said, indicating the body on the floor, "was hushed up by the leader when he started to question the killing. It wasn't part of the plan, and he was clearly upset by it."

Upset enough to seek out the victim's son?

"Mrs. Seabright's identity hasn't yet been printed in any newspapers. There is no chance this man would have known how to track down her son this morning unless," Jasper said, his mind assembling a patent certainty, "they already knew each other."

After speaking to Sir Eamon and learning about Gavin Seabright's questionable character while at the orphanage, Jasper wouldn't have put it past him to have known about the robbery at the benefit dinner. It might even be why he decided not to attend.

"Which means Mrs. Seabright may not have been a random victim," Leo said, her expression lighting with familiar curiosity. "It was the very thing I was considering this morning. The leader of the masked men took several strides toward her when he could have selected anyone closer. Including me."

The comment touched off a smoldering wick inside Jasper's chest. He didn't need to hear a reminder of how close she'd been to death yet again, or how he would not have been able to prevent it.

"Could the leader have been Gavin Seabright then?" Warnock asked.

"If so, he certainly wasn't wearing that scent last night," Leo replied, indicating the bottle Jasper had placed on a shelf.

"Gavin was here, according to Mrs. Beardsley," he said. "She locks the door promptly at eleven, whether her lodgers are in or not. Gavin ate with the others and retired to his room afterward."

His alibi for last night was secure; however, that didn't mean he hadn't been aware of the planned robbery. He very well may have been waiting for word of how the break-in went, and when he heard of his mother's murder, he could have gone to the morgue to be certain it was true. Had the landlady heard a brawl after Gavin's return to his lodgings at a quarter past ten, Jasper would assume he flew into a rage and killed this unidentified man. But as she reported not hearing anything amiss, Jasper was more apt to believe his death occurred while both Mrs. Beardsley and Gavin were out. Someone else had come to this house during that time.

Jasper explained his thinking to Leo and Warnock.

"Another one of the masked men? Perhaps their leader?" Leo supposed.

"Warnock, speak to the neighbors. Ask if they saw anyone arriving or leaving between eight and ten o'clock this morning," Jasper said, then also instructed him to arrange for a cart to transport the body to the morgue. The detective sergeant left with more enthusiasm than the tasks warranted, likely relieved to get away from the dead body.

Jasper crossed his arms, peering down at it. "This man will lead us to the others. We just need to find out who he is."

"Gavin Seabright may also be able to do that," Leo said, then called for Mrs. Beardsley. Again, the landlady appeared in a blink.

"I got things to be gettin' on with," she complained. "What now?"

"Has Mr. Seabright had any visitors lately? Anyone you would see regularly?"

Jasper held his tongue against reminding Leo whose investigation this was and who should be asking the questions. It was already too late. Once she had that gleam of determination in her eyes, there was no going back. It was as frustrating as it was endearing.

"He kept to himself mostly," Mrs. Beardsley answered. "Though, he did step out with some bird not too long ago."

"A woman?" Jasper asked. "Do you know who she was?"

The landlady shook her head. "But it were backward. *She* fetched *him* in a hired hansom and dropped him off again a short while later."

"Did you see her?" Leo asked.

Mrs. Beardsley lifted her shoulder. "I were at the window when she dropped him off. Seen her then, sittin' in the cab. Pretty and young. Dark hair. Dressed too fine for the likes of him. Now, right, I got rooms need doin'. Is that all?"

"Thank you, Mrs. Beardsley," Leo said, and the woman departed with haste. Leo then turned to Jasper, her chin raised, her hands clasped behind her back.

"You're about to ask for something," he said.

She affected a look of injury. "I was merely going to offer my time looking through prisoner albums, searching for our John Doe here."

"Out of the question," he replied.

"But you summoned me—"

"To give a positive identification," he cut in. "I need to move swiftly, and I don't dispute that you can assist, but not at the Yard."

"Detective Chief Inspector Coughlan's orders, I take it." Her lips pursed with indignation. Jasper's attention lingered on them an extra moment before confirming with a nod.

"Very well." Leo pushed down her shoulders and started for the exit. "I'll return to the morgue to await the body."

She was unhappy, certainly, though for once, her displeasure didn't feel directed toward him. Letting her go was for the best. She should return to Spring Street and to Connor Quinn, where they would work together just as efficiently and as affably as she used to work with Claude.

Christ, he loathed the idea of it.

"Esther Goodwin."

The name was off his tongue before he knew what he was doing. Regret instantly followed. Leo paused at the threshold, her dark sable brows pinching together.

"Who is Esther Goodwin?" she asked.

He fell mute for a moment. What the bloody hell was he thinking? He'd only known he wanted to stop her. Keep her from going back to Quinn.

It was too late to reverse course now.

"Martha Seabright's sister. Gavin's aunt, though from what Sir Eamon said, he and Martha hadn't been on speaking terms with Esther for some time. She lives on Gray's Inn Road, at Gunnerson's Rest Home."

Leo squinted at him. "Why are you telling me about her?"

The truth was humiliating, so he reached for another reason—one that wasn't entirely a lie. "I think it would be safe and helpful for you to pay her a visit. She, along with Gavin and Martha's daughter, Paula Blickson, were invited to the dinner, but none of them attended. Initially, Gavin accepted but then changed his mind. I'd like to know why."

It was a rare thing to see Leo truly startled. A softness stole over her brow and released the tension in her jaw. For several seconds, the vulnerability she kept well-hidden shone through. It made him want to reach for her as she gazed at him, circumspect.

"And I'm to inform her that her sister is dead?" she asked.

"You may." The task wouldn't bother Leo. She was more experienced than even he was in telling families the worst of news. "Find out what you can about Martha and her children, and their experience with the orphanage. You should know that one of the children died there. An infant."

Leo's wonderment snapped off, her lashes fluttering as she blinked. "How awful." She then cocked her head. "I don't know if it has anything to do with the death, but I found a letter in Mrs. Seabright's handbag. A letter dated from 1871, giving Mrs. Seabright an agreed-upon sum of money and saying she'd done the right thing. It was only signed N. C. R."

"Nothing more was written?" he asked.

She shook her head. Jasper would see the letter when it arrived at the Yard with Mrs. Seabright's other personal possessions, which would all be logged as evidence. How it could relate to the death of her baby, however, wasn't clear.

"I'll see what Esther Goodwin knows," Leo said and then disappeared into the hall.

He followed. "Remember, Leo, you are going in an unofficial capacity. I don't want anyone at the Yard to learn of it."

He would be skewered, not just by Coughlan but by the superintendent and the police commissioner, should word of it get out.

She'd already reached the stairs and started down. "Right. Good. I'll report back later today."

As she disappeared, Jasper scrubbed a hand through his hair. He'd opened a door that could lead straight to trouble, and he was already sorry for it.

Chapter Eight

Gunnerson's Rest Home was one of many fine homes along Gray's Inn Road. The Georgian style manse, constructed of yellow limestone, had once been the home of the Earl of Gunnerson, according to the plaque next to the front door. Leo glimpsed the brass plate as she stood at the top of the front stoop, reading that the earl had gifted the residence to St. Mary's Hospital to provide a "respectable home for esteemed elders." It was a rare thing to find a home for the infirm that wasn't an almshouse or asylum, which were more akin to workhouses. The elderly, for the most part, were cared for at home and were the responsibility of family. A place like Gunnerson's was not the norm. Nor was it inexpensive.

As Leo brought down the lion's head knocker on the front door, she thought of her aunt, Flora. Over the last year, her aunt's deteriorating mind had stripped her of memories and rational thought. Most of the time, it was as if Flora existed in a world no one else could see, a world filled with people from her past, who were almost all deceased.

Now that he was no longer a city coroner, Claude cared for her each day in their home on Duke Street. The nurse he'd most recently hired and who had been one of the few to tolerate Flora's sometimes wrathful outbursts, Mrs. Boardman, had been relieved of her duties. There was simply no money for it, and there wouldn't be until Chief Coroner Giles agreed to Connor's request and took Leo on as a morgue clerk in an official capacity. Until then, she would be *un*official, just as she was to be here while paying a call on Esther Goodwin, per Jasper's instructions.

While it grated somewhat, she chose instead to focus on the fact that he had asked her to speak to someone connected to the victim. To gather information and report back to him. After feeling unsettled all morning, identifying the body in Gavin Seabright's room as one of the masked men had helped to center her and clear her mind. So, too, had speaking with Jasper, even if it was about the aspects of the case.

She had missed him. It was difficult to put into words the feeling of ease, of frank reassurance, whenever she was with Jasper. Even when they didn't agree, or when he was being obstinate, Leo would rather be squabbling with him than not speaking to him at all. After she'd discovered the truth of who he really was, she'd spent months avoiding him. Months uncertain if she could ever trust him again, or herself. As much as she felt justified to hate him, deep in her soul, she knew she could not.

Leo keenly recalled the mixed emotions of relief and guilt when she and Jasper had, after some time apart, found themselves working together again on one of his cases. After kissing him several weeks ago, those same tangled emotions had overwhelmed her on an even grander scale.

A part of her wanted to pretend their kiss had never happened. Another part of her, however, and perhaps a larger part, would not be satisfied by that.

She needed to knock a second time on the front door to Gunnerson's before someone came to answer. The arrival of a woman in starched uniform lifted Leo's mind from her whirling thoughts.

"May I help you, madam?"

"I hope so. I'd like to pay a call on Mrs. Esther Goodwin," Leo replied.

The woman, who appeared to be a nurse of some sort, narrowed her eyes. "Is she expecting you?"

It was a prudent question, one meant to keep away unwanted solicitors.

"No," Leo answered honestly. "I'm afraid I've some news about her sister. I believe she would want to hear it."

This seemed to give the woman even more suspicion. "Mrs. Goodwin just returned from one of her walks and appears tired, but I will speak to her. What is your name, madam?"

"Miss Leonora Spencer."

"And what is your connection to her sister?"

Leo had expected to be questioned before being allowed in to see Esther. However, she hadn't prepared for this question. The honest answer—*I was seated next to her at a benefit dinner where she was murdered, then assisted in her autopsy*—would likely result in the door being slammed in her face.

She licked her lips and said the next most honest thing: "I am here on behalf of the Metropolitan Police."

It worked, though she well imagined Jasper's scathing glare for ignoring his remark about her being there *un*officially. There was no reason anyone at Scotland Yard should learn of it, however, so as the nurse allowed her into the foyer, Leo set aside the twinge of guilt. She was shown to a nearby chair and asked to wait there, while the nurse went upstairs, presumably to speak to Mrs. Goodwin. Leo sat, taking in the entrance hall, decorated in cool tones of blue and perfumed by bouquets of colorful flowers. Everything was clean, tidy, and serene, though not in any spartan way. Residing here almost certainly came at a dear expense, and she wondered how Martha Seabright's sister had come into her wealth.

The nurse returned in short order and, with a nod, indicated Leo should follow her. Esther Goodwin's rooms were located upstairs at the end of a wide hallway, which had been adorned with thick, blue Aubusson rugs, fine paintings, and more vases of flowers set on pedestal tables. The home must have been large enough for at least a dozen residents, and as she was shown into Esther's room, an unfamiliar tug of envy pulled at her stomach. If only she and Claude could afford for Flora to be in such a place as this… Then again, the residents here might not appreciate Flora's confused and frightened outbursts.

"Thank you, Irene," a woman, whom Leo presumed to be Esther Goodwin, said once she'd turned into a small sitting room. The older woman was seated on a pretty, green settee in front of a wood-burning hearth.

The nurse hesitated a moment before leaving, clearly worried for her charge.

Esther smiled tentatively. "Miss Spencer, I'm told?"

She appeared to be roughly the same age as Martha Seabright, though her dark brown hair had fewer streaks of gray than that of her deceased sister. She seemed relatively young for a rest home; in her early fifties, Leo would guess. But she fit in well with her tasteful surroundings. Her high-necked walking gown was of a current fashion, she wore a touch of rouge on her cheeks, and she held an elegant posture as she gestured for Leo to join her.

"Yes, thank you for seeing me, Mrs. Goodwin. I'm told you've just returned from a walk and may be tired, so I won't take up much of your time."

Leo selected the matching upholstered green chair next to the settee. In her own dark, serviceable dress, she felt pointedly somber in the room. Like a dark spot in a pastel-heavy Impressionistic painting.

"Irene is overly cautious," the woman said. "I'd like to hear the news of my sister. Irene said you're from the police?"

Esther kept her hands clasped in her lap, gripping a linen hankie. Her skin was not calloused or chapped like Martha's had been, though her knuckles were whitened with nervousness. There was nothing visibly infirm about Esther Goodwin, as Leo had presumed there would be when she heard she resided in a rest home.

"I'm afraid I do have sad news," Leo said, then, taking a deep breath, divulged Martha Seabright's fate.

She kept back the more gruesome details of the murder. Just the same, Esther hung her head and cupped her cheek as Leo spoke.

"I'm so sorry, Mrs. Goodwin. I know this can't be easy

to hear." She'd said the phrase countless times in the past, when family and friends of the deceased would arrive at the morgue, full of hope that they'd been given incorrect news.

With her chin still tucked, Esther dabbed the hankie under her eyes. She sniffled and shook her head. "It isn't easy. I think what is worse is that I hadn't spoken to Martha in, oh, seven years? Maybe eight. I've lost track of time."

She straightened up, lifting her head and pushing back her shoulders while drawing in another deep breath. She then settled her composed gaze on Leo. "You say this happened at a benefit dinner?"

"Yes, for the Metropolitan and City Police Orphanage."

Esther blinked and looked away, her brow furrowed. "I was sent an invitation for that dinner."

"You declined, I'm told," Leo said.

She shifted on the cushion. "I did. In fact, I was quite stunned that the governors on the Board planned to celebrate Martha last evening. I don't think they would have if they'd known the truth about her."

The comment sparked interest, and Leo leaned forward. "How do you mean?"

Esther waved a hand, her hankie fluttering. "I shouldn't speak of it, not now. Please, forget I said anything."

That would be impossible, of course. Whatever Esther had been referring to could have been the very sort of thing that might aid Jasper's inquiry.

"Mrs. Goodwin, I should tell you," Leo began, worrying her bottom lip a moment as she considered how much to reveal. "The detectives working on this case suspect your sister may have been targeted. They are looking to understand why."

Esther's dark brown eyes sharpened. In a breathy voice, she asked, "Targeted? How do you mean?"

Leo hesitated to reveal anything more detailed. Instead, she applied a tactic she'd witnessed Jasper employ numerous times: She danced around the question with another one of her own.

"Can you tell me why the two of you fell out?" At the flash of affront on the other woman's face, Leo continued, "I understand it is an intrusive question, but it could help the detectives determine why anyone might wish to harm her."

After a shrewd narrowing of her eyes, Esther asked, "What do you do for the police, Miss Spencer? Are you employed by them?"

The tricky question wasn't one she could evade.

"I…consult, from time to time, on inquiries." Then, before Esther could ask another question, she added, "For this inquiry, I've offered to help gather some information about Mrs. Seabright's family. You said you hadn't spoken to her in about seven years?"

Esther blinked, taking in Leo's answer and considering the tacked-on question. "Yes. We saw each other briefly seven years ago, but it was by chance. Before that, we hadn't been in contact for several more years."

Leo waited in silence, hoping the woman would continue speaking. Being patient worked.

"When we were girls, my sister and I were close. She was different then. Oh, she certainly had a deviousness about her that would infuriate me. Always taking my things and hiding them away in places I never thought to look. I remember her as selfish, but I thought—hoped—she would grow out of it." Esther shook her head as she fiddled with her hankie.

"I couldn't countenance it," she went on. "Handing over her children to an orphanage. What kind of mother would do such a thing?"

"Her husband had been killed," Leo said. "Perhaps she couldn't care for them alone."

Esther scoffed at the suggestion. "Martha would have had plenty of help from others, myself included. My husband and I would have taken the children in, done anything, anything at all to support her. But she would not be swayed. No, my sister wanted to be rid of them, and the orphanage was the answer to her prayers."

She gave a small moan and pressed the square of linen to her nose, obscuring her quivering chin. An uncomfortable moment of quiet stretched on as Leo sorted through what Esther had just revealed. In the scant amount of time she had been in Martha's presence—while she'd been alive, at least—Leo had observed a hardness to her. But to give her children, including an infant, to an orphanage with the eagerness Esther was describing put a cramp in Leo's chest.

"How long were you and your sister close?" she asked.

Esther's flare of temper had cooled, and she nodded morosely. "Until she married. Dan—that was her husband—changed her."

"In what way?"

She sighed heavily. "He was cruel, and it made her small. Scared. She shut me out completely, though she did allow the children to see me from time to time. I appreciated that, at least."

The healed, circular burn scars on Martha's body had undoubtedly been inflicted by the burning end of a cigar. If her husband had abused her, Leo wondered if he'd also harmed their children.

"When Dan was killed, I wasn't sorry," Esther said, speaking tremulously as if the confession embarrassed her. "And I don't believe my sister was sorry, either. I think in her heart, Martha hated him. She hated any piece of him, any reminder."

Looking upon his children every day would have made it impossible for Martha to forget him, Leo imagined. Perhaps her solution had been to rid herself of them, so she could rid herself of him completely.

"What were the children's ages when they were sent to the orphanage?" Leo asked, feeling sorrow for the confusion and pain they must have suffered.

At the thought of the children, a small grin emphasized the round apples of Esther's cheeks. "Paula was the eldest, at fourteen. Her brother, Gavin, was eleven. Oh, he was such a scamp! Not in any devious way. At least, not before his mother sent him away." The grin faltered. "And there was little Edward. Just four months old when Martha shunted him off to that unfeeling place. He was there a month before a fever took him. He was so little. I can't even remember what he looked like."

She touched the creased hankie to her nose again, eyes squeezing shut.

The mention of the baby put Leo in mind of the worn letter in Martha's handbag, dated May 1871.

"When were the children placed in the orphanage?" she asked Esther.

When the woman opened her eyes, they were watery. She'd been fighting tears. "It was in April of 1871."

So then, the infant boy would have died around the time of the letter.

"How did Martha handle the news of Edward's death?" she asked next.

"It still hurts to think about it, if I'm honest. I cried more than she did, I can tell you that. I made the trip down to Twickenham to visit Paula and Gavin, and to lay flowers on the baby's grave. Their mother hadn't come, they told me. My heart broke for them."

The picture Esther had painted of her sister so far was not generous. Leo found herself slipping in her sympathy for Martha Seabright. But, as cruel and selfish as she allegedly had been, she had not deserved to be murdered in cold blood.

"Did Paula or Gavin resent being sent to the orphanage?"

Their rejection of the benefit dinner invitations would indicate they did.

"Oh, yes," Esther answered without hesitation. "As soon as Paula turned sixteen and became too old to remain there, she came directly to me. She wanted nothing to do with her mother."

"And Gavin?"

Here, she bobbed her head to the side. The sunlight coming in through her sitting room's window tapered as clouds thickened in the sky. It cast Esther's face in gray shadows.

"Gavin was torn. Still is, I think, though we've fallen out of touch. He made excuses for his mother's choices, just like Martha did for her husband's abuse. I think

Gavin wanted so much to believe she loved him, but deep inside, he must have known it wasn't true. He and Paula seemed to fall out over her too. It's all so sad. Poor boy."

If he'd been eleven years old when he entered the orphanage, Gavin would now be twenty-four. Much too old to be seen as a boy any longer.

"Did Gavin not come to you then, like Paula did, when he left the orphanage?"

She shook her head tightly, giving the impression of disappointment. "He went straight out into the world, that one."

"Not back to Martha?"

At Esther's deep inhalation, Leo thought she might have pressed too hard with questions. The woman answered succinctly, "He tried. It didn't last."

"Do you know why it didn't?"

Again, Esther adjusted her position on the settee cushion, looking distinctly uncomfortable. "Surely that isn't anything the police need to know."

"I don't wish to seem rude, but in a murder inquiry, it is better to share more than less," Leo urged.

The wrinkles bracketing Esther's chin deepened as she tucked her chin in a show of defiance. Leo waited it out, and the older woman relented.

"Very well. My sister had started to entertain gentlemen friends, if you understand my meaning." She avoided looking directly at Leo as she spoke. "After Gavin returned home and found out, he refused to stay under the same roof with her any longer."

Her meaning was clear enough. Martha Seabright had prostituted herself, and when Gavin learned of it, he'd left.

"I see." Leo imagined such a revelation might have angered him. But that had to have been roughly eight years ago now. "Did he keep in contact with her after that?"

"Here and there, I believe."

What more Leo could ask eluded her. It didn't shock her that Martha would have turned down the path of prostitution, not really. If her surname was still Seabright, that indicated she hadn't remarried. She would have needed to support herself somehow. Leo couldn't fathom such a route for herself. But then, she'd always had Claude and Flora for support. She'd had the Inspector too. And of course, Jasper.

In the fall of silence, she turned to peer around the room. The fireplace mantel held a few framed photographs; one was of a much younger Esther and a man who was not her equal in looks but had a kind smile. Her husband, perhaps. The two others were of a little boy in a sailor's suit, posed next to a chair, and of a young man seated with his elbow propped on a desk. They appeared to be of the same person; in both photographs, his bright-eyed stare seemed to burrow through the photo paper and challenge Leo.

"That is my son," Esther explained, having followed Leo's gaze to the photographs. "Felix. Handsome, isn't he?"

"Very. Do he and his cousins get on at all?" Leo asked.

"Only with Paula. She's like my daughter now," Esther answered, again cheering visibly. She gestured to the room around them. "All this is thanks to her. My own husband, well…he was a shopkeeper. A good man, but never rich. Paula, however, married a man who could provide."

And he'd apparently provided well for Esther too.

"Blickson, is that right?" Leo asked.

"Archibald Blickson," she said with a proud nod.

He must have been very well off indeed to have afforded her rooms at Gunnerson's Rest Home. Leo wondered if Jasper might permit her to visit Paula next. Right then, however, she was supposed to be gathering more information about Gavin.

"Before I leave you, Mrs. Goodwin, I was hoping you might know where the police could find Gavin to inform him of his mother's death," Leo said, the fib light and hopefully believable.

Esther's expression returned to the shadowed one she wore when speaking about her nephew. "Last I knew, he had lodgings in St. Bride."

"We have the address for those and that of the hospital where he works, but the police couldn't find him this morning. Is there anywhere else he might go?"

The woman looked baffled and lifted her shoulders. "I'm afraid I've no idea. Like I said, I don't see him often."

"So, you wouldn't know if he was seeing a lady friend?" Leo asked, thinking of the woman Mrs. Beardsley had mentioned. The one who'd picked him up in a hired hack.

"I'm sorry, no," Esther replied.

Leo stood from the chair, her legs stiff from having sat so tensely. "Thank you for speaking to me, Mrs. Goodwin."

At the top of the stairs, Irene was waiting to see her out. She followed the nurse to the front door, which was shut practically on her heels once she was out on the stoop.

Leo breathed in the warm, mineral scent of a coming rainstorm. A drop of rain struck the bridge of her nose; the clouds would soon break open. She hurried from the manse toward a cabstand. She'd been away from the morgue all afternoon, and Connor must certainly be wondering what had become of her.

Chapter Nine

Rain drove toward the pavements outside Scotland Yard in sheets and pelted the window of Jasper's office. His coat and bowler hat hung drenched on the stand, a puddle forming on the floor beneath. The storm had caught him outdoors, capping off a wasted trip to Marylebone, where Paula Blickson lived on the edge of Regent's Park. The upscale residence on Park Crescent was the sort that would have rather seen police officers go down to the servant's entrance, and the maid who'd answered his knock on the front door scowled when he'd held up his warrant card. Mr. and Mrs. Blickson were out, he'd been informed, and when she'd shut the door, he'd gritted his teeth at the wasted trip.

Jasper stood at his office window, rubbing his eyes from fatigue and thinking of Leo. She said she'd report back by the end of the day, and she wasn't one to not see something through to completion. He only hoped she would not come here to the Yard. He'd been a fool to give her that assignment. Not because she wasn't capable; he trusted her more than most of the detectives in the CID to gather information and to ask the questions that needed asking.

However, each time he remembered uttering the name *Esther Goodwin* to her, he cringed. He hadn't sent her there because he'd wanted her help; it had been a result of his jealousy. A spur-of-the-moment, unthinking, and amateur reaction, meant to stop her from returning to the morgue and working alongside Connor Quinn. Now, Leo would expect to be given more to do. And when Jasper refused, she would be angry and disappointed.

He'd set himself up for the fall.

A set of knuckles rapped on the frame of the open door to his office. He recognized the knock as Roy Lewis's.

"How did things go at Sir Eamon's home?" Jasper asked as he turned.

Rain had plastered the detective sergeant's clothing to him, and Jasper had to hold back a grin at how much he resembled a cat crawling out of a river.

"Aye, it went about the way it looks." Lewis shook off each leg, splattering water on the floor. "Spoke to the footman, Marcus Gibson, like you requested. Pressed him hard, but he swears up and down he didn't know a thing about the armed men who barreled into the house when he opened the door. Got knocked on the head and doesn't remember much after that."

"You think he's telling the truth?"

Lewis nodded, though he didn't look pleased by it. "He's honest. So's the staff. No one knows a thing. But I might have found something with the catering service that was hired."

Jasper perked up, hopeful.

"One of their servers disappeared during the ruckus, after Miss Spencer was taken," Lewis explained. "A man by the name of Philip Green. He was hired on last week. I've got a constable checking on his address."

It could be something, Jasper granted, but it also wouldn't be completely out of the ordinary for the server to have left out of fright. Plenty of the guests had done the same.

He briefed Lewis on the body found in Gavin Seabright's lodgings and how Leo had identified him as one of the masked intruders.

"Gavin's involved then," the detective sergeant said. "And now, he's missing. He's got to be guilty of something."

"We turn our focus to finding him tomorrow," Jasper said, checking the time on his pocket watch. It was nearing six o'clock, and his eyes were burning. Last night's commotion and lack of sleep were catching up with him.

He took down his coat and hat from the stand, along with his umbrella.

"Grab a pint, guv?" Lewis asked.

Jasper paused. The invitation was a first from his detective sergeant. Lewis had a family in St. Andrew, across the river: a wife and two young sons. Most nights, he was eager to get home to them.

Though he was dead on his feet, Jasper heard himself agreeing. They jogged across the street to the Rising Sun pub, where inside, a dozen or more officers were having a few beers after hours. The air was warm and sticky from the rain, and smoky from a peat fire in the hearth. Jasper bought a couple of pints for them and made his way to a pitted table by the window, where he and Lewis sipped their ale. Kept at cellar temperature, the cool ale built a layer of sweat on the glasses.

"You said Miss Spencer was at Gavin's lodgings?" Lewis asked. His attempt to sound casual failed.

"I sent for her, yes," Jasper said.

"She could've identified the man's body at the morgue."

Jasper lowered his mug back onto the ring of condensation on the table. His detective sergeant wasn't wrong. She certainly could have, once he'd had the corpse transported there.

"Waiting might have set me back a few hours. I'm trying to move quickly on this case," he replied. The excuse was paltry, even to his own ears.

"You don't think you're chasing trouble, bringing her in?"

He began to regret accepting Lewis's invitation for a pint.

"I'm not bringing her in, exactly," he answered, though sending her to question Esther Goodwin would be seen that way. "I'm being careful."

Lewis sat back in his chair, his hand still wrapped around his glass. "I'm not against her. She's useful."

Jasper waited for his sergeant to tack on a warning. That Jasper was risking his job, or that Leo wasn't trained as a detective, or some other valid reason to do as Coughlan had insisted—to cease associating with her.

But Lewis stayed quiet.

"I agree," Jasper said warily after a moment. It was on the tip of his tongue to mention that she had gone to see

Martha Seabright's sister. But he didn't want to press his luck.

Lewis sat forward, forearms resting on the table, and lowered his voice. "Coughlan's asked some of the men to keep an eye out. Make sure Miss Spencer's out of the picture. And if she isn't, to report back to him."

The deception shouldn't have been surprising. Jasper had received plenty of warnings from the chief inspector over the last handful of months to keep Leo at arm's length when it came to Scotland Yard investigations. But hearing this felt like a wallop to the gut.

"Which men?"

"That I know of? Wiley and Drake." Lewis took a sip of his beer. "And me."

Jasper stiffened in his seat. He was now glad he hadn't confessed about sending Leo to interview Esther Goodwin. "I see."

"I'm no rat, guv." Lewis's lip curled at the thought. "But we both know Wiley is and that Drake was born without a spine. So be careful. And maybe tell Miss Spencer to be too."

Jasper thanked him with a nod. He appreciated Lewis letting him know he was being spied on. It turned his thoughts to the orange-hatted man who'd been following him the last few weeks and whether he might have anything to do with Coughlan's initiative.

After finishing their pints, he and Lewis parted ways outside the Rising Sun. Jasper popped open his umbrella. It had grown dark with the rainstorm, and the lamplighters were out early to light the gas mantles on the posts. The walk to Charles Street wasn't far, but in the rain and gusting winds, which caught the silk of his umbrella time and again, it felt like twice the distance.

As he reached the bustling convergence of Northumberland Avenue and Charing Cross Road at Trafalgar Square, he considered stopping at the morgue to see if Leo was there. The skittering sensation of beetles crawling over his back stopped him. He was being tailed. Checking over his shoulder, he didn't see the man from that morning, but the poor lighting and busy pavements could have easily obscured him.

If he was correct and someone was following him, Jasper wouldn't lead him to the morgue or to Leo. He kept on, toward Charles Street, and checked behind him again before climbing the steps to his home. Lampposts showed a few people on the pavements, but Jasper's eyes didn't pick out a man in an orange bowler. Clenching his jaw, he opened the front door with his key and let himself in.

At the warming scents of beef and herbs, and the promise of Mrs. Zhao's cooking, his stomach grumbled.

"Mister Jasper," the housekeeper said as she bustled into the front hall. She looked at him aghast as he folded the umbrella and dumped it into the urn next to the door. The muggy air in the Rising Sun hadn't helped to dry him out.

"I know, I know, Mrs. Zhao. I'll change before dinner," he said, starting for the stairs.

"See that you do, but first, Miss Leo is here."

Jasper stopped with his hand on the knob of the newel post. Mrs. Zhao hadn't commented on Leo's absence the last month, but she was an intuitive woman and must have noted something was amiss. She now lifted one of her graying eyebrows, watching for his reaction. He tried to keep his expression impassive as a stirring in the center of his chest—and then lower, in his groin—set him back on his heels.

"In the study?" he asked, hopeful Mrs. Zhao hadn't sensed his jumbled reaction.

She looked to the sitting room entrance. Only then did he notice the room was lit. He frowned.

"Why have you put her in there?"

Mrs. Zhao peered at him as if he'd gone daft. "It was where she wished to wait for you," she answered, then motioned impatiently for him to join his guest.

Jasper went to the half-closed door and pushed it ajar. Several rooms in the house were little used, and the sitting room was one of them. The dated furnishings and decor were kept polished and free of dust, but the room still had a sad, disused air to it. The last time Jasper had been in there, he'd just been beaten to a pulp by four Spitalfields Angels, who'd warned him to stop investigating the Scotland Yard bombings in May. He'd been moved from the kitchen to the sitting room sofa, where Leo had tended to his injuries.

Now, finding her in there again, standing by the glass-fronted bookcase, threw him afield. A few paraffin lamps had been lit for her to see by, and she had opened one of the bookcase's glass doors. She pulled out a volume.

"You don't mind if I borrow this, do you?" she asked by way of greeting. Her attention slipped over his drenched appearance, but she didn't comment on it. "Charles Darwin is something of a hero to Mr. Quinn, and I haven't yet read *On the Origin of Species*. He does go on about it, and it would be good to know how to discuss it with him."

At the mention of the new city coroner, the hot, stirring sensation Jasper had felt just seconds ago turned into a hard coil.

"Take it," he said, more sharply than intended. She went to her handbag and put the book inside.

"I said I'd report back, but I figured you would only shout at me if I dared come to the Yard."

"I wouldn't have shouted," he said, inexplicably irritated as he walked toward the center of the room, searching for a decanter of whisky. There wasn't one in sight.

She eyed him with apprehension. "Maybe not, but you would have certainly growled at me like you're doing now."

"What did you learn from Esther Goodwin?" he asked, wanting to get on with it.

Leo's expression went flat as she turned from him and commenced her report. "No one liked Martha Seabright," she began. "Not her sister, nor her children. Esther was appalled when Martha gave her children to the orphanage. She'd offered to help care for the children, but Martha was insistent on sending them away. Esther suspected Martha did it to be rid of them. Possibly because they reminded her of her husband, whom she'd hated and who had been abusive—Connor and I found old scars consistent with cigar tip burns all over her body."

Jasper grimaced. Those sorts of injuries were common among abused women and children, and they never failed to sicken him.

"Esther took in Paula once she left the orphanage at sixteen, but Gavin went back to his mother, only to leave shortly afterward because he'd discovered Martha was prostituting herself."

Jasper forced himself to focus on the information rather than the way Leo had walked around one of the two armchairs, her fingers trailing along the top seam of the faded rose-pink fabric.

"She hadn't spoken to Martha in about seven years. Esther isn't in contact with Gavin, but she's close with Paula, whose husband pays for her placement at Gunnerson's Rest Home," Leo continued, her hand falling away from the chair as she walked toward the window.

The curtains in the room weren't drawn, leaving an open view of the street. Thinking of the orange-hatted man, Jasper overtook Leo, reaching the window first.

"That fits with the Blicksons' residence on Park Crescent in Marylebone. It's a nice place," he said, while tugging the rope on one of the maroon drapes. Freeing the next rope, he let the curtains fall forward to shutter the window.

"You spoke to Paula?" Leo asked, peering sideways at him as he moved to the other window.

"No. She was out."

"Or she was avoiding you."

He'd considered that. If Paula Blickson still wasn't in when he went first thing tomorrow, he'd try another tack. He loosened the cords on each of the drapes with more force, irritated that his day had turned up so little other than a new dead body.

Descriptions of the stolen jewels would print in tomorrow's *Police Gazette*, and once distributed to other divisions across London, there could be word from constables checking in at pawnbrokers. The men Jasper had sent out to some of the finer jewelry shops, however, had come back that evening with no matches to the stolen items.

"You never said if Sir Eamon was able to tell you what he and Mrs. Seabright were discussing so seriously just before she was killed," Leo asked. "Was it anything useful to the case?"

"I'm not sure," he answered. After finding the body in Gavin Seabright's rooms, Jasper hadn't pondered his discussion with Sir Eamon any further. "She wanted to know if a nurse at the orphanage was still employed there but didn't explain her interest. A Nurse Radcliff."

"That is curious," she replied. "I wonder if Gavin or Paula would understand why she wished to know about the nurse." Leo crossed her arms, her fingers tapping her elbow in thought. "I also wonder if Gavin might be at his mother's home, hiding."

Empty as Martha's home would now be, it was an obvious place for him to hunker down. However, if Gavin was wise, he'd know it was *too* obvious.

"I have constables keeping an eye on the place," he replied.

"Has it been searched? There might be something there that could explain—"

"Leo." He turned sharply from the shrouded window, ready to tell her to let him handle the investigation. Her challenging glare hinted she expected that very response. "It has been searched. Nothing of importance was found."

The glint in her eye eased off, and she accepted his answer with a nod. She crossed her arms again, her fingers drumming her sleeves in a quick rhythm. Jasper knew many of her tells, and this one implied that she was thinking of something but choosing not to voice it.

"What is it?" he asked.

The drumming stopped. "Nothing," she said, much too quickly. "Though I was thinking about the woman Mrs. Beardsley saw with Gavin. She might be connected to the robbery at the benefit dinner. Perhaps they were planning it together."

Jasper pinched the bridge of his nose, exhausted. He was cold, wet, and hungry and felt as if he'd accomplished little except gaining a new dead body. "That is pure speculation."

"How can we not speculate? We don't know anything for certain just yet. There are too many questions and not enough people to give answers."

"That is a common occurrence in inquiries, unfortunately. It just means we need to look harder."

His mistake in saying *we* blared in his ears, and he knew Leo had heard it too. He braced himself for her to jump on it. But when she spoke, it wasn't about his blunder.

"Why did you pull the drapes?"

He didn't want to tell her about the man who'd been following him. She would only worry and then set her mind to figuring out who it was and what he wanted. Jasper already had his suspicions, and he didn't want Leo anywhere near it.

"Privacy." At the parting of her lips, he realized the word sang differently aloud than it had in his head. "This is a ground floor room. The pavements are busy this time of evening."

She seemed to weigh his logical answer as she turned

back toward the glass-fronted bookcase, her fingertips again skimming the tops of the chairs. Her hands were slim and graceful, and though it wasn't wise, Jasper easily recalled what they had felt like, pressed flat against his chest.

He licked his lips. "There is no whisky in here."

Leo reached for her handbag. "I just wanted to let you know what I learned today. It sounds like the rain is letting up. I'll go."

Without thinking, Jasper stepped toward the door. He didn't want her to leave. Not yet. "Why are you in here and not the study?"

He thought he knew, and if she answered honestly, it would mean broaching the topic they'd both been avoiding. It was time.

Leo slipped her handbag into the crook of her elbow and fidgeted with the beaded strap. "I didn't think it would be…appropriate."

Her gaze met his but then averted toward the covered windows. He saw her suspicion in the tense hold of her shoulders: that he'd drawn the drapes for unprincipled reasons. The stirring Jasper had felt earlier returned, only this time, it had a ravening edge. He wasn't going to back away from the matter.

"Because the last time we were in there together I kissed you?"

Leo's eyes slammed into his. He watched her draw a deep breath, a pink tint blooming on her ivory cheeks. A strangely mercenary feeling of triumph gripped him.

"Yes," she answered. The succinct reply wasn't like her.

He took a step toward her. "You said you needed some

time to think. I've given you time. We need to speak about it."

Leo's throat worked as she swallowed and nodded. "You're right. We do."

In the next drop of silence, Jasper watched her: her fingers, fiddling with the beads on her handbag; her stare meeting his and then darting away, only to come back again. Her usual composure quavered. He prepared himself, a stone settling in his gut.

She cleared her throat, however, and surprised him with her next statement. "I liked kissing you, Jasper." Her rosy coloring deepened. "But I feel guilty for it."

Jasper nodded, understanding why. "Because I'm a Carter. Because I was there that night." He'd seen her family killed. Hidden her from the men who'd broken into the darkened home on Red Lion Street to slaughter the Spencer family. It was Leo's worst memory, and Jasper was a part of it.

"Did I betray them," she whispered, "by kissing you?"

He drew in a long breath, a blistering heat building under his collar. In the hours, and then days, after kissing her, he'd come up with a dozen reasons why it had been a lapse in judgment: Maybe he'd confused feelings of protectiveness with feelings of desire. The Inspector would surely be disappointed in him. Mrs. Zhao too. Not to mention what his superiors and fellow officers at Scotland Yard would think or say.

But the reasons had fallen through him like hollow excuses, while one truth continued to burn steadily: He cared for Leo. He wanted her, as a man wanted a woman.

Jasper stepped forward. "Do you wish you hadn't kissed me?"

She worried her bottom lip, deliberating. His attention drifted to her mouth and lingered for a few thudding heartbeats.

"No," she said softly. "But I'm not sure…"

He braced himself, hands clenching into fists. "Is Connor Quinn one of the reasons you're not sure?"

Leo startled. "Connor?"

It pained him to ask and reveal his jealousy. But he needed an answer. "Is there something between the two of you?"

The corner of her mouth curved into a bewildered grin. "No. We're friends; that is all."

Jasper let the tension out of his hands, the release lightening a burden in him. He hadn't realized his jealousy had been so heavy.

Leo's composure seemed to rebound as she took a bracing breath. "I was going to say that I'm not sure we should change things between us."

He shook his head. "Things have already changed. There is no going back."

"What if it's a mistake?" she asked, slightly breathless.

"It isn't a mistake, Leo. I want to kiss you again," Jasper said softly, holding her stare. "It's all I can think about. I need to know if you feel the same way."

Leo's blush had tempered, though now, a torrent of pink lit the apples of her cheeks.

"I…" She blinked, and her glimmering hazel eyes went slightly unfocused. "Yes."

The single word burrowed into his chest. A hot surge jolted through him, terrifying and thrilling in its ferocity. Jasper moved toward her, drawn by some irrepressible force.

The complications and excuses for why he shouldn't want the things he did dissolved in the answering heat of her gaze. What the Inspector would think, had he been alive…what Mrs. Zhao or Claude might say…the scrutiny at the Yard…none of it mattered more than the promise of her mouth under his.

Movement in his peripheral vision knocked cold sense into him instantly. Mrs. Zhao's small frame appeared in the sitting room's doorway.

"Miss Leo, will you stay for dinner?" she asked, oblivious to what Jasper had been two strides away from doing.

Rather than come to an abrupt stop, Jasper sidestepped Leo. And instead of dragging her to him and devouring her mouth, he exhaled sharply and raked a hand through his damp hair as he pretended to have been walking toward the window instead of her.

Mrs. Zhao's question hung in the air, unanswered. She peered between them, waiting. Leo recovered first.

"I'm…afraid I can't, Mrs. Zhao. Claude and Flora are expecting me." She started for the front hall, then seemed to remember her manners and turned back to him. "Goodnight then," she said shakily, without making eye contact. She then spun back around and departed the room.

Mrs. Zhao, dazed by the swift departure, jerked her head as the front door shut behind Leo.

"What on earth did you say to her?" she demanded.

Jasper pulled aside the drape and watched as Leo descended to the pavement and turned for the cabstand. In the rain, now reduced to a drizzle, he searched for the man in the orange bowler. If he was there, Jasper couldn't see him.

"Nothing," he answered, too provoked, his blood too high, to conjure a better excuse. "I'll be to dinner in a few minutes."

Jasper edged past the housekeeper, uncertain if he should be agitated by the untimely interruption or grateful. He had never felt such an intense, craving desire for a woman before. As he climbed the stairs, he was certain that if he had kissed Leo again, he wouldn't have wanted to stop.

Chapter Ten

Leo stood on the front step of the morgue, her hand up to shield her eyes from the glaring sun. At the end of Spring Street, a young messenger boy in short pants and a patched newsboy cap, with a large leather bag slung across his body, was collecting a letter from a man in a business suit. Matty was one of the many messenger boys traversing this street and the others around Trafalgar Square nearly every day, waiting to be hired. Leo signaled him now, waving her hand high above her head. In her grip were two manila folders; one held the postmortem report for the John Doe found in Gavin Seabright's room, and the other was a detailed description of the deceased. The first would go to the CID at Scotland Yard, and the second, to the editor of the *Police Gazette*.

No word had come from the Yard regarding the identity of the dead man, so Leo presumed his photograph had not been found in any of the convict albums. For several months, she'd been providing descriptions of John and Jane Does to the *Gazette* in the hope that they would be recognized by police in other stations throughout London. Well over a dozen entries in the publication had led to successful identifications, so she figured it would be worth a try with this John Doe too.

Connor had performed the autopsy that morning, concluding that the cause of death had been lethal impalement to the temporal lobe. The deadly object would have been pointed and triangular in shape. When Leo described the bloody finial on the top of the coal stove in his room, Connor had nodded. "That sounds right."

"Might he have struck it while falling?" Leo suggested. "If he were to have tripped?"

With details of the small room sealed into her memory, she noted that the braided rag rug on the floor had been flipped up at the corner.

"He would have needed more momentum than a simple trip and fall to inflict damage this severe to his temporal bone," Connor said without reservation.

"So, he was pushed. That would align with the state of the room. There had been an obvious scuffle. Though, even if he'd been given a push, his death still might have been an accident."

The new city coroner had pursed his lips, looking as though he wanted to say something more. But he'd turned back to the body, preparing to restore the organs to their rightful places before closing with sutures.

Leo had let it go. Connor had either been going to remind her to include only medical findings, not theories, in the postmortem report. Or he wished to ask about her summons to the lodging house the day before. Granted, it had been a first. So had Jasper's request that she speak to Esther Goodwin.

Last evening, after arriving at 23 Charles Street to deliver her report of the interview with Martha Seabright's sister, her refusal to wait for Jasper in the study had made Mrs. Zhao suspicious. Leo had thought the cold and unwelcoming front sitting room might keep them from discussing the kiss when he arrived. But it hadn't.

Her pulse continued to stutter whenever she indulged in the vision of Jasper, stalking across the sitting room, intent on kissing her. Of how fiercely she'd wanted him to. A full month of indecision on the matter had been shattered effortlessly. Countless times since leaving his house last night, Leo had envisioned how Mrs. Zhao would have found them if she'd entered the sitting room just a few seconds later than she had.

An electric skittering along her skin both distracted and thrilled her as she dug into her pocket for the twopenny bit Matty would charge for delivering the report to Scotland Yard.

"To the *Gazette* office?" the boy asked as he took the other folder from her.

He'd delivered numerous descriptions of John and Jane Does to Constable Murray there in the past. "The top one, yes. The one on the bottom goes to Inspector Reid."

Under different circumstances, Leo would have gone herself. But she didn't want to see Jasper. Not because she was upset about the night before or his blunt confession that he wished to kiss her again. On the contrary, the promise of it the next time they were alone together kindled an acute flame in her chest. No, the reason she didn't want to see him was because she feared he would somehow read her mind and know what she was planning to do.

Back in the postmortem room, she found Connor lifting the gray tabby cat that lived at the morgue from where it had curled up to sleep—on the chest of a dead man. The fact that the corpse reeked of fish had drawn Tibia from her usual contented sleep on an empty autopsy table.

She complained with a yowl as Connor set her onto the floor. The cat swatted his ankle with her paw before dashing for the office.

"Must we keep that animal?" he asked dolefully.

"Yes, we must," Leo replied. "Give Tibia time to get used to you."

She didn't mention that the cat had never taken to Jasper. But it wasn't all men she objected to. Tibby adored Claude, though perhaps that was because he'd been the one to permit her inside one cold winter. He'd noticed the skinny, distrustful stray haunting the dirt lane behind the morgue and lured her inside with dishes of cream and sardines. Once she'd ventured in, he'd fixed her a box in which to sleep next to the cottage range in the office. Since then, she'd grown round and content. Tibia would nap on Leo's lap while she typed reports, and whenever she was feeling particularly needy, she found her way onto Leo's shoulders, stretching across them like a furry mink wrap.

Connor indicated the next corpse for the day. "I'd like to get the fishmonger here finished as soon as possible, for obvious reasons," he said, scrunching his nose.

Leo clasped her hands together before her. "I know I was out most of the day yesterday," she began, feeling even more guilty now. "But I have another errand that I was hoping to see to."

He bore her a look of inquisitiveness rather than annoyance. "What errand?"

She couldn't tell him the truth, nor could she lie. So, with a remote shrug, she replied, "It's… private."

Connor puckered his brow and smoothed his neatly trimmed mustache as he gave her request thought. Three corpses had been delivered to the morgue overnight, not to mention the backlog from the previous day.

"Well, as you are not strictly employed here," he began, "I suppose you don't need my permission. *Yet*."

Connor sighed and continued, "I plan to speak to my grandfather tonight and make the official request to bring you on as my assistant. If that is still what you want?"

Leo released the stranglehold on her clasped hands. "Yes. Very much."

It would mean the world to her to finally be employed officially because of her ability and talent, and not just at the behest of the late Gregory Reid. She'd forever be grateful for the Inspector's support and for his belief in her, but knowing that she was valued and wanted by someone who had no stake in her happiness felt inordinately more consequential.

Connor nodded and, with his hands resting on his hips, looked at the fishmonger's corpse. "I suppose I can manage here alone for a little while."

She thanked him and, promising to return as soon as possible, removed her apron as she hurried to the back office. The morning had dawned with clear skies, and the bright sunshine didn't hint toward another temperamental rainstorm, so she left the umbrella in the urn by the door and set out with just a wide-brimmed hat to block the sun. With her handbag tucked into the crook of her elbow, Leo walked to Charing Cross Station, where she boarded the District Railway train. Hailing a cab would have been simpler, but at a dearer cost, and so she settled on a hard bench and endured the slow, crowded rail ride to Moorgate Street.

The letter from the orphanage that Leo had found in Mrs. Seabright's handbag had been stored within its original envelope, a posting address printed on the front. A key had also been inside the handbag. Before sending the woman's possessions to the Yard that morning, Leo had taken the key.

Jasper had said her home was searched by constables, with nothing of importance found, but Esther's comment about Martha as a young girl, hiding the things she'd stolen from Esther, had given Leo an inkling. It had prickled at the back of her mind all night and into morning, however dully in comparison to her more stirring thoughts of Jasper.

The detective inspector would not have responded well to her suggestion that he have constables search the house again. As it was, it had been on the tip of his tongue last night to tell her to stay out of the inquiry.

So, she'd made up her mind to have a look for herself.

Leo stepped off at Moorgate Station, the barest reservation tingling through her. From Fore Street to Cripplegate, she kept a steady pace, slowing only when she found Well Street. A row of red-brick, terraced housing lined each side of the street, numbered brass plates on the front doors of each. She came upon No. 19, which belonged to Martha Seabright, but didn't stop. Glancing up and down the street, she failed to see any constable in a blue uniform and hat, but she was still wary. So, she continued to the end of the street, turned the corner, and then, after several strides more, turned again to enter the narrow alleyway behind the terraced row.

She was grateful for the sunshine as she walked along the alley. Laundry lines were strung overhead, creating a warren of long underwear, petticoats, dresses, shirtwaists, and cloth diapers. She passed a few women bent over washbasins and shouting at little tots playing. A few peered suspiciously at her but said nothing as she passed.

Leo counted off the back door of each home, her eyes skipping ahead to the one that would belong to Martha Seabright. The key she'd pilfered was in her handbag, but before she could reach for it, the back door to No. 19 opened. Leo skidded to a stop along the grass-and-pebble lane as a woman draped in a dark, sapphire-blue cape emerged. She had pulled the hood of the cape up to obscure her face. The velvet material was much too heavy for summer, but the voluminous hood was effective at concealing her features. Leo presumed that had been the intent as the woman lowered her head, then gripped the side of the hood with one white-gloved hand to keep it in place. She closed the back door and started briskly down the alley, heading in Leo's direction.

Leo whirled in between two sheets hanging from laundry lines. Could this be the woman the landlady, Mrs. Beardsley, had seen with Gavin? Holding her breath, as much to silence herself as to not inhale the musty odor of the poorly washed linens, Leo's pulse skipped madly at the base of her throat. She waited for the woman to pass by, her cape rippling and her head still down as she went.

Waiting another few moments, Leo slowly peeled back one sheet and watched the woman's retreat. Whoever she was, she was not being furtive or unassuming in the least. Everything about her, from her fine cape to her liquid, graceful movements, shouted that she was in a place where she didn't belong even less so than Leo.

Casting a look over her shoulder toward Martha's home, Leo made the decision to abandon her plan to search the house. If this woman was the one associated with Gavin, it would be more crucial to find out who she was and where she lived.

Leo stepped out from the hanging laundry and hurried to keep the woman in sight. If the lady was cautious, she would have looked over her shoulder to see if she was being followed. But she disappeared around the alley entrance, back toward Fore Street, without a backward glance.

When several seconds later Leo turned out of the alley, the mysterious woman was still moving along the pavements at a businesslike clip. Her hood was still up as well. Leo stayed far enough behind so that if the woman did turn, she would not startle at seeing someone so close on her heels.

The train station wasn't her destination. Instead of turning in the direction of Moorgate Street, the woman strode toward a line of cabs. Leo gnashed her teeth. If the woman got into a cab, the only way to follow her would be to hire one as well.

Sure enough, the woman approached a cabbie. She angled her head just enough for Leo to see the very tip of her nose. But then it disappeared again into the hood, and the woman climbed into the hansom.

Leo broke into a run now and reached another cabbie at the stand, panting.

"Can you follow that cab?" she asked, pointing to the one that had just drawn into traffic.

"Where's it goin'?" the cabbie asked.

"I don't know, but I need to follow it."

He grimaced. "How's it I know you got enough to cover the fare?"

Suppressing a groan of exasperation, Leo opened her handbag and pulled out all the money she had: a single shilling. "Take me as far as this will cover, but please, we must go now."

His brushy brows leaped up. "Six pence gets a mile."

She put the coin into his palm. "Just drive."

He pocketed the coin, while she climbed up into the forward-facing seat. During the colder months, most of these open hansom cabs had a leather curtain to block the cold, rain, and snow, but in this fine weather, Leo's view was unobstructed. She kept her eye trained on the cab the woman had climbed into as her own pulled into traffic. As Leo instructed, the driver didn't follow too closely. A coach and an open wagon separated them for a short while, but as they traveled west along Holborn Street, the woman's cab was straight ahead.

"Your shilling's up," the cabbie called from his high bench behind her. He pulled the traces and slowed his two horses.

"It can't be. We've been less than a mile!"

"We've been *one mile*," the cabbie insisted.

There was no time to waste arguing. The woman's cab had pulled farther ahead already. Leo leaped from the cab and started following on foot. She had no choice but to run, and as she did, she drew quizzing looks from those she passed. Bracing one hand on the top of her hat to keep it from flying from her head, and the other gripping her skirt to lift the hem just enough so that she wouldn't trip and make a complete spectacle of herself, Leo grew breathless as she kept a taxing pace.

The cab slowed as it met with traffic, giving her a chance to catch up. She was still at least twenty yards behind it when the cab turned toward Bloomsbury Square and disappeared.

Sweat streamed down her neck and back and dampened her forehead as she hurried to reach the busy garden square. When she did, she stopped to both draw breath and search for the cab. Most hansoms and their drivers looked alike, but the horses pulling the one she wanted were dappled-gray mares and easily spotted across the square. To her relief, they'd come to a stop along the curb. Had the cab continued away from the square, Leo wasn't sure she would have been able to trail it any longer.

Bloomsbury was home to only the wealthiest Londoners, and the terraced homes boxing in the lush, green square were unlike any Leo had ever visited. Even 23 Charles Street was shabby in comparison. As the blue-caped woman stepped from the hansom, her hood still in place, Leo slowed to a brisk walk, though her pulse still hammered.

The woman went to one of the whitewashed terraced homes, but she did not need to knock or wait at the front door. After a moment spent fitting a key into the lock, she let herself straight in and closed the door behind her.

She lived here, at Bloomsbury Square.

What in the world had a woman of her status been doing at Martha Seabright's home?

The perspiration that had built up during her run now stuck to the cotton chemise under her corset. Leo evened her breathing as she walked toward the home the woman had entered. She needed to find out who lived there. However, if she were to knock upon the front door and ask, she would surely be turned away.

Close to the townhouse, Leo spotted a twist of rose and white checkered steps leading down to the servant's entrance, hidden beneath street level. If she wanted answers, it was that door to which she would need to apply. Of course, she would need to devise a reason.

Leo took a handkerchief from her handbag and wiped the perspiration from her brow. She then tucked a few strands of hair that had come free from her combs behind her ears and repositioned her hat. With a bracing breath, she opened the wrought iron gate at the top of the steps and descended to the swept landing, all the while cobbling together the reason for her knocking at this particular servant's entrance.

After three purposeful raps upon the door, she stood back and waited, her pulse still irregularly high in her throat. When the door opened, an older woman in uniform and a mobcap met her with an expectant stare. "Well, what is it?"

Leo cleared her throat. "I'm here to answer the advertisement in the paper."

The woman squinted as she wiped her hands on a towel. "What advertisement is this?"

Mind scrambling, Leo replied, "For a new maid. A lady's maid."

The servant's perplexed expression remained. "We've nothing in any papers for a maid."

"Isn't this the Rupert household?" The name of the dead fishmonger back at the Spring Street Morgue was the first one that came to mind in her moment of need.

"Rupert? No, no. You've the wrong house, missy," the woman said, then moved to close the door.

"But this must be the Rupert home. It's 10 Bloomsbury Square, isn't it?" Leo pressed.

The woman sighed and opened the door again. "It is, but this here is the Hayes residence, not the Ruperts', whoever they are."

A shudder snapped Leo back a step, her skin prickling. "Hayes, you say?"

The woman's patience dried up. "That's right. Hayes. Now, off you go."

The door shut, and Leo was left staring at her startled face reflected in the pane of glass.

Chapter Eleven

Detective Sergeant Warnock was waiting outside Jasper's office at eight o'clock when he arrived, a surly mood already setting in for the day. He'd slept, though poorly, and only after apologizing to Mrs. Zhao for not eating most of the dinner she'd prepared. After Leo had left, his thwarted desire for her still stringing him tight, he'd been impossible to please.

That morning, before leaving for the Yard, Jasper had gone to the kitchen and apologized to Mrs. Zhao again.

"Did the two of you argue, Mister Jasper?" she had asked, her forgiveness clear when she poured him a cup of coffee at the kitchen table.

"No." He'd considered leaving it at that, but the truth was he'd wanted someone to talk to. Rubbing his jaw, he'd continued, "Mrs. Zhao, there is something I should tell you."

The housekeeper pulled out a chair and sat, her grin effusive. "Does it have to do with Miss Leo and how you would like to court her?"

Jasper's shock had him spilling the coffee over the rim of his cup.

"How the blazes did you... I have not asked to court her." His defensive reply had only made Mrs. Zhao chuckle.

"We are not courting," he'd insisted as he'd risen to find a towel. She'd taken it from him and mopped up the spill, smiling widely.

"How did you know?"

Mrs. Zhao shook her head. "The way you look at her."

"And what way might that be?"

At this, the housekeeper had leveled him with a stare and tucked her chin, her answer all too clear in the chastising arch of her brow.

"Forget I asked," he'd said, before making his way out of the kitchen.

Now, meeting the eager, new detective sergeant outside his office door, Jasper questioned if other people had noticed the way he looked at Leo. Constance certainly had.

"What do you have for me, Warnock?"

The young man followed him into his office. "Two hansom companies are registered in London with the word *Best* in them: London Best Carriage and Frank's Best Livery and Cab."

"Good. Look into them. Miss Spencer mentioned the cab appeared dated. You have her description of the interior?"

Warnock nodded. "I'd like to check into Frank's Best first. There was something I noticed with that one when Sergeant Brooks gave me the files."

Jasper arched a brow, waiting for him to go on.

"It's registered to a Francis Green," he said. "Yesterday, I heard Sergeant Lewis say the server who ran off after the murder at Sir Eamon's home was Philip Green. I wondered if there is a relation."

"Excellent work, Warnock," he said, impressed. It could be something indeed. "Take Price with you." Two men would make quicker work, and if either Francis or Philip Green was connected to the masked thieves, he didn't want to send the sergeant in alone.

Shortly after Warnock and Price left the Yard, a wire came in that noted a sapphire necklace matching the description of one stolen from the benefit dinner had been located at a jeweler near Picadilly Circus. However, when Jasper arrived there to question the proprietor, he was told an old widow who had fallen on hard times had pawned it. The piece had been a gift from her late husband, and she'd parted with it tearfully. Jasper examined the necklace, and while it looked like one that had been worn by a woman at the dinner—the woman flirting with Commissioners Danvers and Fraser—he couldn't be certain. Besides, he was looking for men who had pawned jewelry, not old widows.

Annoyed, he returned to the Yard in time to update Chief Inspector Coughlan, who had not been pleased that another body had been found in connection with the benefit dinner robbery and initial murder. His instruction to Jasper to make some headway, fast, had not been helpful in the least. He had held his tongue and prepared to go out to Marylebone to try the Blicksons' home again. However, before he could put on his hat, two visitors arrived to see him: Mrs. Paula Blickson and her cousin, Mr. Felix Goodwin.

Jasper welcomed them into his office, taking note of Mrs. Blickson's mourning dress. A brimmed hat with a veil obscured her face, though the lacy tatting was sheer enough to provide him with a view of her features. She was pretty, with dark hair and eyes, thick, black lashes and eyebrows, and a striking mole on the side of her right cheek.

"My servants informed me that you had stopped in yesterday, Inspector," she said as she took a seat, clutching a black lace handkerchief in her hand. She did not provide any excuse for where she'd been.

Leo had failed to mention the cousin, Felix, in her report. He, too, was dressed somberly, though the black suit was a little snug for his tall, athletic frame. Jasper guessed it was not his own but one that had been borrowed.

"Thank you for coming in, Mrs. Blickson." He had not left any request for her to do so; she'd taken it upon herself, it seemed.

Felix Goodwin settled into the chair next to his cousin. "My mother informed us that a woman had stopped by her rooms yesterday. She claimed to have been sent by Scotland Yard."

Jasper clenched his molars. It was precisely what he'd hoped Leo would not say, but apparently, *unofficial capacity* meant something different to the stubborn woman.

"I authorized Miss Spencer to call on Mrs. Goodwin," he said, grateful that no one else was in his office right then. "However, I do have questions for you, Mrs. Blickson, regarding your mother. My condolences," he added when the young woman reached underneath her veil to touch the lace hankie to her nose.

"Thank you, Inspector. I wasn't close with her," she admitted. "But I find what happened horrific."

Witnessing it certainly had been, Jasper thought, though he kept that to himself.

"You were extended an invitation to the orphanage benefit dinner," he began. "But you chose not to attend."

Mrs. Blickson lowered her hankie. "I couldn't stomach the thought of celebrating that awful place."

"It was unconscionable of them to ask my cousin," Felix said, his voice low and gruff. He grasped Mrs. Blickson's hand, which was resting on the arm of the chair, as if to show support. "How could they think she would look back upon her time there with happiness and gratitude?"

Jasper didn't disagree with him entirely. The orphanage was a charitable fund and did some good for the wives and children of fallen officers, but the idea of displaying Martha Seabright and her children as indebted recipients smacked of arrogance.

Mrs. Blickson stiffened her back and slid her hand out from under Felix's. Jasper sensed she didn't want her cousin's pity.

"I also did not wish to see my mother or speak to her," she said. "If I am honest, that is the main reason I declined the invitation."

"You bore your mother ill will?" Jasper asked.

"Why the hell wouldn't she?" her cousin snapped loudly, causing her to startle in her seat. "Paula never should have been sent there. None of them should have been."

Mrs. Blickson angled her head down, the lace veil obscuring her face.

"Your mother would have helped care for them?" Jasper asked Felix, recalling what Leo had imparted about Esther Goodwin.

"My mother offered numerous times, and yet Martha refused. I think she was envious of my mother. Paula and Gavin preferred our home to their own." Felix reached over to cover his cousin's hand with his again. "I'm sure Edward would have too. Had he been given the chance."

Paula Blickson put her hankie to her nose again, wracked with new tears. She stood up from her chair quickly and paced away, putting her back to them.

"Did Gavin decline the invitation to the dinner for the same reasons?" Jasper asked.

She turned and with a tremulous voice, replied, "I don't know. I haven't seen or spoken to my brother in a long time."

"Why don't you ask him yourself?" Felix demanded, his temper still high.

Jasper wasn't inclined to relate the trouble at Gavin's lodgings the previous day. "As soon as I can locate him, I will."

Paula walked back toward Jasper's desk. "You can't find him?"

"He has not returned to his lodgings since yesterday morning." A rotation of constables had been placed on watch outside Mrs. Beardsley's home. So far, there had been no sighting of Gavin.

"That is curious," Felix said. "Right after Martha's killing, he's nowhere to be found?" He scrunched his forehead, skeptical. Jasper was as well.

At least one of the masked intruders had known Gavin and gone to his room, ostensibly to inform him of his mother's death. Jasper thought it highly likely Gavin was involved with the robbery, even if just the planning of it.

"Can you think of any specific reason your brother would hold a grudge toward your mother?" he asked.

"The same reason I held a grudge, I suspect," Paula answered plainly.

"Where were you on the night of the dinner?" he asked.

The lace veil could not obscure her frown. "At home, with my husband. Why?"

"I'm trying to build a picture of that evening," he said vaguely. He peered at Felix, curious as to why he had accompanied Paula and not Mr. Blickson. Archibald Blickson had been absent from the house yesterday as well.

"And yourself, Mr. Goodwin?"

"I was not invited to the benefit dinner," he replied.

"I'd like to know where you spent the evening, just the same."

After a loud sigh of annoyance, he tossed up his hands and answered, "I went to Evans in Covent Garden for some entertainment."

Jasper knew of the music and supper room. It catered to men only, and while some of its acts were mild, its license had once been revoked for a full year before being reinstated due to an overly lewd entertainer.

"Inspector, my aunt informed me that Scotland Yard believes my mother was targeted at the dinner," Mrs. Blickson said. "Are you saying this wasn't a robbery that went wrong?"

He gritted his molars again. *Leo.* Telling Esther Goodwin that had been premature. For all Leo knew, the woman could have gone to the press and spouted off everything she'd shared with her. Had that happened, Coughlan would have skewered him.

"It is a robbery, Mrs. Blickson, but we are also looking into the possibility that the assailant chose to shoot Mrs. Seabright on purpose."

"She was a horrible woman, but to murder her…" Felix sighed heavily, head shaking.

"Have you any idea where Gavin might have gone to lay low awhile?" Jasper asked.

Mrs. Blickson shook her head, as did her cousin. "As I said, we're not close," she replied. "I'm sorry. I wish there was more I could do to help."

She went toward the office door, and Jasper stood from his chair. Apparently, she was ready to conclude the interview.

"One last thing," he said, thinking of what Sir Eamon had told him the day before at the Law Courts. "Do you remember a Nurse Radcliff from the orphanage?"

Mrs. Blickson went stone still for a moment and then whirled to stare at Jasper. The glistening of her eyes was visible through the lace veil. By her startled reaction, it was evident she did remember the nurse.

"I haven't heard that name in…in years." She gasped as emotion swarmed her again. Standing next to her now, Felix Goodwin touched her elbow. Mrs. Blickson blinked rapidly, appearing to battle more tears.

"Your mother mentioned the nurse to someone the evening of the dinner," Jasper provided. "Do you have any idea why she might have been asking about this Nurse Radcliff?"

Paula Blickson lifted her chin, her gloved hands curling into tight fists. "She was the nurse who was caring for my baby brother when he died. I don't know why my mother would have been curious about her now, all these years later. Forgive me, Inspector, but I'm finding it difficult to think. I've spent so long trying to put that place behind me."

Felix wrapped his arm around her shoulders, which were now trembling as fresh tears cut down her cheeks. Paula appeared to sink inward, as if trying to escape the memories Jasper had dragged up for her.

"Of course, my apologies," he said. He could understand the desire to keep the past firmly in its place. "The Spring Street Morgue will release your mother's body to you or to whatever funeral service you choose."

Paula and her cousin turned to leave without comment, and Jasper wondered if they would even bother to claim the body. Felix's arm was still holding her steady, and as Jasper watched them go, he felt no closer to answers. Paula had despised her mother, just as he'd already known. She had not attended the dinner, as he'd already known. And the distance between her and Gavin would give Jasper little to go on in his search for her brother.

He went to stand in the doorway of his office, agitation threading through him at the lack of progress. Looking into the department, the stirring of tension amplified when he saw he had yet another visitor.

Chapter Twelve

Traversing on foot from Bloomsbury Square to Scotland Yard in the full light of day wasn't nearly as wretched as being taken from the benefit dinner by masked robbers and then dropped off in Battersea Park on a dark and stormy night. But by the time Leo reached Scotland Yard, she was perilously close to tears of frustration.

Without a farthing in her handbag, she'd been made to walk a near half hour to Met headquarters. The heat and humidity of the June sun had baked her as she'd trekked toward the Thames, and her short lady's boots proved unserviceable as the blisters that had formed on her heels while chasing the cab to the Hayes residence earlier grew untenable.

Leo tried to distract herself from her painful feet by piecing together any plausible reason why the Hayes family would be involved with the murder of Martha Seabright. Jasper had once mentioned that Constance's family had a home on Bloomsbury Square. As such, the caped and hooded woman had to have been either Constance Hayes's mother—or Constance herself. But why would either of them have been snooping inside Martha's home?

Jasper had ended his courtship with Constance in May. At the time, Leo had felt slightly guilty for the delight it had brought her. Not so any longer.

The Hayes family was rich and powerful. What connection could they have with the widow of a police sergeant, dead nigh on fourteen years?

Hot, thirsty, and inordinately frustrated, Leo at long last crossed the threshold at Scotland Yard. She sighed at the cool shade of the lobby, closing her eyes in relief.

"Are you well, Miss Spencer?"

She collected herself and met Constable Woodhouse's concerned stare. "Well enough, Constable, thank you. Is Inspector Reid in?"

"Far as I'm aware."

Leo hesitated, looking in the direction of the CID. "And what of Detective Chief Inspector Coughlan?" It was half two in the afternoon. Too early for him to have gone home for the day.

The receiving desk constable chuckled, interpreting her caution. "He's left for a meeting with the superintendent." Constable Woodhouse winked, and Leo shot him a grateful smile before heading to the detective department.

There, however, her reception wasn't nearly as hospitable. Constable Wiley was at his desk, a bored expression turning down the corners of his mouth. When he saw her, his sneer only increased.

"He's busy interviewing someone important," the

constable said before Leo could even step foot into the room. "You'll have to wait."

Leo expected him to say more, perhaps call her *LeoMorga*, as he too often did. But he only slumped in his chair, his round cheek pressed into his fist as he leaned an elbow on the desktop. He fell back into his thoughts, ignoring her completely.

Before Chief Inspector Coughlan had turned serious in his threats to sack Jasper, Leo would have bypassed Wiley's desk and proceeded to Jasper's office, usually with the complaining constable on her heels. However, such an action now would only reflect poorly on Jasper, so she gathered her patience and stood still.

"Who is Inspector Reid interviewing?" she inquired.

"Daughter of the woman who got shot at that dinner," he answered, still sulking.

"Paula Blickson?" Leo asked, brightening.

"If that's her name."

She could take it no longer. "Constable, what is the matter with you today?"

He blinked and lifted his cheek from his knuckles. An imprint had been left behind. "With me? What are you on about?"

"You're not yourself," she replied. "Not that I'd like you to return to your unfriendly ways, but there is clearly something bothering you."

He scowled at her, then returned to his slouch. "Mind your own business, *LeoMorga.*"

She rolled her eyes. That was more like it.

Across the department floor, Jasper's office door opened, and Leo stood at attention, ignoring the ache of her feet. A man and woman emerged, the woman wearing mourning black, including a stylish hat dressed in dark purple flowers, with black lace billowing from the narrow brim. The veil obscured most of her face, though she had shifted it aside to press a handkerchief to her nose, exposing her smooth, pale cheek, an artful curl of black hair, and a noticeable mole on her cheek, close to her bejeweled earlobe.

At her side, a tall man in a dark suit and bowler kept his arm around Paula's shoulders, leading her toward the department exit. Leo stood aside as they approached. The man guiding her maintained a stoic expression. His sapphire eyes met Leo's as they passed. He gave a polite, detached nod, a greeting one might give a stranger passing by on the street. He might not have known Leo, yet she knew him. It was Esther Goodwin's son, Felix.

They turned into the narrow corridor and were gone.

"You can see the inspector now," Constable Wiley said.

They were words Leo had never heard him say before. She eyed him curiously as she started for Jasper's office. The detective inspector stood in the doorway, watching her with clear admonition for having come to the Yard.

The ache of her feet and the soreness of her calves dissipated with each step she took toward him. For a fraction of a second, his expression opened, revealing what else he was thinking of: last evening. Their thwarted kiss.

But then he blinked, and he was once again the irritable inspector from Scotland Yard.

"What is the matter with Constable Wiley?" she asked, trying to deflect whatever scolding he had in mind. "I've never seen him so morose."

"He requested a secondment to Liverpool," Jasper answered as they moved into his office. "It was denied."

Leo felt sorry for it, though not for Wiley in particular. It would have been lovely to have someone else as desk constable. "Maybe you could put in a good word for him in the telegraph room. Or in some other department far from here."

He stepped behind his desk to close a folder. "Leo—"

"That was Paula Blickson?" she asked, cutting him off again. "And her cousin, Felix Goodwin."

Jasper sighed. "Yes. She decided to come in."

"How did she seem?"

He crossed his arms. "Upset. Leo, you know that it would be better if you did not come here any longer."

She peeled the gloves from her hands, the cotton damp. "I know, and I'm sorry, but this was important. It couldn't wait."

His chest expanded as he dragged in a fortifying breath. "Close the door." She did as he bade, shutting out the rest of the department.

"Tell me what has happened," he ordered next.

On her walk from Bloomsbury Square, she'd tried to organize what she would say once she arrived at her destination. The only conclusion she'd reached, however, was that nothing would adequately protect her from Jasper's wrath.

Leo held up her palms. "You might be angry with me, but hear me out."

Tucking his chin, he practically growled, "What have you done?" with such vehemence, the small hairs on her arms stood on end.

She lowered her hands and clenched them into fists. "I believe Mrs. Stanley Hayes was at Martha Seabright's home on Well Street. She was inside the house, alone, and she most certainly did not want to be seen there."

Though his expressions were not often readable, this one of stunned confusion couldn't be mistaken. Jasper's arms dropped to his sides. "Mrs. Hayes?" But then, he cocked his head. "What the devil were *you* doing there?"

Leo turned away from his forbidding stare and headed for the corner of the small office, where shelves were filled with books, maps, and case files. "I think we are better served concentrating on Mrs. Hayes right now," she said, adding, "to avoid becoming distracted."

"Damn it, Leo." He shoved his chair hard under the desk. "I knew I shouldn't have asked you to talk to Esther Goodwin."

The doubt and disbelief she'd felt when he'd asked her the day before reared back up again. "Then why did you?"

He lowered his head and, with his hands hitched on his hips, looked to be taking even breaths. "Fine. For now, we will discuss Mrs. Hayes. But eventually, you *will* tell me what in God's name you were doing there."

She could only hope his resolve would fade or that more pressing matters would crop up in the meantime.

"How can you be sure it was Mrs. Hayes?" he asked.

"At first, I wasn't." She explained how she'd followed the unknown woman, her face well covered by the hood on her cloak, from near Moorgate to Bloomsbury Square.

"I saw her enter a home, not as a guest, but as someone who resided there," she said. "So, I went to the tradesman's entrance and applied for a position that didn't exist so that I might learn the name of the owners."

He groaned and rubbed his face, massaging his eyes as he did.

"The home belongs to Mr. and Mrs. Hayes," Leo concluded. "I can only reconcile that the hooded woman was either Mrs. Hayes or Constance."

At Jasper's pause and his contemplative brow, Leo began to suspect something. "Did you already know of their connection to Mrs. Seabright?"

The sash of his window had been lifted, letting in the myriad noises of Whitehall Place. Shod horses' hooves on the cobbles, clattering wagon wheels, whistles, shouts of newsboys hawking papers. It all filled the office as Jasper slowly came out from behind his desk.

"Not of their personal connection, but Mr. and Mrs. Hayes were on the guest list for the benefit dinner. They were supposed to have attended. At the last minute, they canceled."

"Just like Gavin Seabright," Leo said.

It couldn't be a coincidence. It was almost as if they all had known the robbery would take place and wished to avoid it.

"Are the Hayeses regular contributors to the orphanage?" Leo asked.

"Stanley was on the Board of Governors years back, when the orphanage first opened." Jasper looked out the window, then shut the sash to lock out the noise.

"That was when the Seabright children were there," Leo said, a small quiver of excitement growing just under her skin. It was entirely plausible that Stanley Hayes had met Martha at that point in time. Had Mrs. Hayes as well?

Earlier, Leo had wondered if the woman wearing the cloak could have been the dark-haired lady Mrs. Beardsley had seen with Gavin. But when she posited this with Jasper, he shook his head right away.

"I've never met Constance's mother, so she might have dark hair, but she is surely too old to match the landlady's description."

Leo found she could agree with Jasper on that point. Unfortunately, she also found the stabbing sensation in her lower stomach at the mention of Constance's name unsettling. Jasper had courted her for several months, and while Leo had never truly liked Constance, she now understood it was due to jealousy more than anything else.

"Maybe something untoward happened between the Hayeses and Martha Seabright back then," Leo mused. "Though, I can't imagine why Mrs. Hayes would have snooped around Martha's home. She didn't leave with anything in her hands, though she could have put something into one of her pockets."

Jasper scrubbed a palm down his face and turned a look onto Leo that she knew well. "You shouldn't have gone anywhere near that house. What were you intending to do there?"

The key in her handbag felt even more criminal now. She couldn't bear to admit that she'd pilfered it from the dead woman's possessions with plans to do the same thing Mrs. Hayes had been doing. Without warning, shame doused her head to toe. Sneaking about, breaking into homes wasn't commendable in the least.

Leo eyed the office door, eager to leave. "I just wanted a look. Call it a hunch. Now, I should be getting back to the morgue."

Jasper moved, blocking her direct path to the exit. "I'm grateful for this lead, Leo. Truly, I am." He gritted his teeth, and she knew a *but* was on its way. "But I am asking you to stay away from this investigation from this point forward. If any of the other masked assailants learn you've been sniffing around their tracks, they might regret letting you go and return for you."

The worry was oddly reminiscent of the one that had been dogging her for the last month or so, ever since Eddie Bloom, the owner of Striker's Wharf nightclub and the head of a criminal racket on the Lambeth wharves, had warned her away from asking more questions about the murders of her family. The killers hadn't forgotten the little girl they'd failed to find that night. If she started looking into the past too deeply, they might suspect she knew more than they were comfortable with.

The warning had chilled her interest in what her father had done to betray the East Rips criminal syndicate. She'd stored her father's account ledgers and the old letters her aunt had sent to Leo's mother, detailing Flora's concerns for the safety of her sister and her family, under her bed, alongside the thick file on the Spencer family murders that she'd been given by the Inspector. Every time Leo entered her room or got into bed, she would think of them. But at the idea of reaching for them and disturbing the detritus of the past, Eddie Bloom's warning would sound in her ear.

Not only did Leo not want to draw the interest of the East Rips, she also didn't want them looking any closer at the Scotland Yard detective inspector who had once been a runaway from the Carter family.

Leo nodded. "I understand."

Jasper waited, a skeptical brow raised as if expecting her to tack on some dispute. When she didn't, he seemed to be at a loss.

"All right. Good, then," he said.

He still blocked her path to the door.

"Might I get by?" she asked. "There are several corpses at the morgue, and I've already been away too long."

After the torturous walk from Bloomsbury Square, it seemed like days had passed since she'd left Connor rather than just a handful of hours.

Jasper stepped aside swiftly. "Right. Yes."

She passed him, a smile she could not suppress tugging the corner of her mouth. He really was quite charming when he was ungainly. She opened the door, allowing in the hum of activity in the busy department.

"Leo?"

She turned back at his voice, predicting another warning to stay out of the investigation. Instead, Jasper had his hands in his trouser pockets, something he only ever did if he felt discomposed. After parting his lips once without making a sound, on the second try, he managed to say, "Will you have dinner with me?"

Heat reached like a tidal swell from her stomach to her throat, and then back down again. She prayed the flush stayed clear of her cheeks as she tried to maintain some degree of poise.

"Tonight?" she asked, her voice slightly rough.

"If you don't already have plans."

She pinned her lower lip with her teeth, biting back the giddy grin threatening to break forth. It felt altogether foreign and more than a little alarming.

Forcing some composure, she nodded. "I'll be home by seven."

A grin began to emerge on his mouth, and before her

own involuntary smile could take shape, Leo swiftly turned to leave.

Somehow, the walk to the morgue didn't pain her feet at all. The fatigue and frustration weighing her down when she'd arrived at the Yard had dissipated completely, and taking its place was an exhilarating thrum that seemed to lift her from the pavements as she walked. Jasper's invitation to dinner had been like a cup of strong black tea to her system, waking her up and electrifying her brain.

It was nothing like how she felt when Constable Elias Murray had asked her to dine with him a few months ago. Those invitations had made her squirm and perspire. She'd accepted once, but even then, she'd had her reservations. Did she like him well enough to encourage him? And what would they discuss for the duration of dinner?

However, the idea of dinner with Jasper filled her with a trembling of anticipation, not doubt. To calm her flittering pulse before entering the morgue, she turned her mind to practicalities, like what she should wear and where they might dine. Leo had seen Jasper in a fine suit and tie when he'd been courting Constance. The vision of him turning up at her front door on Duke Street in such clothing gave her stomach an unruly swoop as she neared the back door to the morgue's office.

Instinct flared up Leo's back and alerted her to a presence behind her. Too late. A hand wrapped around her arm and jerked her back. Something dull and hard pressed firmly into her back, just below her right shoulder blade.

"Don't shout," the male voice said, and at the pungent waft of neroli and bergamot shuttling up her nostrils, Leo knew exactly who had sneaked up on her.

"Mr. Seabright."

The door to the morgue was close. Connor would be inside, waiting for her to return.

"How do you know that?" the man asked, his breathing choppy with panic.

"You ought to have a lighter hand with your cologne," she replied. "And for someone who is a prime suspect in at least one murder, you are unadvisedly close to the Metropolitan Police headquarters."

"I'm no murderer," he said through what sounded like gritted teeth. He was strong, his grip severe, and he was tall; in her limited side vision, he stood a good head taller than she did.

"If that is true, then why are you thrusting the barrel of a revolver into my back?"

He emitted a soft growl of aggravation. Then, his grip on her arm loosened. With some bewilderment, Leo stepped away and turned to face him.

Gavin Seabright resembled his mother in many ways, from the grim slash of his thin lips to the bold, high forehead and hard, gray eyes. But when he showed her his weapon—an empty glass beer bottle, the tapered neck of which had doubled as a revolver's barrel—his maladroit hands revealed the truth: he wasn't a killer.

Leo exhaled, and while not exactly comfortable, she was at least relieved.

"You have much to answer for, Mr. Seabright. There was a dead man found in your lodging room," she said. "This man was part of the criminal party that robbed the benefit dinner and killed your mother. How did you know him?"

As if recognizing he no longer needed the bottle, he dropped it onto the gravel path. "I didn't know him from Adam." He said it emphatically enough for her to believe him. "The first time I'd ever seen him was at Mrs. Beardsley's door before breakfast. Said he had bad news about my mum, that he needed to speak to me alone."

"You invited a stranger to your room?"

Gavin snorted. "What, and chum up an extra six pence to use Mrs. Beardsley's private sitting room? No, thank you."

Leo stepped closer to the exterior of the vestry, into the strip of cool shade cast by the roof's eaves. From there, she saw the man much better. Smears of dirt on his clothing and face hinted that he'd slept outside overnight, perhaps in a park or cemetery.

"What did the man tell you?" she asked, then more eagerly, "His name, perhaps?"

"Said his name was Harry."

"Did he give a surname?"

"No." He checked over his shoulder, glancing toward the street. There was no one there, but it was clear he was worried about being followed. "Just said my mum had been killed. That he'd seen it and knew who'd done it."

"Who?"

Again, he shook his head and shrugged. Leo reeled in a dash of annoyance. "How did he find you?" she tried next. "How did he know the victim was your mother?"

"He just said the man who killed my mum had asked him to keep an eye on my lodgings for a few weeks. When I asked why, he wouldn't say. Just that he'd explain everything and that I could go to the police with what he said," Gavin said. "But first, I had to help him."

"Help him how?"

"He wanted money and a place to lay low until he could get out of London."

A bold request, coming from a stranger who'd just confessed to being present when Gavin's mother was killed. How was Gavin supposed to trust what he said? But then, she worked it out.

"You came here to the morgue that morning for proof that your mother was indeed dead," Leo surmised. "But why would you allow him to stay in your room meanwhile? He was a stranger."

"I've nothing in there worth stealing. Got my money in a bank, where no nosy landlady or lodgers can sniff it out when I'm not about. In fact, the bank's where I went after here," he said, jutting his chin toward the vestry. "Took out a pound note and put it in my shoe, but I wasn't giving it to him until he told me who killed my mum and why."

"But when you arrived, Harry refused to talk," Leo guessed. "And then you fought?"

He snarled, "No, I didn't do a thing to him. He was already dead, lying there on the floor, when I returned."

Leo cocked her head. "Mr. Seabright, all indications are that he fell and hit his head during a fight. It was an accident. There is no need to lie."

Crimson flashed over his cheeks in a blink, and his muscles tensed. "I'm not lying. I didn't push him! He was dead already, and that's the truth."

"Then why run?" she pressed. "Why not call for a constable?"

He grimaced. "It's obvious, isn't it? There was a dead man in my room. My landlady, the other lodgers at breakfast, they all saw him go upstairs with me. Who do you think the police would accuse?"

His reasoning wasn't entirely unsound. Jasper was a thorough investigator and would take into account the approximate time Harry had been killed, but there really was no solid evidence that Gavin had been gone from the lodging house at the time of the man's death. Only a strong, distinct odor in the morgue could point to Gavin having been there. No one had seen him, least of all Leo. The evidence against him was condemning.

"Why have you approached me?"

He lowered his head in what might have been bashfulness. "Saw you yesterday morning. First here, when you nearly came upon me when I was leaving. And then later at Mrs. Beardsley's, with that detective."

Leo cocked her head. "You were watching the lodging house."

He nodded. "You've got to tell the coppers I didn't kill that man. That I didn't have a thing to do with it!"

"It doesn't matter if I believe you. Running away did you no favors, Mr. Seabright," she said, annoyed by his request. What did he think? That because she was a woman she would be soft and willing to be his advocate?

"It also doesn't look good for you since you chose to skip the disastrous dinner at the last minute," Leo said. "Why didn't you attend? You'd accepted the invitation but then changed your mind."

He lifted his chin, covered in dark stubble and a smear of dirt. "I had my reasons."

"It is suspected that you knew the robbery was going to take place."

"That isn't true! I didn't go because…" He grimaced. "Because Paula said I'd be a traitor if I did."

Leo stepped out of the shade. "Your sister?"

Esther Goodwin had said the two siblings had been estranged for years. So, when had Gavin and Paula seen each other? The answer came to Leo in a rush.

"Your landlady saw you with a dark-haired young woman recently. She picked you up and dropped you off again in a hansom cab." Paula Blickson was pretty and young, with dark hair, as Leo had seen earlier at Scotland Yard.

The muscles along his jaw tensed. He nodded.

"She'd rejected the invitation extended to her," Leo deduced. "Then she sought you out and implored you to do the same. Why would she have called you a traitor for attending?"

He clenched his mouth shut and hitched his chin, his expression turning chary. "What does it matter?'

"Every detail matters when nothing is known for certain," she replied.

He backed up a few steps, his heels dragging through the gravel. "Because of Edward. Our little brother. He was a baby when he died at the orphanage."

She nodded. "Yes, I know about that. What then? She blamed the orphanage for his death?"

His heavy brow furrowed as he pulled down the brim of his hat in a nervous gesture. "Paula never believed he died. She thought we were lied to."

It was an extraordinary claim. Leo drew in a breath

and wondered why Esther Goodwin had not thought to mention it.

"Lied to by whom?"

He shook his head and shrugged. "Everyone. All the adults. They were all the same, treating us like troublesome pests."

Leo couldn't imagine what it had been like to grow up in an orphanage. She'd often considered that, if not for the Inspector and then Claude and Flora, she would have been turned over to one. Either that, or to a workhouse. She'd been enormously lucky.

"What did your sister believe happened to Edward?"

Gavin again looked over his shoulder. He'd tarried too long, and evidently, he was agitated by it. "That he was taken. Said she knew it in her gut."

Leo gazed at him, appalled and confounded. To give away the infant, then lie to Martha Seabright and tell her the baby had died… It was too cruel and diabolical. Leo had trouble believing it.

"She had a point," he said, as if seeing her doubt play out in her expression. "We'd seen Edward the day before at Sunday sermon. He seemed perfectly fine, babbling like always. And then, Tuesday morning, we were told he died the night before of a fever. Came up out of nowhere, though none of the other little ones were ill. They'd already buried him, just to be safe, they said. But we never saw him. His body, I mean."

It was irregular that none of the other small children had been ill, as fevers were known to spread. There should have been at least a few others afflicted. And to not allow Edward's siblings the chance to say goodbye to their infant brother was also strangely callous.

"Paula never got over it," Gavin said, his frown pinching his brow. "Losing him haunted her."

"Did she share her suspicion with your mother?" Leo asked.

Gavin bounced on his toes, then started to retreat. "What does any of this have to do with the dead man in my room? I've explained why I didn't go to the dinner. Now, will you speak to the detective? Will you tell him I'm innocent?"

Her annoyance with Gavin increased. "You must speak to him yourself, Mr. Seabright. You must tell him everything you've told me—"

"No. This was a mistake," he growled and then, before Leo could plead with him not to run, disappeared down the dirt lane and into the street, leaving nothing but a cloud of dust in his wake.

Chapter Thirteen

As Jasper approached 10 Bloomsbury Square, he eyed the recessed steps to the servant's entrance, tucked underneath the main entrance. He would not descend and knock upon that door, even if the residents within the home would have preferred it.

On his way to Bloomsbury from Westminster, Jasper had been struck with conflicting moments of buoyancy and dread. Buoyancy, because asking Leo to dinner, and the smile she'd tried to hide when she accepted, had given him an unexpected sense of victory. Dread, because the notion of calling upon Stanley Hayes weighed on him like lead ballast.

Stanley had been an arrogant prig in Sir Eamon's office the day before, and his opinion of Jasper had been clear. However, the revelation that either his wife or his daughter had been seen emerging from Martha Seabright's home needed to be addressed. Jasper required answers, and though that lead ballast shifted down to his feet now that he was climbing the front steps, he had a duty to perform.

He lifted the shiny, brass Hand of Fatima knocker and brought it down twice. He released it quickly; he'd never liked the door knocker style of a small hand clutching an orb. To his mind, it had the appearance of someone reaching through the door, despite its alleged ability to ward off evil and bring good luck to the household. He considered, too, that the heat was making him more irritable than usual. The day's humidity had turned the air in London into a Turkish bath, heavy and still. He found himself wishing for another rainstorm, if only to clear away the rising stink of horse dung, rotting food, sweat, and sewage.

When the door opened, he was met by a short man in footman's livery. His hair had been curled purposefully at the nape to give the appearance of a justice's powdered wig.

"The servant's entrance is directly below." He sniffed, then began to close the door.

"Detective Inspector Reid from Scotland Yard," Jasper said, simultaneously holding up his warrant card and stopping the front door with his foot. The servant glared in offense but pulled the door open again. "I'd like to speak to Mr. Hayes."

"Mr. Hayes is out," he snapped.

"Then I would like to speak to Mrs. Hayes. This is a matter of some importance."

"Jasper?"

His attention diverted from the servant's stern disapproval to where Constance was descending the staircase into the foyer. Jasper drew in a bracing breath and tucked his warrant card away. He hadn't known if he would see her, but he'd come prepared for the possibility.

"It is all right, Gerard; let the detective inspector inside," Constance commanded in the smooth, cultured voice of someone who was accustomed to giving orders to servants.

Jasper entered the bright and spacious entrance hall.

"Thank you, Gerard," she said, and after a sharp nod, the servant left them.

"Why have you come here?" she asked Jasper once they stood alone. She didn't invite him into the front sitting room like any other guest would be, but he didn't take offense. He wasn't technically a guest of the family's and had, after all, thrown her over. By her cool expression, she hadn't yet forgiven him.

"I'd like to speak to your mother. It's regarding an inquiry. Is she in?"

Constance clasped her hands before her, and her brow formed a haughty arch. She was quite beautiful, with blonde hair fashioned in an elegant, upswept twist, blue eyes fringed by dark lashes, and a figure that had, on occasion, set his pulse racing. However now, his heartbeat remained steady. Seeing her again had not inspired more than a twinge of guilt for his having waited so long to end their courtship.

"My mother?" Constance asked. "How can she possibly be of interest to you in one of your inquiries?"

"That is a discussion I'd like to have with her." Jasper was aware that he sounded rude, and yet he was unable to avoid it. "Is she in?" he inquired again.

"No," Constance bit off. "She is not."

He swept a look up the staircase. "Are you staying here now?"

The question was meant to tip her off balance, and it seemed to work. Her expression softened. "I'm only paying a call. I still have rooms at the ladies' boardinghouse."

Jasper had wondered how her parents handled the news that their daughter was working as a typist for *The Times*—women of their ilk did not work, and they certainly did not live in boardinghouses. But it seemed Constance had stood up to her parents and maintained her independence. He found that admirable.

"When do you expect your mother to return?"

She folded her arms. "I don't expect her at all. She has left London."

Alarm sharpened its claws in his back. "When was this?"

"An hour ago, or so."

Somehow, he managed to suppress a frustrated groan. So, Mrs. Hayes had snooped in Martha's home and then fled town right away? She'd found something, perhaps.

"Your father left with her?"

At her open glare, he guessed the barrage of questions was not welcome. "He and my brother left yesterday morning. Why are you so rabid to speak to them?"

"What was their destination?" he asked rather than answer. She wasn't pleased. Her lips pressed thin, and her blue eyes flared.

"How is that any of your business?"

"Miss Hayes, I must insist you tell me where they've gone."

Either their voices had carried, or the servant she'd

dismissed had stayed close behind a door because Gerard returned to the foyer, a questioning glance thrown between Constance and Jasper.

"Is there a problem, Miss Hayes?" He likely hoped he might be allowed to show Jasper the door.

She held up her hand. "Everything is fine. But I do think the inspector will be leaving shortly."

"Constance." The use of her given name snagged her attention and her ire. Before she could rebuke him, he continued, "It is imperative I speak to them."

She drew out the moment until Jasper expected that she would turn him out after all. But then she exhaled, and her tensed shoulders dropped as her resistance melted away. "My father and brother left for Beechwood, our home in Hampshire, yesterday. I arrived here an hour ago to learn that Mother had followed them. Her note to me said that she needed to take the country air."

Why they had not all gone together stood out as odd to him. From the muddled expression Constance wore, she felt the same.

"They left unexpectedly without saying goodbye to you," he presumed. When she nodded, Jasper looked to the servant still waiting to toss him out. "Did Mrs. Hayes leave here earlier today, alone, for an hour or two, and was she wearing a hooded blue cloak?"

"What an odd question," Constance exclaimed. "Did someone see my mother out somewhere and tell you?"

He would not, under any circumstances, reveal who had seen her mother or where it had been. Constance already despised Leo, and Jasper didn't want anyone in the Hayes family to know who had seen Mrs. Hayes. "I need an answer," he said, deflecting Constance's question.

Gerard sought instruction from Constance. She nodded, albeit reluctantly.

He replied tartly, "Yes. She was out, and she was wearing the cloak you describe."

"What happened when she returned?" Jasper asked.

"She ordered her maid to begin packing and alerted the rest of the staff that she was leaving London posthaste. We are to send the rest of the belongings behind them."

"Was there anything that happened that could account for her and her husband's impulsive departures?"

Again, the servant sent Constance an imploring look. She gestured toward Jasper with an impatient flick of her fingers. "I'm curious myself, Gerard. Tell the inspector what you might know."

What Gerard thought of the order was plain on his face, but he relented. "Two nights ago, Mr. and Mrs. Hayes had quite a row. We could hear their shouting from where we were belowstairs."

That had been the night of the benefit dinner. Stanley claimed they hadn't attended because his wife was ill.

"What were they arguing about? Did you hear anything specific?"

The servant shook his head. But as with so many people Jasper had questioned in his career thus far, Gerard's lie showed in the twitch of a facial muscle and the lack of eye contact with him.

"What aren't you telling me?" Jasper asked.

"Gerard?" Constance said, her tone clear: He was to speak. And she appeared to be just as curious as Jasper.

"I did go up, but only to be certain all was well," he confessed. "They were in Mrs. Hayes's bedchamber, and when she raised her voice, I heard…" Here he paused, as if torn. But he sighed and went on. "I heard her ask, '*How could you lie to me?*'"

"What else did you hear?" Constance asked, alarmed.

"Not another word. I knew straightaway that I shouldn't be listening and returned downstairs."

For once, Jasper wished the servant had done what many servants were wont to do: eavesdropped.

Constance dismissed him with a prim nod. Then, with a circumspect glance toward the retreating servant, she gestured Jasper toward the sitting room. Once they were inside, she lowered the haughty shield she'd erected around herself when he'd first arrived.

"I called on my mother yesterday afternoon," she began. "She had been weeping. Her eyes were swollen and red, and though she claimed she was only feeling ill, I suspected it wasn't that. Now, after what Gerard overheard, I know for certain it wasn't."

The argument between Stanley and his wife had been the cause, surely.

"And at the time of your visit yesterday, your father had already left London?"

Constance nodded. "And George, with him."

Her younger brother. By a good ten years, if he wasn't mistaken.

"Did she say anything of note to you yesterday? You must have asked why your father and brother had gone without saying goodbye."

"I did, of course," she said. "Mother said Father had unexpected business to attend to and that George yearned for the country and his horses."

She shrugged, as if she had easily believed her mother's reasoning. Jasper, however, did not.

"Where is your family's home in Hampshire?"

She balked. "You're not going there, are you?"

If he did, he would have to take the train. It would be several hours of travel. However, he needed to speak to Mrs. Hayes; he needed to know what she was doing in Martha Seabright's house, and if the argument the servants overheard had anything to do with why they did not attend the benefit dinner.

"Your mother may have information that is crucial to my inquiry," he said, "so if I must go there, I will."

Constance relented and gave him the address in Hampshire and directions.

"Jasper," she said, slowing him as he reached the front door. "Are my parents in any sort of trouble?"

He held his tongue against the truth: He was becoming ever more certain that they were. The last thing he wanted was to give Constance a reason to send a telegram ahead of him, alerting her parents to his interest in them. It was what he would have done if his father were alive, and a police inspector came calling.

"I only want to put some questions to them," he said, then tipped his hat and left.

The day's hazy sky and oppressive heat broke as Jasper was stepping down from a cab outside Scotland Yard. The windows in headquarters were bright with gaslight, the warm glow welcoming as rain began to fall in earnest.

Jasper started for the doors, and as he went, he swept a look around the courtyard for the stranger in the orange bowler. There was no sign of him, and he could only hope that would remain the case when he went to pick up Leo for their evening out. However, with or without Leo, should Jasper set eyes on the man again, he would confront him, come what may.

He rushed inside the lobby as the storm intensified with a reverberating clap of thunder.

"A lad delivered a message for you, Inspector," Constable Woodhouse said from his place at the front receiving desk.

Jasper took the familiar buff-colored envelope, sealed with black wax—stationery used by the Spring Street Morgue. He was walking toward the CID while breaking the envelope's seal when Sergeant Warnock came upon him.

"Frank's Best Livery and Cab was shuttered a few years back," he said, his excitement evident. "Francis, or Frank as he was known, was the original owner, and when he died, his son, Philip, inherited the business but closed the place almost immediately, according to neighbors."

Jasper lowered the envelope. Philip Green, the server who ran from the dinner. "He's our link. Philip provided the getaway carriage and was the inside man at the dinner, informing the robbers of the details they would need." He clapped the sergeant on the shoulder, impressed again by Warnock's good police work. "Put out a notice for Philip Green's arrest, then go to the catering service again. Get people talking. Someone may know something about Philip that could lead us to him."

Warnock dashed off toward the telegraph room, where the operators would send notice to all divisions, along with a description of the suspect. Jasper returned to opening the envelope, elated by the break in the case. As he took out the notepaper folded within, however, his pleasure dipped. For a bare second before reading the inked handwriting, he wondered if Leo had changed her mind about having dinner with him. But then, he stopped in his tracks as he read the note: *Come to the morgue. G.S. was here.*

He crushed the paper in his hand and swore under his breath. *G.S.* Gavin Seabright. Turning around, he pulled up his coat collar, passed Woodhouse, and went straight back outside into the rain. Without an umbrella, his coat and hat were soaked by the time he arrived at the morgue. He entered through the front lobby door, setting off the bell that hung attached to it.

"Is that you, Jasper?" Leo called, her voice raised to be heard from within the postmortem room.

He pushed open the door and slammed into a wall of stink. The day's heat had quashed the scant cool temperature the vestry held onto during the summer. The warm weather had sped up the decomposition of corpses, and the resulting odors were more than a little unpleasant.

Leo stood at a large steel sink, rinsing a pair of elbow-length rubber gloves he'd seen Claude use during examinations. A calico kerchief, tied at the back of her head, covered her nose and mouth. She twisted to see him.

"Oh, good, you received my note," she said with perceptible cheer.

Leo usually only sounded cheerful when she'd figured something out and was eager to tell him.

He took the handkerchief from his breast pocket and placed it to his nose. It didn't help much. "When was Gavin Seabright here?" he asked, then looked around the large room. "And where is Quinn?"

There was no sign of the new coroner.

"Gone for the evening," she replied as she shook off the rinsed gloves and clipped them onto a line of wire for drying. "And Gavin was here earlier, just after I left you at the Yard."

"Were you here alone with him?"

"I was perfectly safe," she said, goading him with a crafty glance over her shoulder. "He isn't a murderer."

"Are you sure of that?"

"Yes. He didn't do it." She wiped her hands on her apron as she explained, "The John Doe's given name is Harry, surname unknown, and he was a stranger to Gavin."

Leo removed her apron and hung it on a hook, then smoothed her skirt from her hips down. Jasper followed the motion, and his pulse kicked into a rapid tattoo.

He cleared his throat, which suddenly felt like a cord had cinched it tight. "What did he say to you?"

"That Harry promised to confess the name of the man who killed Gavin's mother in exchange for money and a way out of London," she replied. "Gavin doubted his mother was dead, so he came here to see for himself."

"He knew her body had been sent to Spring Street?" Jasper asked, wondering how. But then thought of Philip Green. He'd disappeared in the commotion after the shooting, but he might have stayed long enough to have heard where Martha's body was to be taken and conveyed the information to the other members of the group, including Harry.

"Yes, somehow," Leo said. "But what is important is that Gavin was going to agree to Harry's demands. Unfortunately, he was killed while Gavin was at the morgue. Gavin ran, knowing how bad everything looked for him."

With one party dead, there was only Gavin's word for it. "You believe him?" Jasper asked.

She nodded firmly. "I do. It aligns with how Harry acted in the carriage with the other masked intruders. He was upset and nervous about Martha being killed that night."

Jasper grimaced at the reminder that Leo had been abducted that night as well, if only for a short while. He wondered if the memory would ever fail to affect him this way.

The fetid odors of rotting flesh had seeped through the weave of his handkerchief. "Do you mind if we go to the office?"

She nodded, her own kerchief still in place. Once they had left the postmortem room, closing the door behind them, they lowered their linens and drew in breaths. The air was only marginally better here.

"Where is Gavin now? He should have come to Scotland Yard and pled his case to me, not you."

Leo moved toward the desk, where the gray tabby morgue cat had draped itself across the blotter. "I suggested Gavin do just that, but he became spooked and ran off."

Tibia mewed when Leo scratched her fingers into its neck fur.

"What spooked him?" Jasper asked.

She scratched the cat's neck another moment, then answered, "I think it was the mention of his sister, Paula Blickson. It turns out she was the dark-haired woman Mrs. Beardsley saw."

That caught his interest and his suspicion. He took a step toward the desk but stopped when Tibia hissed at his approach. "When I interviewed Mrs. Blickson this morning, she claimed she hadn't spoken to either her mother or Gavin for a long time."

"And yet, she was the one who asked him not to attend the benefit dinner. She said he would be a traitor if he did go."

Paula had mentioned nothing about this earlier. Though he hadn't been able to say why, there had been something disingenuous to her wearing mourning black, her dramatic black lace veil, and the trembling of her hand when she touched the handkerchief to her nose. Her red, glassy eyes had been real, however, and so Jasper had left his suspicions alone for the time being.

"Why would he be a traitor?" he asked Leo.

She pressed her lips together, as she did whenever she was about to say something he might not like. "That is why I sent for you. It couldn't wait. I think I've figured out how Mrs. Hayes is connected to Martha Seabright."

He braced himself.

"It's Edward," she went on. "The baby."

"I remember. What about him?"

"According to Gavin, Paula never believed that he died of a fever. She was convinced that her infant brother was instead taken."

A large morass seemed to grow inside Jasper. The death of the baby brother had prickled through him with some sense of significance when he learned of it, but he hadn't understood why or if he'd been reacting out of pure pity.

"Taken by whom?" he asked, even though an instinctive answer was already there, waiting to be pulled forward. Leo did just that.

"I believe by Mrs. Hayes."

Chapter Fourteen

A growl of thunder filled the pause that dropped between them. That afternoon, after Gavin Seabright's departure, Leo had entered the morgue in a fog, her mind spinning over the beginnings of her theory. That's all it was. She had no proof for any of it. And yet, the more she thought of it, the more confident she felt that she was onto the truth.

Jasper's immediate apprehension wasn't unexpected.

"You think Mrs. Hayes *took* Martha Seabright's infant? How in the world did you reach that conclusion?"

The back door to the office had been propped open most of the afternoon, and now, light gusts of wind and rain blew inside, wetting the threshold stone. Leo gravitated toward the fresh air as she gathered the reasons she'd accumulated during the afternoon. They were piteously few.

"Gavin explained that Edward hadn't been sick when he and Paula had last seen him. However, he apparently died the next night of a mysterious fever."

"Gavin and Paula were young, just children themselves. Maybe the baby was ill, and they simply didn't realize it," Jasper said, following her toward the open door.

It was something Leo had considered too and was a valid argument.

"And fevers can claim the very young and the very old quickly, I am aware," she said. "But we can't dismiss the fact that they never saw the infant's body. Edward was buried before dawn of the following day before Gavin and Paula were even alerted."

"If the nurse believed the fever could be contagious, she might have wanted the burial to be done as quickly as possible," he said, citing another possibility Leo had weighed. But she'd found it unlikely. Unless the baby had been afflicted by smallpox or some other plague, there was no reason to bury the victim so swiftly, and a nurse would have known that.

"Mr. Hayes was a governor of the orphanage at the time, was he not?" she asked.

Jasper nodded as he eyed the storm outside. "He was."

"As such, his wife would have also held a position of authority," Leo said.

He crossed his arms. "And you think she ordered the nurse to give her the baby and tell Martha Seabright her infant son had died?"

"Sir Eamon said that Martha asked about a particular nurse at the orphanage," Leo pointed out. "This could be the reason why."

"What about the other employees, like the groundskeeper who would have dug the hole for burial?

Surely, the matron, too, would have seen the dead child before he went into the ground."

The quick barrage of reasoning battered her theory, riddling it with holes. And yet, she knew instinctively that something about Edward's supposed death was not true.

"I can't help but think of the cryptic note Mrs. Seabright had in her handbag at the time of her murder," Leo began. "She was given a sum of money for a choice she'd made. It had been a business transaction, and the author had assured her she'd done the right thing."

Jasper closed his eyes and pinched the bridge of his nose. "You're suggesting she was paid in exchange for her son?"

"It is an awful notion. However, Esther Goodwin said her sister was eager to be rid of her children. If Martha was made an offer for her son to be taken in by another family, to be given a better life, maybe she accepted it. The note in her handbag would make sense if that were the case. And perhaps Mrs. Hayes sneaked into Martha's home for a reason related to the baby."

He shook his head, a stutter of lightning accentuating his disagreement. "That letter could have been about anything. There were no details, not even a name. Furthermore, what would Mrs. Hayes have wanted with a baby? She already had two children of her own."

That is where Leo struggled too. Mrs. Hayes couldn't have simply shown up at home with a baby and not been questioned. Still, Leo wasn't ready to abandon her theory.

"Perhaps she brought the baby to someone else she knew. A friend. I don't know," she admitted, which felt too much like defeat for her liking. "But Paula always believed Edward was taken from the orphanage."

"Mrs. Blickson identified Nurse Radcliff as the one who was caring for Edward when he died," Jasper said, still shaking his head. "She never breathed a word about believing he was alive."

"I think it would be prudent to speak to her again."

Next to the sound of rain assailing the roof and splattering in the puddles along the dirt lane, Leo barely heard his grunt of assent.

There was nothing more to present to him regarding her theory. All she could do now was wait to hear what Paula said when he did question her. Tomorrow, most likely. And so long as they met here afterward, rather than at Scotland Yard, Leo suspected he would share the results of the interview. She'd brought him the lead, after all. Just as she had earlier, about Mrs. Hayes being inside Martha Seabright's home.

"Did you go to Bloomsbury Square?" she asked, eager to know what the woman had to say for herself.

"I did. I spoke with Miss Hayes."

Miss Hayes. *Constance.* A twinge of disappointment and something else Leo didn't quite like traveled their way through her, from belly to throat. It had been some months since Leo had last seen Constance Hayes, but she hadn't forgotten how striking she was, how stylish and sophisticated. Leo raised a hand to pat the back of her head. Wisps of her dark brown hair had come loose from several pins over the course of the afternoon while assisting Connor with the autopsy of a middle-aged man. She had been so preoccupied with thoughts of Gavin Seabright, Mrs. Hayes, and little Edward that she had not stopped to consider how untidy she might appear.

She lowered her hand, hoping Jasper hadn't noticed her insecurity. "Was her mother in?"

"Mrs. Hayes left London immediately after returning from her outing to Martha Seabright's home. A servant confirmed she'd gone out for a few hours and was wearing a hooded blue cloak, just as you noted."

"She has left London?" Alarm pitched her voice higher. "Where has she gone?"

"According to Constance, to their family home in Hampshire. Her father and younger brother departed for the country yesterday unexpectedly, and today, Constance discovered her mother had gone too. There were no goodbyes."

"There is no question, then. Something must have happened," Leo said, thinking of Martha's home. Had Mrs. Hayes found something there? Something worrying enough to make her flee London?

"The servant I spoke to said Mr. and Mrs. Hayes had argued the night of the benefit dinner," Jasper said. "Mrs. Hayes was heard accusing her husband of lying to her."

"Gracious," Leo murmured, her mind spinning with this new information. "I wonder how it connects to Martha Seabright."

"It might not connect at all," he warned. "I won't know until I question them."

"Are you going to Hampshire, then?" Leo eyed the clock on the wall. It was nearly six o'clock. "Not tonight, I hope?"

They were supposed to have dinner together this evening. She'd been anticipating it all afternoon, even if the promise of it made her feel a bit wobbly.

Jasper formed a slow, crooked smile. "Not tonight."

Again, conscious of her bedraggled appearance, Leo pushed a loose strand of hair behind her ear; it had been coming forward, tickling her cheek for a few hours. She hadn't cared enough to pin it back into place, though now she regretted the decision.

"Are we still dining at seven?" she asked, next running her palm over her narrow belt and the rumpled green shirtwaist tucked into the band. "I'm not sure I'll be ready so soon. I'm rather a mess."

Jasper only continued to grin, his attention slipping down the length of her body, from where she held a palm to her stomach to the tips of her boots. When his eyes met hers again, she felt pinned in place by them.

"You don't look a mess, Leo. You look beautiful."

A gust of wind blew in, sprinkling her lightly with rain. She didn't blink or flinch. She could only stare up at him, befuddled. Her first instinct was to deny the compliment. Beautiful wasn't how she would have ever described herself. Awestruck as she was, however, she paused long enough to recognize sincerity in the way Jasper gazed at her. He'd meant it.

"No one has ever called me that." Only once she'd spoken did she hear how pitiful the confession sounded. Embarrassment warmed her. Or perhaps it was pleasure from his flattering remark. She wasn't certain.

"Never?" Jasper appeared doubtful.

Leo shrugged, wishing she hadn't said it now. "Trust me, I would remember if someone had."

Just as she would always remember this. Jasper, holding his bowler by its dampened crown, his honey-blond hair a shade darker from the rain that had soaked through the wool felt on his walk to the morgue. His dark green vest, the one that accentuated the color of his eyes. His brown tie, the knot loose after a long day.

He moved closer, narrowing the space between them. When his hand reached for the stubborn curl of sable hair that had slipped forward once again, his fingertips brushed her cheek as he tucked it behind her ear. Standing this close to him, breathing in the scent of his clothing, of his skin, was all so new and thrilling and terrifying. And yet, as overwhelming as it was, nothing could have induced her to back away when Jasper's warm hand cupped the nape of her neck. Or when he angled his head nearer, and his lips lowered to hers.

He tested the kiss with a gentle press of his mouth, and after a heart-stopping moment, Leo met it with an answering nudge. Her palms lifted to the damp lapels of his coat, and she gripped them lightly. Through half-lidded eyes, she saw a flicker of lightning. The scent of ozone mingled with his musky sandalwood.

The details of their first kiss were locked as vividly in Leo's memory as everything else, and yet she was surprised by what she'd forgotten—the galvanizing sensation of Jasper's arm, hooking her waist and pulling her against him. How curiously small and delicate she felt in his embrace. The magnetic need to rise onto her toes and meet his seeking lips.

The rolling thunder, the spray of rain against them as they stood near the open doorway, those things didn't matter right then. And, as if the meeting of their mouths allowed her to read his mind, Leo knew Jasper did not care either. Her hearing went a bit muffled, the world muting beneath those sounds that were closest: Jasper's uneven breathing and her own. The rustle of his coat under her hands. The scuff of his shoes as he slowly guided her away from the door's entrance in the direction of her desk.

Whether he'd been kissing her for one minute or five, she didn't know. Nor did she care. She'd become lost in the lovely marvel of it, of allowing him to pull her flush against him. Leo wanted the kiss to go on and on. Forever would have been acceptable.

As such, the pointed clearing of a throat took a prolonged moment to register in her awareness. Then, in a sharp and disorienting flash, Jasper's mouth and the arm around her waist were gone. Leo staggered back a step as he released her to face the interloper.

Standing just outside the open doorway, holding an umbrella above his head, was Detective Sergeant Lewis. Mortification seared her, and Leo turned away, though not before glimpsing Sergeant Lewis's chastened, though somewhat amused, expression.

"Roy," Jasper said, his voice low and rough. There was no mistaking his annoyance even before he snapped, "What is it?"

"Sorry, guv. Woodhouse said you'd run out earlier. I thought you might be here."

Leo ran her thumb over her lower lip and pushed back the rogue curl of hair again before daring to face the detective sergeant. Her ears burned, and her cheeks would surely be glowing. There was no chance of concealing her embarrassment, however, so she gave up.

Sergeant Lewis carefully avoided meeting her gaze as he said to Jasper, "I need a word," then stepped away from the door as if to indicate that Jasper should join him under the umbrella.

Jasper slapped on his hat and went outside under the dome of black silk. As Sergent Lewis spoke in low tones, Leo's curiosity increased while Jasper's expression hardened. Then, he closed his eyes as if he'd been dealt bad news. With a curt nod of acceptance, he hurried back inside the office. Drops of rain flicked off the brim of his hat as he removed it.

"What's happened?" she asked, her lips feeling swollen. His were a shade more pink than usual too.

"I'm sorry, Leo. We'll need to dine together another evening." He kept his back to his waiting sergeant. "Lewis and I have been called away."

"To where?"

His jaw shifted as if in aggravation. "Twickenham."

The discomfort over the detective sergeant coming upon them in such a private moment dissipated. "That is where the orphanage is located," she said.

Jasper glanced over his shoulder toward Sergeant Lewis, then nodded. "A nurse there has been found dead. Murdered."

Her head went a bit dizzy, though not in the same pleasurable way it had when Jasper had been kissing her. "Nurse Radcliff?" she asked, breathless.

He nodded grimly.

"The murders are connected," she said. "They must be."

While he didn't agree, he also didn't dispute her deduction. Instead, he reached for her hand. His palm was coarse and warm, and he brought her a little closer. "It's a distance, even by train. We'll be staying over, and I'm not sure when I'll be back. I don't want you involved in anything while I'm gone. Promise me you'll stay clear of this case, Leo. And if Gavin Seabright comes to see you again, send him to Sergeant Warnock. He's in charge now until we return."

As much as she hated being given orders, she understood his reasoning. She also understood the twinge of worry pulling his brow taut as he watched her, waiting for her to reply. It was ridiculous, but she, too, felt a prickle of unease at the thought of Jasper boarding a train and leaving her. It shouldn't have given her pause at all. He was a detective inspector. Murder inquiries were his stock-in-trade. He wasn't in any danger. At least, not that she was aware of.

Leo gave a nod. "All right."

His answering grin drew her eyes to his lips. She could still feel the phantom pressure of them against her own.

"Write down your statement about your meeting with Seabright. Word for word. Then give it to Warnock," he said. After tensing his hand around hers an extra moment, he released her and stepped back out into the rain. He put on his hat and turned up his collar as he joined Sergeant Lewis under the umbrella, and the two of them set out at a swift pace.

Letting out a long exhalation, Leo closed the door and went directly to her desk. She gently scooted Tibia from the blotter and prepared her typewriter. Detailing her brief interaction with Gavin Seabright helped to draw her mind from the last several perplexing minutes. It would be so easy to simply close her eyes and return to the memory of Jasper's kiss. However, she prided herself on being neither daft nor prone to daydreaming and she also took pride in writing thorough reports.

After typing her statement, Leo locked the morgue's front doors, put out the gasoliers, and fed Tibby a couple of tinned sardines for her dinner. She went out the back, grateful the rain had ebbed to a light drizzle, and by the time she reached Scotland Yard, she barely needed her umbrella. Another constable was at the receiving desk, as Constable Woodhouse had left for the evening, and this officer asked her what her business was.

Leo started to explain when the building's doors opened, and Lord Oliver Hayes and his cousin, Constance, entered. In a drop of silence, the three of them peered at one another. Constance's eyes flared when they settled on Leo, and though they were filled with dislike, that wasn't what bothered Leo most. They were also swollen and red from crying.

All the envy she'd felt toward the young woman dissipated. "Miss Hayes," she said, stepping away from the desk constable. "What is the matter?"

Lord Hayes removed his hat and, with some visible apprehension, replied, "We are looking for Inspector Reid."

"I'm sorry," Leo replied. "He's left for the train station."

"No!" Constance's voice broke. "He can't have gone. We need to speak to him!"

She turned to her cousin, as if pleading with him to snap his fingers and make Jasper appear. He tried to calm her with a hand to her shoulder, but she only shrugged it off in a huff of temper. The viscount turned to Leo.

"Do you know if he has gone to Hampshire?"

"Not to Hampshire, but to Twickenham," she answered. "He won't be back until later tomorrow, I expect."

Oliver swore under his breath.

"We don't have time to wait," Constance cried, nearly shouting in her panic.

"Madam, sir, would you like to report something? Some crime?" the desk constable asked.

Constance grunted in frustration, a sound which somehow managed to be graceful.

"What has happened?" Leo asked.

"As you are not a detective, Miss Spencer," the other woman snapped, "I fail to see how you can help."

Leo stiffened.

"*Constance*," Lord Hayes said, his tone commanding. She crossed her arms and looked away but didn't say anything more.

"Miss Spencer," the viscount began in a conciliatory manner. "I am aware that you've worked with Jasper in the past on some inquiries…even though it was surely in an informal capacity," he tacked on, with a guarded look toward the listening desk constable. "I'm not sure if you can assist, but I don't see the harm in telling you that yesterday, my uncle, Constance's father, arrived at my home in Kensington."

"I thought Mr. Hayes was traveling to Hampshire," Leo said.

Constance peered at her. "How did you know that?"

"That may take too long to explain," she answered, not wanting to divert from what Lord Hayes was saying.

"He was stopping over on his way to Beechwood," the viscount continued. "The strange thing was that Stanley was unnerved. So was George."

"My brother," Constance said, then added more sharply, "Or perhaps you already knew that too."

"Yes, in fact, I did," Leo replied, growing impatient

with her attitude. "Unnerved how?" she asked, turning back to Lord Hayes.

"Stanley wouldn't say much, just that he was tired with Town and wanted to retreat to the country. But there was something more he wasn't telling me. I could sense it." The viscount exhaled slowly. "Anyhow, it was around eleven o'clock this morning when Stanley came to me, asking if I'd seen George. I had not, not since the evening before. Neither of us had. We searched the house and the grounds. We scoured Holland Park near my home and even went round to my neighbors' homes to see if they had seen him. No one had."

Alarm shuttled up Leo's back to her scalp. "Are you saying George is missing?"

"That is exactly what he is saying," Constance replied, her voice quavering with dread. "My brother is gone."

Chapter Fifteen

As he stepped off the train onto the platform at Twickenham Junction just past nine o'clock, Jasper breathed in the cool, sweet scents of clipped grass and fresh air. Even the clouds of smoke billowing from the train's coal-burning engine could not subdue them. It had been years since he'd left London. Truly left it, that was. Oliver Hayes's home in Kensington, which Jasper had viewed as a kind of country retreat from the city, did not have this same tranquil stillness. His ears had become so accustomed to the turbulent cacophony of city life that its absence, now replaced by the melodic chirp of crickets, was a little overwhelming.

The late summer twilight had slipped away while he and Lewis rode the train southwest from Charing Cross Station. The rickety ride had lasted a good two hours, with stops made at every rail station along the way. The uncomfortable wooden bench, its cushion worn into a thin, lumpy state, had probably bruised Jasper's backside.

"Detective Inspector Reid?" A uniformed police constable was waiting near the Twickenham station doors. By the gas jets of the station lamps, he appeared young. Probably no more than twenty or twenty-one years of age. He stepped forward, wearing an open, somewhat eager grin to greet the Scotland Yard detectives.

"That's correct," Jasper said, then introduced Lewis as his detective sergeant.

"PC Landry, sir. Sergeant Tinsdale sent me to escort you to the orphanage at Wellesley House. He and Matron Westover are waiting for you there."

Jasper and Lewis followed the young police constable to a wagon in front of the station. The dirt road was dark and empty, with only a few spots of light emanating from nearby structures.

"Is there an inn or lodging house that might be able to give us rooms for the night?" Jasper asked. "My sergeant and I will likely be staying here until morning."

"Mrs. Barnston usually has rooms at her place," Landry replied. "She runs an inn and tavern. I'll arrange for it after I take you to the orphanage."

With any luck, the tavern would also set aside supper for them. Jasper's gnawing hunger had grown as they'd traveled toward Twickenham, and it had likely been the reason why, after enduring Lewis's smirking glimpses for as long as he could stand them, he'd snapped at the detective sergeant, "All right. Out with it."

He knew exactly what the smirks were regarding.

Kissing Leo had been impulsive, and doing so within view of the open back door to the morgue's office, reckless. His blood had simmered high and hot the second he'd had her in his arms, crushed against him. When her lips parted against his, allowing him to deepen the kiss, he'd tumbled well past caring where they were or who might see them. Thankfully—and irritatingly—the detective sergeant had interrupted before Jasper could completely lose control of the moment, and of himself.

"Nothing to say, guv. Nothing at all," Lewis replied, still grinning like a fool. "Except that you and Miss Spencer are a good match."

Jasper had shifted on the hard bench, uncertain how to respond. He and Leo weren't *matched*. They weren't courting. What they were was too fragile to define just yet. Still, he knew kissing her the way he had and the desire building within him for her only led to one place.

"She's smart, serious," Lewis had gone on conversationally. "Like my missus."

The compliment had left Jasper dumbstruck. He'd known Lewis didn't dislike Leo, as the other men at the Yard might, but he hadn't realized the detective sergeant thought enough of her to liken her to his own wife.

"That is high praise," Jasper said, slightly uncomfortable. He attempted to steer the conversation away from Leo. "I haven't yet met your wife."

Lewis had kept his life and his work at the Met separate, so much so that Jasper didn't even know his wife's or sons' names.

"We'll have you around," Lewis replied with a firm nod. "You can bring Miss Spencer—so long as she doesn't talk about dead bodies at the dinner table."

Jasper feigned annoyance with the caveat, but truthfully, the invitation from his sergeant pleased him. He'd wondered for some time if Lewis even liked him or was only being courteous because of their different ranks.

The pleasurable image of him taking Leo to dinner at Roy Lewis's home had reminded him of their foiled dinner plans for that evening. He supposed that was just how it was when one was a police detective. Thankfully, she hadn't seemed overly upset.

PC Landry drove them to Wellesley House, the main building of the Metropolitan and City Police Orphanage. As the police forces increased their numbers, so too increased the number of officers either killed or seriously wounded in the line of duty. With more children affected, the need for additional space had grown. Jasper recalled his father speaking of the orphanage's recent purchase of another building across the street.

Both domiciles were dark and quiet when their wagon arrived. Lanterns flickered in a few windows of Wellesley House, and two gas brackets at the main door spluttered, but otherwise, the large manor looked to be abed for the night.

Landry drew the horses to a stop, and Lewis whistled softly. "Remind me to be more cautious while I'm on duty," he said. "I can't stomach the thought of my boys being sent here if I were to cark it."

"They wouldn't be sent here. Your wife would never part with them, I'm certain." Jasper's thoughts immediately turned to Martha Seabright and her sister, Esther Goodwin. The older woman had informed Leo that Martha had been eager to be rid of her children. The sentiment left him cold.

"You're right," Lewis said as they approached the main entrance. "Her mother would take her and the boys in."

That Lewis would have to consider any alternative to living long enough to raise his two children was a reality of the job. At the hollow clangs of the door knocker, Jasper thought of all the children housed here, many of whom had lost their fathers.

The front door was opened by a man in police uniform who introduced himself as Sergeant Tinsdale. He was older, graying around the temples, and he had a rigid, rule-following bearing as he took over from Landry and led them inside. The interior was airy and cold, without hangings on the walls, rugs on the floor, or any other décor. Spartan was the word that came to mind as Sergeant Tinsdale held a lantern aloft, lighting their way up a set of wide marble stairs to the first level.

"The body hasn't been moved from where it was found earlier today in the infirmary," he reported. "Matron Westover was not pleased, as we had to close off the room and post a man outside the door."

The Matron was the top authority at the orphanage, and Jasper held a vision of what she would look like. Older. Stern and draconian.

"Thank you for adhering to protocol, Sergeant," Jasper said as they followed him. He had worried on the way there that the body would have been moved, the immediate area cleaned, with helpful evidence swept away.

"I heard about what happened the other night in Town at the benefit dinner for this place," Sergeant Tinsdale said once they'd reached a landing. "The robbery and the woman who was shot. So, when I saw the nurse here had been stabbed, I thought it best to contact Scotland Yard. Two murders connected to this place had me suspicious."

"You were right to be," Jasper said. The sergeant was to be commended. There were plenty of officers who would not have wanted to turn the reins over to someone else, out of pure pride. "Stabbed, you say?"

Another lantern brightened the hallway ahead, and as they walked along the corridor, a woman exited a room. Seeing them, she hurried in their direction. Tall and lithe, she had an elegant, feminine figure that set Jasper back on his heels. Lewis, too, by his staggered expression.

"Matron Westover," Sergeant Tinsdale said in greeting, though he sounded irked. It must have been a long day holding her off from having the nurse's body removed. "Detective Inspector Reid and Detective Sergeant Lewis from Scotland Yard have arrived."

Jasper's expectations were not usually so thoroughly upended. The matron, wearing a dress of somber dark blue that reminded him of the fashions Leo wore to the morgue, was probably no more than forty years of age. She was quite pretty, with a long, swanlike neck and golden hair done up into a soft twist.

"Inspector, Sergeant," she said in greeting, her expression stark, though not severe. "I am glad you've come. It's been an awful day, as you can imagine, and I would very much like permission to attend to Nurse Radcliff as soon as possible. It's indecent, leaving her there upon the infirmary floor."

"Matron Westover, I appreciate that it's been a difficult day for you, but Sergeant Tinsdale was correct to leave the deceased where she lay. If she has been killed, it is best for us to view her where she fell."

The matron's chin lifted, and she challenged him with a glare, one that Jasper imagined many children would cower under. But she did not argue.

"If you will take us to her, please," he urged.

Without a word, she held out her arm to direct them, then began down the corridor. Tinsdale fell into step beside her, with Jasper and Lewis following.

"What time was Nurse Radcliff found?" Jasper asked.

"Ten o'clock this morning," the matron replied, her pace brisk, the soles of her shoes clicking along the bare stone. "She was absent at breakfast, but as she had been tending to a sick child, it was presumed she was taking breakfast in the infirmary instead."

"A child was present when she was killed?" Lewis asked, echoing Jasper's own surprise. And hope. If there had been a witness to the stabbing, it could help their investigation considerably.

"Yes," Matron Westover said, "however, the child is but two years old, so you won't be able to question him as a witness. With any hope, he was asleep at the time."

"No one else was in the infirmary overnight?" Jasper asked.

"No one," the matron answered. She and Tinsdale turned a corner into a short extension off the main corridor. A uniformed constable sat in a chair, arms crossed over his chest and chin tucked. Asleep, it appeared.

"Constable," Tinsdale barked in reprimand. The young man leapt to his feet so quickly he nearly knocked over the chair.

"Sir." The constable's glazed eyes rounded in further mortification as he saw the Scotland Yard detectives they'd been waiting on.

Matron Westover brought out a key from the chatelaine at her waist and unlocked the door. She stood aside, allowing them to enter first. The large open space held several beds in an orderly line along a wall of windows, some partitioned off by privacy curtains. Several paraffin lamps had been lit in preparation, allowing Jasper to see the nurse immediately; she'd come to rest on the floor between two of the beds, one of which looked to have been knocked askew. A small table at the foot of that bed had been overturned, folded linens spilled onto the floor.

She lay on her front, one arm raised by her head and the other tucked down by her hip. As he approached, he noted the pool of blood in which she lay. It was dark and viscous. It had been nearly twelve hours since she'd been discovered, and the ashen pallor of her skin reflected that.

"Why did the telegram to Scotland Yard arrive so late in the afternoon?" Jasper asked as he observed the body and the evidence of a struggle surrounding it. The pushed-aside bed, the streaks of blood upon a white blanket, apparently transferred from the dying nurse when she reached for it.

"Apologies, Inspector. I'd spent the night at my brother's home in Putney, a few towns over from here," Sergeant Tinsdale said. "It took some hours for my constables to reach me and additional time for me to return and view the body. And then, the telegraph line out of the constabulary was down. It took some time to repair."

In a small town like Twickenham, only a few police officers were typically stationed there at any one time. Jasper nodded, annoyed but understanding that they couldn't operate as fastidiously as a larger London division could.

"Matron Westover," Jasper said, turning. He'd thought she would be in the room with them, but instead, she lingered by the open door. She swiped at her cheeks as if to brush away tears.

"I'm sorry, Matron, but I have to ask: Who discovered Nurse Radcliff?"

"Nurse Peters," she said, her chin trembling briefly before she took a breath and composed herself. "She resides in town and usually comes in at eight o'clock in the morning to relieve Nurse Radcliff from her shift."

"Why wasn't she here at eight today?" Jasper asked.

"Her son has been ill this week. Pneumonia. I've allowed her to come in at ten o'clock the last few days. When she arrived today" The matron didn't finish her sentence. It wasn't necessary. Nurse Peters had found Nurse Radcliff on the floor, dead.

Jasper crouched by the body. The back of her dress was blood-soaked, and as the blood had dried, the light gray cotton had turned dark red and brown. He counted four visible entry points—inch-long tears in the fabric—where a knife, slim by the looks of it, had been plunged into her back.

"Looks like she might have struggled with her killer," Lewis observed from where he stood at the victim's feet. "Knocked a few things over as they fought."

"Was a weapon found?" Jasper asked, directing the question to either Tinsdale or Matron Westover—whoever could answer first.

"I saw none," the matron replied, her voice quavering.

"We searched the orphanage over," Tinsdale reported. "Nothing, sir."

The killer must have taken it with him or her then.

Jasper straightened. "When was the last time Nurse Radcliff was seen alive, and by whom?" He directed this question specifically to the matron, who was still hovering near the door. She clearly did not wish to be any closer to the dead nurse, though he didn't sense it was out of disgust. Her fair cheeks were damp, her large eyes shimmering with more tears.

"Miss Jones, one of our teachers, came to the infirmary at midnight for some headache powder. She said Nurse Radcliff was rocking little Vinny to sleep in the chair." She gestured toward a rocking chair beside a baby's crib. Vinny was the ill two-year-old witness, he presumed. "Miss Jones stayed a few minutes before returning to her room."

He looked to Tinsdale. "You spoke to Miss Jones?"

The sergeant nodded. "She was in shambles when I did."

Jasper wanted a look at her room and her clothes for any evidence of blood. No one could be ruled out as a suspect at this point.

"Would she have had any reason to harm Nurse Radcliff?"

Though he hadn't asked this of Matron Westover, she stepped forward. "Of course she wouldn't. What an awful question, Inspector. Everyone here adored Aunt Charlotte—"

Her voice squeezed off, and she brought her hands up to cover her face as it crumpled.

Jasper exchanged a glance with Lewis, then asked the matron, "Nurse Radcliff is your aunt?"

She sniffled and nodded, again trying to compose herself. This tearful state was likely a show of too much emotion for her. As matron of an orphanage, she would be looked to as an example of strict and stern consistency.

"Her name is Charlotte Radcliff?" Lewis said, writing in his notebook as the matron confirmed it with a nod.

"Excuse me," she said, unable to look in their direction any longer. "I will wait for you in the hall."

Matron Westover's skirts whirled as she fled. As the victim was her aunt, Jasper understood such a reaction. He turned back to Tinsdale.

"What else can you tell me, Sergeant?" he asked.

"No staff or child has left the premises since this morning, after the body was found. PC Landry, he's a good copper. Make a fine detective one day, I'll wager. He knew to keep everyone penned in while he had me sent for."

Tinsdale went over the number of staff (eighteen) and children (fifty-seven) at Wellesley House and confirmed that he'd had a look inside Miss Jones's room. She didn't have bloodied clothing or shoes, or anything of a suspicious nature, though Jasper conceded she could have disposed of them well before the sergeant arrived.

"When are the doors locked for the evening?" Lewis asked.

"They're locked at all hours," Tinsdale answered, sounding as if that should have been obvious. "Can't have the little ones running off. And they would, mind you. A few manage it every now and again. Though, they're never very good about getting far."

It reminded Jasper of Gavin Seabright and his reported escape attempts when he'd been a boy here. With his mother still alive and living at home, he must have wished to return to her. It wasn't so surprising that other children would attempt to do the same. When Jasper had fled his Uncle Robert and Aunt Myra's home, he'd been prepared to live rough on the streets. It would have been preferable to him going back to the unyielding clutches of the Carter family. Perhaps the children Tinsdale had needed to track down and return to the orphanage all felt the same way as Jasper had.

"Were there any visitors yesterday?" Jasper asked, thinking of ways someone might have slipped inside the walls of the orphanage.

"As far as I know, there weren't any visitors. The groundskeeper said he found a damaged cellar window this morning, as if a housebreaker took a crowbar to it."

An intruder during the night, then.

"Was anything taken?"

The sergeant shook his head. The medicine cabinets looked undisturbed, and Jasper couldn't imagine the orphanage would keep a large quantity of money or valuables anywhere on the premises.

Jasper took another look at the body and wished Leo had traveled with them. She would have been able to determine a more exact time of death. As it was, sometime between midnight and ten o'clock in the morning was their window. However, taking into consideration the groundskeeper's discovery of the broken cellar window that morning, the coagulation of the blood pool around Nurse Radcliff, and the lividity of the victim, Jasper was confident that the killer had struck the previous night, while it was dark and everyone else was asleep.

The question was why target Nurse Radcliff at all? Martha Seabright had been asking questions about her the night of the benefit dinner, and the nurse had been the one to declare Edward Seabright dead. Now, Leo's theory that Edward had *not* died echoed in the back of his head.

Jasper instructed Lewis and Tinsdale to arrange for the body to be removed and then joined Matron Westover in the hall outside the infirmary.

"I have some questions for you," he said.

The matron nodded, as if in resignation, and led him back through the darkened corridors. Her office, she claimed, would be the best place to speak.

"The children were sent to bed earlier than usual this evening, though I don't trust they are asleep just yet," she said, her voice subdued so as not to carry. "They are aware something has happened, but I didn't want them crossing paths with detectives from London. As you know, they have family ties to the police, and many of them are newly grieving."

He understood. To see police roaming the corridors, causing a stir, would likely upset the children.

Using her chatelaine again, she opened the door to her office. A lamp was still lit, and the dim light gave the small room a snug atmosphere. It was different from what he'd seen of the orphanage so far. Matron Westover went not to her desk, but to a pair of striped cushioned chairs near a small hearth, inset with a coal stove. A half-full cordial glass of spirits—sherry, if he were to guess by the golden chestnut color—had been left on an occasional table next to one chair. The matron retook her seat and held out a hand to indicate he take the one across from her.

Jasper preferred to stand when asking questions related to an inquiry. However, realizing it might be too intimidating for him to loom over her, he perched on the edge of the chair's cushion after relenting.

"I'm sorry for your loss," he offered.

She accepted his condolences with a pert nod and then picked up her small glass of sherry.

"Sergeant Tinsdale mentioned a damaged cellar window that appeared to have been pried open," Jasper said. "Did your groundskeeper find anything of note in the cellar? Or elsewhere on the grounds?"

She shook her head after sipping her drink. "He must have gotten in through that window. There is no other way he could have entered the building. I keep all the doors locked at all times."

"He?"

"I'm assuming the intruder was a man," she replied.

The physical strength needed to pry open a window and to violently attack a woman led Jasper to suspect a man as well. The violence was itself a clue, too.

"Whoever killed your aunt, they seem to have targeted her specifically. No one else was harmed as a result of the break-in, correct?"

The matron nodded, her throat working against another sob.

"That tells me that the killer had a grievance with your aunt. Or perhaps needed to silence her for some reason."

Leo's theory—that Edward Seabright had not died of fever but had been taken—played well here. He'd dismissed it earlier, thinking it too far-fetched. However, the orphanage nurse had been killed just days after Martha Seabright. And he could not discount the fact that the letter Leo found in Martha's handbag, the one indicating a sum of money had been enclosed and that she'd made the right choice, had been signed with the initials *NCR*.

Nurse Charlotte Radcliff, possibly.

"I cannot fathom who would have had such a grievance against my aunt," Matron Westover replied.

"How long had she worked at the orphanage?"

"Since its inception. This was her home." Her voice broke on the last word. She turned her head, covering her lips and nose with a trembling hand. It was only when she fought tears that the fine lines around her eyes and on her forehead became visible. Jasper found himself wondering if she'd ever married, and if not, why. She was the sort of English rose men would have flocked to and women would have been envious of.

"Tell me about your groundskeeper," he said after allowing her a moment to compose herself. He was again thinking of Gavin Seabright and the accusation that he'd killed the groundkeeper's dog as a boy. Jasper also considered how the man would have needed to dig a grave for Edward Seabright.

"Virgil Clooney," she answered. "And before you ask, no, he would not have heard anyone breaking into the cellar. The window in question is on the opposite side of the grounds from his cottage."

He raised a brow, impressed by her perceptiveness. Or perhaps she had merely asked Clooney the same question earlier. "I'd like to speak to him nevertheless."

"Tomorrow, Inspector. Virgil is quite old and has been abed well before now," she replied.

As he and Lewis were staying the night in Twickenham, he wouldn't complain. He would speak to the elderly groundskeeper in the morning.

"Did your aunt ever speak to you about her time here, when the orphanage first opened?" he asked.

Matron Westover's eyes narrowed on him. "Why do you ask?"

"Have you heard about the events at the orphanage's benefit dinner a few nights ago in London?"

Her trembling sorrow seemed to clear for a moment. "I don't often have time to read the London papers, but Sergeant Tinsdale mentioned that there was a disturbance. It was a robbery, wasn't it? And a woman came to some harm?" Matron Westover shifted in her seat, crossing her ankles. "What does that have to do with my aunt's murder?"

"Are you familiar with a woman named Martha Seabright?" he asked the matron instead of answering.

The matron's posture stiffened, though only for a heartbeat. "The name sounds familiar."

"She was the wife of a police sergeant killed in the line of duty. Her three children were taken in here in 1871."

"*Was?*" the matron echoed, having astutely latched on to his use of past tense when speaking of Martha.

"Mrs. Seabright was the woman shot and killed at the dinner," he explained.

Matron Westover's ankles slipped free, uncrossing. Her wariness subsided to shock. "She was shot? Gracious." She blinked and looked at her nearly empty cordial glass. She drained it in a backward toss of her head.

"Are you aware that Mrs. Seabright's youngest child, an infant boy, died here less than a month after arriving?" he asked.

The matron set down her glass, her hand trembling before the base met the table with a hard *clink*.

"No, I was not aware," she replied after clearing her throat. "And I'm not sure what an infant's death so long ago could possibly have to do with what happened to my aunt *today*."

"The two crimes could share a connection," he allowed.

The matron let out a huff of air as if flabbergasted. "What sort of connection?"

As he wasn't going to answer the matron's question, he pivoted again. "I would like to see Martha Seabright's file as well as any records the orphanage might have on her children, Paula, Gavin, and Edward."

If he could, he wanted to try to match the handwriting on the note Leo had found in Martha's handbag to any writing made by Nurse Radcliff in the files.

Matron Westover's sad, weary welcome quickly evaporated. She braced her hands on the arms of her chair and pushed herself up to standing. Jasper rose as well.

"The records of the wives and children we assist are confidential. I cannot just hand them over to you, and besides, are you not here to solve the murder of my aunt?"

"I am, and that is why I need that file," he replied evenly, intrigued by her sudden change in demeanor.

The matron held firm. "I will need permission from the orphanage's Board of Governors to release it to you."

That would require contacting the president of the board, Sir Eamon Giles, with the request. A telegram would need to be sent, and then, Jasper would have to await a response. Considering the late hour, he imagined he'd have to wait until morning anyhow.

"Very well, if that is necessary," he replied.

"It is," she said brusquely. Then, she moved toward the door. "Now, it is quite late, and it has been a wretched day. I will allow you to collect your detective sergeant, and then I ask that the two of you take your leave."

The hasty dismissal might have meant nothing, but as he left the matron's office and went back toward the infirmary to see how things were coming along with the removal of the body, he couldn't help but suspect Matron Westover had wanted to shuffle him out of Wellesley House for another reason altogether.

Instinct told him that the matron had known the surname Seabright right away. If she knew the family's history, including the death of little Edward, why lie and claim that she didn't?

He passed the blanket-wrapped body of Nurse Radcliff in the bleak corridor. PC Landry had returned, and he and the constable who had been napping outside the infirmary were carrying her.

"The chap's arranged for rooms at that inn, as he said he would," Lewis said as he joined Jasper, following him downstairs.

"I want to stop at the public stables first," Jasper said. "Stanley Hayes left London late yesterday, and I'd like to know if anyone matching his description was seen here in town. His driver might have stopped in for fresh horses."

He and Lewis reached the bottom of the stairs. "You think *Hayes* came here to kill the nurse?"

Jasper couldn't quite see the man sneaking in through a cellar window, but his unexpected departure from London was suspicious. If what Leo theorized was true, and Edward Seabright had been given to Mrs. Hayes, Stanley may have wished to tie up any loose threads.

Or perhaps Gavin Seabright, who'd been on the run for over a day, had come here to speak to the nurse his sister had accused of taking their baby brother. A discussion between them could have turned into a violent attack. Gavin might have known of a way to sneak into the building since he'd once lived here. He could have taken the first train back to London that morning and arrived in time to meet Leo at the morgue.

"I don't know what happened to Nurse Radcliff just yet," Jasper said as they left the orphanage. "But it's connected to the Seabrights; of that, I am sure."

Chapter Sixteen

The windows of the house on Bloomsbury Square were dark except for those in a downstairs, street-facing room. As Leo accompanied Constance and Lord Hayes to the front door, the knot in the pit of her stomach kinked more tightly. The carriage ride had become awkward after the first few minutes, during which she'd explained how she'd known that Stanley Hayes had set out for Hampshire.

"It was *you*?" Constance had nearly shrieked. "You were the one who followed my mother this morning and told Jasper about it?"

"I certainly didn't expect the woman I saw emerging from Martha Seabright's home to be your mother, Miss Hayes," Leo replied. "I did follow her, and when I learned who she was, I had no choice but to inform Jasper."

"Wait a moment. Seabright?" Oliver Hayes had asked. "The woman who was shot and killed at Sir Eamon's home the other night?" Apparently, he'd read about her in the newspaper. "Why the blazes would my aunt have been inside a dead woman's home?"

"I couldn't say for certain," Leo had replied, not yet wanting to share her theory about Mrs. Hayes paying Martha Seabright to relinquish her infant son thirteen years ago. Not until she spoke to Stanley Hayes, at least.

Once inside the Hayes home, they were greeted by a servant who turned up his nose at Leo without even trying to mask his disdain.

"Oliver?" came a deep voice from within a room off the entrance hall. "Constance?"

A tall man with fair hair stepped into view. He was wearing a suit, his shirt collar loose, and he clutched a snifter in his hand. When his eyes settled on Leo, he frowned.

"Who is this woman? I sent you to bring back the detective inspector."

Constance finished removing her hat and gloves, then tossed them onto a table. "Ask Oliver. He's the one who thought it would be a splendid idea to have her come in his stead."

She strode past her father and into the room. Lord Hayes sent his cousin an irritated glance before saying, "This is Miss Spencer, Uncle. Inspector Reid isn't in London currently."

He handed his outer trappings to the servant, who continued to stare at Leo balefully.

"Miss Spencer? The deadhouse worker?" Stanley Hayes looked her over with marked revulsion. "What the devil? Why have you brought her here?"

"Mr. Hayes," Leo began, becoming rather tired of being disparaged, "I am here to assist in finding your son."

He balked. "*You* are to assist? You are no detective, young woman. What do you know about any of this? Oliver?" Again, he turned to his nephew, demanding an answer with an open glare.

Lord Hayes held up his hand. "Uncle, you cannot afford to be choosy right now. Inspector Reid has, on occasion, trusted Miss Spencer during his inquiries, and I recommend that in his absence, we do the same."

The suggestion mirrored the one he'd made at Scotland Yard when Constance had argued against bringing Leo to Bloomsbury Square. The viscount's willingness to see how she might be able to help had been unexpected, and Leo had the discomforting sense of not wanting to disappoint him.

Though Stanley was visibly unhappy, he sealed his lips and returned to the sitting room. Lord Hayes exhaled, then gestured for Leo to join them.

The air in the sitting room smelled of cigar smoke and whisky. In the corner of the hazy room, Constance was setting down a crystal decanter, having already poured herself a drink. She refused to look in Leo's direction.

"How is it, exactly, you believe you can help, Miss Spencer?" Stanley Hayes asked. He stood by the flameless hearth, arms crossed, and chin lifted imperiously. He didn't believe she could help them at all; that much was evident.

Leo did not reply straightaway. Three framed photographs set on an occasional table next to a settee had captured her attention. One portrait was of a much younger Stanley Hayes with a woman whom Leo presumed was his wife. They were attired in wedding garb, and Mrs. Hayes was holding an enormous bouquet of flowers. The two other portraits were of Constance and of a young boy who looked to be ten or eleven years old. George, she deduced.

His features were decidedly different from those of his fair-haired sister and parents; he possessed ink-black curls, dark eyes, and thick, dark eyebrows. The photographer had posed him with his elbow resting on the back of a chair, and though his head was angled to show more of the left half of his face, a dark smudge on his right cheek, just beneath his ear, was still visible.

"How old is your son, Mr. Hayes?" she asked as she made her way toward the photograph, her attention riveted.

"Thirteen," he answered, after first rolling his eyes as if the question was irrelevant.

"The night of the benefit dinner, to which you canceled your attendance at the last minute, your wife accused you of lying to her. What did you lie about?"

Her question was met with spluttering outbursts from both Mr. Hayes and his daughter, both of whom spoke over each other in their indignation.

"Jasper had no right to tell you that!" Constance cried out, while her father shouted, "You impertinent shrew, who do you think you are?"

"Uncle." Lord Hayes raised his voice with the clear message for Stanley to calm himself. Despite the difference in their ages, Oliver was Viscount, and so Stanley heeded him—though barely.

"All right, Mr. Hayes," Leo said, lifting her eyes from the portrait of George. "I will tell you what I know, and what I suspect. Perhaps then, you will help to fill in the gaps. First, the victim at the benefit dinner, Martha

Seabright, placed three children at the orphanage in 1871, when you were on the Board of Governors there. Second, among Martha's possessions, I found an old letter in her handbag, mentioning an agreed upon sum of money she had received and acknowledging that she'd *done the right thing*. It was dated May 14, 1871—May was the month her infant son, Edward, reportedly died at the orphanage. However, Paula, Martha's eldest child, never believed her brother had died of fever. She suspected he'd been taken from the orphanage's care and placed with another family."

Stanley Hayes's expression had gone to stone.

"Third, earlier this morning, I saw your wife leaving Martha Seabright's home. Shortly thereafter, she departed London unexpectedly. So unceremoniously, in fact, that she did not even say goodbye to her daughter. Just as you had not the previous day, when you dashed from London with George."

The viscount stepped forward, his hard glare jumping between Leo and Stanley. "Miss Spencer, come to your point, please."

She would, even knowing it would cement her as an enemy in the eyes of the others in the room. Was this how Jasper often felt whenever he was questioning a suspect? In that moment, she longed for him to be here, at her side, rather than hours away in another part of England.

"I believe your son, George was, in fact, born Edward Seabright and that you arranged for his secret adoption, paying Martha a large sum of money to turn him over to you and your wife."

The reaction she expected came to pass, though with

more fervor than she'd anticipated. Constance's shout nearly deafened her.

"How dare you?" She stormed forward as if to better spear Leo with a blistering glare. "You are deranged! My father did no such thing!"

Lord Hayes closed his eyes and swore under his breath as he hurried to the sitting room door and slammed it shut, presumably to keep the servants from hearing anything more. Meanwhile, Stanley Hayes stood still, his eyes searching Leo with intensity.

"At first, I thought it was Mrs. Hayes who must have arranged for the adoption," Leo went on, ignoring Constance. Her father's unflinching reaction was far more interesting. Encouraging, even.

"But then, your servant overheard the row between the two of you the night of the dinner, wherein she accused you of lying to her," she continued. "She knew, of course, that George was not her child by birth, but I suspect there was another element to the adoption that you failed to tell her about. It was this element that upset her."

"That is quite enough, you horrible woman!" Constance cried. She then implored her father with a beseeching look, "Say something, Father. Tell her she is mad and that George is not who she thinks he is."

Lord Hayes held his uncle in a resolute stare, waiting for him to speak. But the seconds ticked by, and Stanley remained voiceless. As if in a daze, he walked to the nearest armchair and gripped the back of it hard, his knuckles turning white.

"Whatever you may think, the adoption was not illegal," he said after another long moment. "I did not steal the boy."

Constance clapped her hand over her mouth, muffling her gasp of horror. Leo felt a twinge of guilt at the shock she must have been experiencing.

"*Bloody hell*," Lord Hayes grumbled as he turned away and raked a hand through his dark hair. "

"Mr. Hayes," Leo said before either Constance or her cousin could lob questions at him. "You are admitting that you paid Martha Seabright to give you her infant son in 1871?"

While adoption itself was not illegal, Leo questioned if the purchase of a child would be.

At his answering nod, Constance let out a sob. She staggered to the settee and dropped onto a cushion, a hand still covering her mouth in disbelief.

"Uncle, how could you?" Lord Hayes said, disgust and horror mingling in his expression.

"All this time, all these years, you've lied to us." Constance's voice trembled violently. "My God—does George know? Did he find out? Is that why he's gone?"

They were all valid questions. However, Leo thought it better for Stanley Hayes to start at the beginning. She asked him to do just that while Constance blotted her eyes with a linen handkerchief that Lord Hayes passed to her.

"After Constance was born," Stanley began, after clearing his throat and adjusting his loose tie, "there were…complications. Doctor Reeves told us that Melanie, my wife, would never be able to conceive again."

"But that can't be true," Constance cut in. "I remember

Mama with child. I was ten years old when George was born."

Stanley nodded, though it seemed to pain him to remember. "Yes, you remember correctly that she was with child. And your mother nearly carried to term. But when she went into labor, it was too early. The babe was stillborn."

Leo lowered her head, feeling deep sympathy for Melanie Hayes for the loss of a much wanted second child. And for Constance, as tears welled in her eyes once again. Lord Hayes paced toward the hearth, his palm scrubbing his cheek and chin as he shook his head.

"I remember now," he recalled. "You sent Aunt Melanie to Beechwood for her confinement, and Constance came to stay with us." The viscount would have been thirteen or fourteen at the time, Leo calculated. "Are you saying she had already lost the child at that point?"

Stanley's answer was in the guilty bowing of his head. "You cannot have any idea how distraught my wife was. She was delusional with grief, threatening to harm herself." He squeezed his eyes shut as if the memory still pained him. "She needed time before facing her friends with the truth. I was protecting her *and* her reputation by sending her away."

"But that wasn't the only reason you sent your wife out of the public's eye," Leo interjected. "You'd already come up with a way to fix the problem, thanks to your connection to the orphanage. How did you know there was an infant there?"

He peered at her as if she was a bothersome gnat that he'd have liked to silence with a swat of his hand. But he'd already started to confess, and there could be no diverting from the truth now.

"Melanie and I toured the home earlier that month. She was still weeks away from her confinement at that time, and she insisted on accompanying me. She has a bleeding heart, always has, and was the one who convinced me to support the fund in the first place." He drained his glass and, finished with it, set it on the table that held the three framed photographs. His eyes lingered on the one of George.

"He was so small. So delicate. The nurse said he was malnourished, but Melanie was utterly enchanted with him. She held him for nearly an hour before I finally insisted that we had to move along."

So, when his wife lost their own baby a month later, Stanley Hayes thought of the one in Twickenham. He must have hurried to conceal that his own child had been stillborn, sent his wife to the country, and then arranged for the adoption.

Leo laid out the supposition for him, and he nodded.

"Melanie understood that this was the only chance we had at having another child," he said. "Admitting to the adoption was out of the question. George would be ridiculed, and we would be judged. There were also legal ramifications; he might not be entitled to his inheritance. No, the easiest thing was to say he was our son."

"Your staff must have known the truth," Leo pointed out. "Both here and in Hampshire."

"A few did, yes," he replied. "But they are loyal, Miss Spencer. They all adore my wife. And for that, I rewarded them with my loyalty in return."

She wondered if that meant an increase in their wages

but thought it might be rude to pry. While some of the staff knew the truth when Mr. and Mrs. Hayes returned to London with a baby, their friends and acquaintances—even their own daughter—were none the wiser. Leo looked at the framed photographs again. It was quite apparent that George looked nothing like the other members of his family. Had he noticed it? Had anyone else?

"Let's return to the argument you had with your wife on the night of the benefit dinner," Leo said.

"How is that going to help us find my brother?" Constance demanded, her eyes swollen and shimmering.

"I don't know yet," she replied honestly. "However, I do know that lies never help. They only hinder."

"Constance, let your father answer the bloody questions," the viscount snapped, though his anger was clearly directed toward Stanley, not his cousin. "I need to know every facet of this scandal if I'm to help mitigate it."

Constance threw a glowering stare toward him before settling back into the cushions of the settee and sealing her lips tightly.

"What lie was your wife referring to?" Leo asked bluntly.

Mr. Hayes shifted as though he wanted to stand but ended up looking too defeated to do so. "I'd learned Martha Seabright would be at the benefit dinner. I could not risk my wife and her meeting."

"Why not?" Lord Hayes interjected.

Stanley's throat worked as he swallowed nervously. "Because I had told Melanie that George's mother died after he'd been admitted to the orphanage. She believed all this time that our son was well and truly an orphan."

The viscount swore more oaths under his breath, and Constance shook her head, staring at her father as if she did not know him.

"I was protecting her from whatever misplaced feelings of guilt she might have felt, taking in a baby whose mother was still alive," he said, the excuse weak and grasping.

"Protecting Aunt Melanie?" Lord Hayes barked. "Or protecting yourself? You took a child that was not your own and passed him off as if he was. If anyone finds out what you've done, the stain upon the Hayes name may be permanent."

His uncle weathered the viscount's rebuke with a stiff chin. "I don't regret it, not for a moment. Martha did not want him. She was a vulture and would have sold him off to anyone. At least we were able to give him a stable home, a family. *Love.*"

He seemed to believe that what he had done hadn't been wrong, and while Leo did not agree with his methods, perhaps it was true that he'd given Edward a better life and home than what the boy would have otherwise had. Martha might have thought so too. If so, Leo wondered why Stanley had worried she might say something to Melanie Hayes at the dinner.

He'd called Martha by her given name and accused her of being a vulture.

"Did she contact you throughout the years?" Leo asked as a suspicion grew. "Did she ask for more money?"

At his long, slow blink, she understood: Martha Seabright had been blackmailing him.

"I would hear from her every few years," he said after several beats passed. "It would be ten pounds or so, whatever she claimed to need at the time. She made it clear that, should I refuse, she would make it known publicly that George was her son. She had letters, she said, from the orphanage, detailing the conditions of the exchange. And over the years, she demanded portraits of George to know what he looked like."

"And you told Mrs. Hayes about these letters and photographs that night?" Leo asked.

When he nodded, she understood what his wife had been looking for inside Martha's home.

"How did Aunt Melanie know where this woman lived?" Lord Hayes asked.

"I had gone there previously to meet and pay Martha. I must have mentioned the address during our argument. I never thought she would *go* there."

But Mrs. Hayes had been worried that some evidence had been left behind regarding the adoption. And with Martha Seabright's murder, she must have also worried suspicion could fall upon her husband. Or herself. The woman had been blackmailing them, after all.

"Now you have it all, Miss Spencer," he went on. "However, I fail to see how it is going to bloody well help me find my son!"

Leo passed Stanley Hayes in his chair and went toward the windows, needing to move, needing to think.

"Do you think it's possible George overheard your argument?" Oliver Hayes asked his uncle after a moment. "He would have been at home."

Stanley rubbed his forehead. "I didn't think we were shouting that loudly, but if the servants heard, I suppose it is possible that he did as well."

"If he found out he was adopted, he might have decided to run away," Constance said.

"If that is the case, he could have gone somewhere he is familiar with," Lord Hayes replied. "Perhaps he is making his way to Beechwood."

Their discussion over where George might have gone gave Leo time to think about the letter in Martha's handbag. It had been signed NCR. And at the benefit dinner, Martha had asked the chief coroner about Nurse Radcliff. The letter N might have stood for Nurse rather than a given name. And, as she'd already theorized with a doubtful Jasper, only a nurse at the orphanage would have been able to pronounce the Seabright baby dead.

"Mr. Hayes did Nurse Radcliff facilitate the adoption of George?" she asked, cutting into something the viscount had been saying about taking the next scheduled train to Hampshire.

Stanley sat a little taller in his chair. "Yes. At the time, it was Radcliff," he answered. "Caroline Radcliff."

Nurse Caroline Radcliff. *NCR.* Her letter to Martha had been about Edward Seabright's adoption after all. It was central to everything that had taken place since the night of Martha's murder. But then, Leo peered at Mr. Hayes.

"What do you mean by her name being Radcliff *at the time?*"

Chapter Seventeen

Dew coated the grass and flower beds outside Mrs. Barnston's inn the next morning, and a low-hanging mist curled up toward the rising sun. As Jasper set out for the orphanage, he was unexpectedly grateful for his coat. The air held a raw chill that would never be present in London in June. Back home, the close, humid air gathered under his shirt before he could arrive at Scotland Yard each morning. He now understood why the wealthy abandoned their city homes and set out for their country estates at the close of May.

Despite it being far more agreeable in the borough of Twickenham, Jasper needed to return to the city. Hell, after the telegram PC Landry had just delivered to his and Lewis's breakfast table a few minutes ago, he began to wish he hadn't left at all.

"What do you think it means, guv?" Lewis asked as he kept pace with Jasper.

The telegraphed message had been sent to the constabulary from Scotland Yard during the night.

However, the constable on duty—the same one who'd been sleeping outside the orphanage's infirmary—had also slept through the arrival of the message. When PC Landry arrived at the station, he'd found the ticker tape waiting, deciphered the Morse code, and brought it swiftly to the inn.

S Hayes admits George is Edward. G now missing. Westover is NCR.

There wasn't room in a brief telegram for context, but Jasper knew the message must have come from Leo and understood what she meant. That she'd gone to Scotland Yard with information regarding his case would not be overlooked by Coughlan or anyone else within the CID. He wasn't looking forward to the complications it would undoubtedly cause, but that was a worry for another time.

"Stanley Hayes must have arranged to adopt Edward Seabright, whom he raised as his own son, George," Jasper explained to his detective sergeant as they walked along Hampton Road, now busy with horse-drawn wagons and carts, children and their mothers approaching the costermongers' handcarts, and a few men in farmer's threads.

"And now the boy is missing?" Lewis asked.

"It appears that way."

Stanley had left London with George two days ago. If Leo had spoken to Stanley, did that mean he was back in London? And if George wasn't with him, where had the boy gone? The questions plagued Jasper. As did the fact that Leo had sent the message. He'd asked her to stand down while he was away, and she'd sworn to do just that. Yet, it seemed she had broken that promise.

"What's this bit about Matron Westover being NCR?" Lewis asked as Jasper tried to calm his irritation.

Quickly, Jasper reminded him about the old letter found in Martha Seabright's handbag. Lewis recalled it, though he admitted to having forgotten about the initials *NCR* being used as a signature. When Jasper went over Leo's theory—that the payment enclosed had been for giving up her child, Edward—Lewis hissed through his teeth.

"She sold her own baby to Stanley Hayes? What kind of mum would do such a thing?"

The kind who wanted to be rid of her children, according to Esther Goodwin.

As Wellesley House came into view, Jasper went on, "Our victim last night was Charlotte Radcliff. *Nurse* Charlotte Radcliff."

Lewis nodded, acknowledging the appropriate initials. "But then how is Matron Westover *NCR?*"

Jasper increased his pace. "That is what we are going to find out."

The manor house was slightly less menacing in the morning light, but with Jasper bringing down the knocker, waiting a long minute, and then knocking again, the place took on last night's unwelcoming impression.

After a few more minutes and another round of knocking, at last, the door opened. An older man with patchy silver whiskers, impressive jowls, and the clothing of a laborer gave them a once over.

"You're the detectives, I take it," he said.

Jasper had an idea as to who this was. "That's correct. And you are Mr. Clooney, the groundskeeper?"

"Aye," he said, stepping aside and allowing them in.

The murmurs of children's voices could be heard in a nearby room, and a woman in a serviceable black gown and white mobcap swept into view from one corridor before disappearing into another. There was a strange friction in the air, and Mr. Clooney's prolonged hesitation after shutting the door added to it.

"Has something more happened since last night?" Jasper asked.

"It's Matron." The groundskeeper clasped his hands together and rubbed his palms nervously. "She hasn't been seen this morning."

The news should have struck Jasper like a hammer on an anvil. But it did not, and he merely shook his head. "I knew something was off."

He should have paid more attention to the matron's change in attitude after he'd brought up the Seabrights.

"What's that? What was off?" Mr. Clooney asked. But Jasper didn't have the time nor the patience to explain.

"Who is in charge without Matron Westover here?"

"That would be me, Inspector," a short, older woman said as she came down the stairs at a brisk pace.

While Matron Westover had moved and spoken with cultured, gentle elegance, this woman was abrupt and direct. She held Jasper's stare as she came to a stop in the entrance hall. "My name is Mistress Richards. I oversee the younger girls at Fortescue House across the street. I must ask what you said to Matron last night."

There was no mistaking her accusatory stare or tone.

"I had questions to put to her regarding the murder of Nurse Radcliff," he answered.

"She was clearly distraught about what happened to her aunt. I knew she should not have dealt with the police," Mistress Richard huffed.

"Do you have any idea where she could be?" Lewis asked.

"None at all. She has never disappeared like this."

"Cherry is missing from the stables," Mr. Clooney interjected.

"Is that Matron's horse?" Lewis asked.

"No, Cherry belongs to the orphanage."

"But can Matron Westover ride?" Jasper's question received a nod of the groundskeeper's head. As the first train of the day from Twickenham station was not leaving for another thirty-five minutes, he presumed the matron had left the vicinity on horseback.

"Most of her clothes are gone," Mistress Richards said, an edge of panic to her already tense tone. "I'm quite concerned for her."

Matron Westover had run, no question. And Jasper was beginning to comprehend why.

"Mistress Richards, I need to see Martha Seabright's file," he said. "Her children were placed here in 1871."

She scoffed at him. "I cannot share that with you. Recipients of the fund are guaranteed their privacy, no matter how far back the year may be."

"Seabright?" Mr. Clooney said. "Now there's a name I haven't heard in an age."

Unlike Mistress Richards's fractious reaction to the Seabright name, the groundskeeper merely looked a bit wistful. It was unexpected, considering one of the children had killed his dog.

"I understand Gavin Seabright gave your dog too much sedative one night so he could sneak out and run away," Jasper said.

Mr. Clooney grimaced and shrugged. "It were an accident. He were a troubled one, that young boy. Especially after what happened with his wee brother."

Clearly, the groundskeeper didn't hold the incident against Gavin.

"Felt right awful for what he done," the man kept on. "Offered to work for me for the whole summer to make up for it. And he ended up staying on as my assistant of sorts until he left here."

Sir Eamon had not imparted that detail. Had he, Jasper might not have worried so much about Gavin's character and his visit to the morgue to see Leo.

"You recall Edward Seabright?" he asked the groundskeeper.

"Oh, aye. I remember every grave I've ever dug for a wee one."

"Mr. Clooney," Jasper began, "did you see the child after he had passed?"

"See him?" The groundskeeper crinkled his forehead. "No, no. I couldn't ever bear it, looking at the dead little ones. No, he were already in his wee casket. I only lowered it into the grave."

"Who then placed the child in the casket?" Jasper asked.

At this, Mistress Richards protested. "Inspector, your questions are quite perturbing. What is their purpose?"

"Forgive me, but last evening, Matron Westover became agitated when I asked about Martha Seabright and her infant son, Edward. Martha was shot and killed a few days ago in London, and my investigation since then has led to the story of Edward's death. Without going into greater detail, I need to know if Matron Westover was ever a nurse here."

Leo's message—*Westover is NCR*—sat like a rock in his gut. It grew in size when Mistress Richards answered.

"She was. Many years ago. In fact, she was our first head nurse. Why?"

He closed his eyes. "And her name at that time?"

"Radcliff. Caroline Radcliff," she answered.

Nurse Caroline Radcliff. Not Charlotte, but Caroline.

"Mr. Clooney," he said, turning back to the groundskeeper. "Was it Caroline Radcliff who prepared the casket?"

He gave a nod. Matron Westover had been the one to declare Edward dead. And yet, she'd sat before Jasper in her office last night, claiming to not recall the Seabright name. Then, after Jasper's inquiries about the family, she'd packed her things and fled in the night.

"Did she marry, then?" Lewis asked, scribbling everything down in his notepad. "Take a new last name?"

"She married one of the masters here, Charles Westover. Sadly, he died, but she remained." Mistress Richards canted her head. "I think, in part, because of her aunt."

Jasper raised his hand, feeling spun around. "Charlotte Radcliff?"

"Yes, Charlotte was Matron here for many years. When she decided it was time to step down, the governors approved the exchanging of their roles."

So, Nurse Radcliff had become Matron Westover, while Matron Radcliff had become Nurse Radcliff.

"The wrong Nurse Radcliff," Jasper murmured.

Lewis lifted his pencil. "Guv?"

The groundskeeper and Mistress Richards stared at him in confusion too. But at last, Jasper had some clarity. Leo's theory had been correct: The baby had not died.

Paula's suspicion all these years had been warranted, and bringing up Edward with Matron Westover last night had tipped her off that her secret could be coming to light.

Caroline Westover had facilitated the sale of Martha Seabright's infant son. Martha had clearly known of the transaction, as she had been paid for her decision. Now, Martha was dead.

If Paula Blickson and Gavin Seabright had learned the truth, if they found out their mother had sold their brother and that Nurse Caroline Radcliff had helped, they would have strong motive to take their revenge on the two women.

But why now? Thirteen years had passed uneventfully.

And surely, Paula and Gavin, had they approached Nurse Radcliff in the infirmary last night with the intention of killing her, would have recognized her as the former Matron. They would have known she wasn't the same Nurse Radcliff responsible for Edward's disappearance.

It led Jasper to think the killer had been someone else. Someone who hadn't resided at the orphanage and who'd only been given a name—Nurse Radcliff—and the place where to find her.

"Inspector, please explain what you are thinking," Mistress Richards urged. He'd been silently sorting through all the pieces of information, leaving the others to wait.

"I am coming upon the reason Nurse Radcliff was killed," he replied. "And possibly why Martha Seabright was as well."

There was nothing more to be done here. He and Lewis needed to get back to London.

Chapter Eighteen

The beaker of strong black tea would not be enough to carry Leo through the morning. Exhaustion weighed on her eyelids and even her bones as she sat at the kitchen table with her aunt and uncle. At least it was Sunday, and as such, the Spring Street Morgue would be closed. She was supposed to be at her leisure on her days off, but after the events of last night at the Hayes home, there were too many things she needed to see to. A second cup of tea would be necessary.

Like usual, Claude had prepared his wife's plate, spreading a thin layer of marmalade on a triangle of toast and cutting her sausage into small, bite-size pieces. Flora stared at her food quizzically and then turned up her nose. She had not been eating much lately, and it was beginning to become worrisome.

"You did not sleep well last night," Claude said to Leo after trying, and failing, to entice his wife to eat a slice of sausage. "I heard you pacing in your room at all hours."

She lowered her beaker to the table, the wood scarred and pockmarked with age. "I'm sorry I kept you awake."

"Not at all," he said with a dry laugh. "I'm awake most of the night anyhow. A result of my age, I'm sure."

Leo wasn't quite sure she believed that. Her uncle was finding it difficult to no longer go into work each day. Though he smiled when she left for the morgue in the mornings, there was a wistful envy in his expression that he could not conceal. Caring for his wife was something Claude would never complain about or resent. But Leo, who had always been closer to her uncle than to her aunt, knew how much he'd loved his job at the morgue. She suspected a persistent longing for his old life was what kept him up during the night.

He was correct, however, that she had not slept well.

After leaving Bloomsbury Square, Leo and Oliver Hayes had traveled back to Scotland Yard. The general post offices were all closed at that hour of the evening, and their telegraph lines would not reopen until eight o'clock the next morning. A message needed to be sent to Jasper without delay, and the only place Leo could think of to do that was the Yard's telegraph office.

Lord Hayes had gone into the building, leaving Leo to wait impatiently in his carriage. As much as it annoyed her, the truth was her presence inside would have only caused Jasper more grief among his superiors at the Met. As a viscount and one of Jasper's respected friends, the operators in the telegraph room were more likely to send the message if it came from him. Leo, however, had composed the telegram, telling the viscount exactly what to have the operator tap out. With any hope, Jasper would question Matron Westover. Perhaps even arrest her.

A second telegram had been sent to the police constabulary in Hampshire, and constables were dispatched to the Hayes estate of Beechwood to determine if George had gone there on his own. Leo, however, did not believe the boy had.

Lord Hayes had been delivering her home when he'd seemed to interpret her silence. "You mentioned earlier that George has siblings."

"Gavin Seabright and Paula Blickson," she replied.

"Could either of them have found George? Approached him?"

Leo would have said yes straightaway, but she couldn't imagine how they would have known where to find him. Unless Martha had confessed something to them before she was killed. Or perhaps the former Nurse Radcliff.

"I'm not sure, but it would be beneficial to speak to them. Gavin is lying low right now. Paula Blickson will be easier to locate to question."

Lord Hayes had nodded. "Reid will be back tomorrow. First thing, I'm sure. I'll mention it to him."

Though Leo had nodded, she'd had the distinct feeling of being shuffled to the side. After all, Oliver Hayes had only permitted her involvement because Jasper had been away.

Across the table, Flora accepted the smallest bite of toast before sticking out her tongue. Claude sighed and turned to his own food, which had already cooled.

"Are you helping Inspector Reid with the benefit dinner case?" he asked.

"He wouldn't like me to say I'm helping, but yes," she replied.

She had not yet told her uncle about the death of one

of the masked men, Harry, and with Flora present, it was better not to talk of murder at all. She was sensitive to the topic. As her aunt had started to live more and more in the past, she often thought of her sister's murder, and those of her nephew and niece. Any time she did, she would devolve into hysterics.

But there was something Leo did want to discuss with her uncle, which she thought her aunt might not react to.

"The investigation has gone in a new direction," she said. "There is a young boy who is missing."

"What boy?"

"It's a complicated tale," she said. "He was adopted in a shady dealing thirteen years ago when he was an infant."

Claude's white brows furrowed behind the rims of his thick spectacles. "And now someone has taken him?"

Leo believed that was the most likely thing, and so did Constance. As cold and peevish as she had been toward Leo the previous night, she refused to believe her brother would run off. "George just isn't like that," she had insisted as Lord Hayes and Leo prepared to leave Bloomsbury Square. "He isn't temperamental in the least. He is a veritable angel compared to me."

"If he has discovered he was adopted, he might react in unexpected ways," the viscount had reasoned.

Leo could not deny that possibility, but what continued to perplex her as they rode toward the river and Scotland Yard was how the masked man who'd shot Martha Seabright might be connected to George. Or rather, *Edward*. If this masked man had wanted Martha dead, was it because of her deal to sell her youngest child to Stanley Hayes?

"Yes, I think someone has taken him," Leo answered

her uncle, then drained the last sip of her now cooled tea. A vague notion of whom George might have gone off with had stayed in the forefront of her mind all night. It was the framed photograph of the young boy on the occasional table in Stanley Hayes's sitting room that had turned her mind in an unexpected direction.

"Uncle Claude, do you recall a pair of corpses that came into the morgue three years ago in late December? The two women were delivered at different times that day," Leo said, remembering them perfectly. One had been younger, wearing a red and black frilly dance hall costume. She had been poisoned shortly before taking to the stage at a bawdy club and had died of acute arsenic poisoning. The other, older woman had been fished from the Thames. Witnesses told constables they'd seen her jump into the river.

"Three years ago?" Claude said with an indulgent laugh. "My dear, have pity on my average memory."

"You remember them," Leo assured him. "They were a mother and daughter. Though at first, we did not know as much."

Recognition lit Claude's eyes, and he nodded. "Ah, yes, now I recall. The matching birthmarks."

It wasn't until the two women were undressed and lay upon different tables at the morgue that Claude noticed they each bore the same dark, pigmented mark on their left shoulder. Claude had known straightaway that the two women were related.

"You explained that pigmented marks, such as moles and port wine stains, are often passed down from mother to child," Leo said, as she poured another cup of tea for herself.

"Yes, that has been my observation," he replied. "And in that case, it proved correct."

It turned out the mother, furious with her daughter for defying her strict edicts and choosing to dance at a bawdy club, had poisoned her. Then, she'd gone straight to the Vauxhall Bridge and leapt to her death.

"Why do you mention these two women?" Claude asked.

"The young boy who is missing," Leo began. "He has a large mole on the side of his face."

"A boy," Flora said, speaking for the first time since entering the kitchen. "A little boy." She lifted her hand and touched the table, petting it as if it was something other than a table. "My little boy."

Then, without warning, Flora's face screwed up into an expression of pure anguish. She let out a low moan, her hands coming up to cover her face.

"My darling," Claude said, pushing back his chair and coming to his feet. "Flora, dear."

But she continued to sob, the heart-wrenching sounds so alarming that Leo did not know what to say or do. Claude took his wife's arm and tried to bring her up from her chair. Finally, Leo snapped out of her stunned stupor and stood to assist him. Amazingly, Flora allowed Leo to touch her arm and help Claude get her to her feet.

"Uncle?" Leo whispered as he began to guide Flora slowly from the kitchen.

"It's all right, Leonora," he told her, readjusting his spectacles. "As for this boy you mentioned, the mole. It isn't always the case, but it would most likely have been passed to him by his mother."

She nodded at her uncle's rushed explanation, and

then, a moment later, she was standing alone in the kitchen. Flora's sobbing grew distant as Claude helped her upstairs to her room. Leo shook off the strange turn her aunt had taken and cleaned up the breakfast dishes before getting ready to go out. She had an important visit to make, though nothing she could explain easily to her uncle.

The flat banking of gray clouds in the sky let only a little sunlight filter through, and once again, the humidity thickened the air. Leo drew her mind from the bothersome perspiration gathering on her skin as she took an omnibus toward Park Crescent in Marylebone. Jasper had not let slip the exact address for Paula Blickson's home, but once there, Leo easily asked a crossing sweeper boy which home belonged to the Blicksons. After giving the enterprising young lad a penny, he pointed to a three-story home across the tidy garden square.

She gazed upon the home's exterior as she made her way through the square toward it. Jasper's voice was lodged in the back of her mind, commanding her to stop and turn around. Leo had promised him not to do anything regarding the case while he was away, and she felt slightly guilty that she was now breaking that vow. But there was no telling when he and Sergeant Lewis would return to London, and with George Hayes missing and her theory about hereditary moles confirmed by her uncle, Leo felt she had no choice but to see if Paula Blickson was at home.

If Leo was correct in her supposition, there was a good chance Mrs. Blickson would not be there. She might be long gone—with her son, George Hayes.

She climbed the stoop and brought down the front

door knocker, her pulse bubbling with anticipation. A maid opened the door and assessed Leo with a lengthy stare.

"Is Mrs. Blickson in?" Leo inquired. Before the maid could answer, she continued, "I am from Tate's, the funeral service handling her late mother's burial."

The lie was no guarantee of entry, but as she'd hoped, the maid was alarmed enough to invite Leo in to wait while she checked with her employer. The maid didn't go far, just down the short hall and into a room, before returning a few moments later.

"Mr. Blickson will see you," she reported.

Leo masked her disappointment that it wasn't to Mrs. Blickson she would be led and followed the maid into a study. However, just because Mr. Blickson had agreed to see her, it did not mean his wife was out. The maid might have decided Paula's husband should handle burial arrangements rather than the mistress of the house.

In the study, a well-dressed gentleman stood from his chair to greet her, and surprise dragged Leo's heels to a stop. With thin, silvering hair and lined, mottled skin, Mr. Blickson appeared to be at least sixty years of age. Perhaps older. Leo didn't know why it startled her as much as it did; women married older men all the time, especially if the match was intended for financial security. But one glimpse of Mr. Blickson, and Leo couldn't help but think of Paula being led from the detective department on the arm of her cousin, the handsome, thirty-something Felix Goodwin. Why her mind touched on him perplexed her, which caused her to delay answering Mr. Blickson's greeting.

"Thank you for agreeing to see me," she said after recovering.

"This is in regard to Mrs. Seabright's arrangements?" he asked, sounding and looking as doubtful as he rightfully should have. It wasn't at all common for funeral services to show up, unannounced, at one's door. Leo only knew which one was servicing Martha's funeral because of their arrival at the morgue the previous day.

The maid stepped out then, and Leo let the ruse drop.

"It is regarding Mrs. Seabright, but the truth is I am not from Tate's. I only told your maid that because I was afraid if I told her the truth, she would turn me away."

The lines on Mr. Blickson's forehead deepened as he raised his silver brows. "Is that so? How intriguing. I suggest you take a seat, miss, and tell me what my maid might find so objectionable."

He gestured toward a leather chair and then folded himself back into the one he'd been sitting in. He crossed his legs and waited. His bemused interest wasn't what she'd been expecting, but Leo did as bade and perched on the edge of the chair.

"The truth, Mr. Blickson, is that I was seated next to Martha Seabright at the benefit dinner when she was shot." At this, his bemusement transformed to alarm. Leo went on. "And I was then taken by her killer, as a sort of hostage, so that no one would chase after him."

He uncrossed his legs and sat forward. "Good God. That sounds utterly harrowing."

It had been, but Leo found focusing on the investigation helped dilute the distressing memories. "I have been assisting Scotland Yard in their work to capture the criminals from that night," she said, even though she knew

Jasper would reprimand her for revealing her role in the investigation.

Mr. Blickson's forehead creased again. "That is admirable, young lady. Quite brave, I'd say. But what brings you here? I was told my wife has already spoken to the detective inspector leading the inquiry."

His commendation of her for helping the police was given so naturally and artlessly that she believed he truly meant it. Even having just met him, Leo's impression was that he was much like her uncle: mild-mannered and kind.

"She has spoken to Inspector Reid. However, I have a few lingering questions. Is Mrs. Blickson at home?"

His open interest shuttered slightly. After lacing his fingers together, he rested his hands on his lap. "No, my wife is out, I'm afraid."

She stopped herself from asking where Paula had gone. It would be rude, and so far, Mr. Blickson had been accommodating. Leo didn't want to push too hard for answers, and yet she also could not back down.

"Do you have any idea when she might return?"

His clasped hands squeezed a little tighter.

"I do not." The succinct answer was guarded and cool. There was something behind it; some knowledge he didn't wish to share with her. If his young wife had disappeared, the man would likely want to conceal it, if only to keep his pride intact.

"How long has she been gone, Mr. Blickson?"

Unsurprisingly, he wasn't pleased with the question. "That is none of your concern, Miss…? What is your name anyhow? You've not said."

"Spencer," she replied. "Leonora Spencer. And it is my

concern since I believe your wife is very likely involved in the disappearance of a young boy."

Shock stiffened his back. His hands unclasped to grip the arms of his chair. "That is preposterous. I won't stand for such an accusation."

As Leo's tenuous welcome had now come to an end, she set aside polite restraint. "Has Mrs. Blickson ever mentioned the name George Hayes to you?"

He had started to rise but then, with a cock of his head, slowly floated back into his seat. "Hayes, you say?"

Recognition softened the older man's scowl, and Leo's skin prickled with excitement. "Yes. George Hayes. He would be thirteen."

He blinked, flummoxed. "Are you saying George Hayes is the boy who is missing?"

Leo leaned forward. "Do you know him?"

"I believe he is the son of one of my clients."

"Your client is Stanley Hayes?"

Mr. Blickson appeared awed that she knew the name. "Yes, well, he is a rather new client." According to Esther Goodwin, Mr. Blickson owned an estate insurance firm. "But you are mistaken, Miss Spencer. My wife has no reason to take the boy. They got along famously when they met."

Leo leapt to her feet. "When was this? Where did they meet?"

"Last month, at a dinner," he spluttered. "The Hayeses invited my wife and me to their home."

And there, Paula had met George Hayes.

Leo could only imagine how she must have reacted when she saw the boy. Had she known right away who George truly was? The prominent mole on his right cheek had been partially hidden in the photograph, appearing more like a dark smudge of ink, thanks to the camera's careful angle, but Paula would have seen it fully. She would have surely recalled baby Edward's same marking and seen George's strong resemblance to herself. And she would have noted, as Leo had, how very little George resembled Stanley and Melanie Hayes. Her old belief that Edward had not died but instead been taken would have resurfaced with a vengeance.

"George Hayes has not been seen in over a day," Leo said. "I must ask you again, Mr. Blickson, how long has your wife been gone?"

For a protracted moment, he lifted his chin as if to refuse to answer. But he must have already been stewing with worry and uncertainty because his resistance summarily fractured. "Since Friday evening."

George was first noted to be missing from Hayes Manor on Saturday morning. If Paula had not been seen since Friday night, that aligned with the timing of George's disappearance.

"Did your wife ever speak of her childhood? Of her baby…" Leo paused. "Of her baby brother, Edward?"

She was certain Paula would not have shared with her husband what Leo now believed to be true—that Edward had been her child, not her brother.

Mr. Blickson squinted, his liver-spotted hands now rubbing at his chin with anxiousness. "The one who died? She mentioned him only once, but…honestly, Miss Spencer, we do not often speak deeply on such matters." Mr. Blickson emitted a defeated sigh, no longer looking as though he wanted to toss her out. "I am not foolish enough to believe Paula is in love with me. I wanted a companion, and she needed security. Stability. I offered her both. Constricting her, trying to make her love me, would have ruined what we have."

A marriage to someone like Mr. Blickson would not be such a bad arrangement, Leo conceded. It was pragmatic, really, and it did seem as if he was a kind and patient husband. He may not have even demanded consummation of their marital vows. Perhaps, at the time, those had been the most important things to Paula.

But a marriage based on friendship could not hope to compete with love. Love in any form, really.

"Do you have any idea where she could be, Mr. Blickson?" Leo asked. "Have you checked with her aunt, Mrs. Goodwin?"

He shook his head. "I had planned to tomorrow, if Paula did not return by then."

Leo knew where to find Esther Goodwin. However, not Esther's son, Felix. He and Paula had to be close, considering he'd escorted her to Scotland Yard. "What about Felix Goodwin, her cousin?"

Mr. Blickson brightened a little. "Ah, yes, Felix. A nice fellow, if a bit of a flatterer. I find thespians usually are."

"Thespian?" Leo echoed. "He is an actor?"

"He no longer takes to the stage, to my knowledge, but he manages a theatre. The Epoch on Whitfield Street."

She knew of the Epoch. It wasn't one of the acclaimed theatres of the West End, but it was known to produce affordable entertainment for the middle class. She and Dita had once attended a production of *Dalilah* there.

"Miss Spencer, I can assure you, Paula doesn't have a thing to do with Stanley's missing boy," Mr. Blickson said beseechingly as Leo started for the study door. "My wife would never harm a child."

"I don't believe she intends to harm George," Leo said, impatient to leave. The Epoch wasn't too far away. "On the contrary, I think she cares for him a great deal. I'll be in touch, Mr. Blickson."

She left through the front door, not waiting for the maid to see her out.

Chapter Nineteen

Jasper's body buzzed with impatience the entire train ride back to Westminster. The cars cut along the tracks with more speed than any horse-drawn coach could have done, but it still felt as if they were curling through the countryside no faster than a stream of honey.

"You're driving me barmy with that leg bobbing, guv," Lewis said more than once as they traveled.

The detective sergeant pointing it out had not cured him of fidgeting, however, and when, at last, their train pulled into Charing Cross Station, Lewis leapt to his feet to disembark almost as quickly as Jasper. Once they were outside the station, they easily spotted DS Warnock and PC Drake. They stood with Oliver Hayes, next to one of the waiting carriages lining the street. Before leaving Twickenham, Jasper had asked PC Landry to telegraph the Yard with their train's expected time of arrival and a request for Oliver, Warnock, and Drake to meet it.

"What has happened since last night?" Jasper asked as soon as he and Lewis reached them.

Usually, Oliver was well put together, his collar starched, his clothing creaseless, his dark hair perfectly combed and pomaded. But not today.

"Nothing promising," the rumpled viscount answered. "The Hampshire County Constabulary says George has not arrived at Beechwood. My aunt has been made aware of what is happening and is returning to London today."

Stanley Hayes stepped out of the carriage, and if possible, he appeared even more haggard than his nephew. "I must have George back before my wife arrives in London, Inspector. I fear for her health."

Jasper suppressed a growl of annoyance. "Don't you mean Edward Seabright, Mr. Hayes?"

The man did not even have the decency to look ashamed. With an impatient wave of his hand, he dismissed the truth about George as a trifling fact. "Yes, yes, I have confessed it all, thanks to bloody Miss Spencer. What happened back then is in the past, and it does not change the fact that I need you to find my son *now*."

Jasper's tolerance for the arrogant man had already been wearing thin, but at the mention of Leo, it deteriorated entirely. As if sensing it, Lewis interrupted.

"Guv, you still want me to head over to the Blicksons' home?"

On the train, they had planned for Lewis to go with Constable Drake to Park Crescent. Somehow, Paula had learned that Edward had been given to Stanley and Melanie Hayes to raise as their own son. How she'd come to know, Jasper wasn't sure, but as George was now missing, and Paula had always believed Edward was still alive, she was almost certainly involved in his disappearance.

Lewis was to take her into custody, should she be at home. If not, he was to track her down.

Meanwhile, Jasper and Warnock would go to Gunnerson's Rest Home. When he'd sent Leo to interview Esther Goodwin, he'd considered it a relatively simple and safe task. He'd regretted his decision, of course, because he'd led Leo to believe she might assist him in future inquiries. But her report detailing the interview gained in magnitude as he'd traveled back to London.

It was plausible Paula had shared her theory about Edward being alive with the two people whom she vastly seemed to prefer to her mother and who had taken her in after she'd aged out of the orphanage. During Jasper's interview with her, Felix had expressed his clear dislike for Martha Seabright. The fact that he'd come with Paula to the Yard rather than Paula's own husband had also been curious. The two cousins were undoubtedly close. If Paula had something to do with George's disappearance, there was a good chance her aunt and cousin knew about it.

However, before he could instruct Lewis and Drake to set out for Marylebone, Stanley inquired, "Blickson? Not Archibald Blickson, surely?"

Jasper turned sharply toward him. "Yes. How do you know him?"

"How is Archie involved?" Stanley asked.

"Answer my question, Mr. Hayes," he barked, drawing the attention of multiple passersby. He did not care. "How are you connected to Blickson?"

Stanley glowered at him. "The man is my property insurer."

The link tolled through him, clear and palpable. This

was it. "Paula Blickson's maiden name is Seabright," he supplied. The color drained from Stanley's face. "She is Edward's sister."

The older man clutched the edge of the open carriage door. "That is… No. Impossible. I had them to dinner last month. How could I have known?"

He couldn't have, and Jasper was willing to wager the chance meeting had been the catalyst for everything involved with this case.

"Blimey," Lewis hissed. "Did Mrs. Blickson meet your boy at the dinner?"

At Stanley's distracted nod, a deluge of answers fell into place. Answers, and yet more possibilities too.

Jasper signaled a nearby driver of a coach waiting for hire.

"Lewis, Warnock, with me. Drake, return to headquarters and request a judge's warrant to search the Blicksons' home. We're going there now, but I want a warrant in case we are blocked from entry."

They would search every nook and cranny of that home for George.

"I'm coming with you," Stanley said as he started to climb back into his carriage.

"I cannot prevent you from following us, but you *will* stand back and allow me and my officers to do our jobs when we arrive." Jasper speared him with what he hoped was a warning stare. Stanley flared his nostrils in contempt, then disappeared into the carriage.

"Jasper." Oliver stopped him before he could join Lewis and Warnock, who had already piled into the hired coach. "I think you should know that last night, Miss Spencer mentioned Paula Blickson."

"She suspected Paula knew her brother had not died," he replied. "It seems she was correct."

"That isn't all," Oliver said with some urgency. "She mentioned that it would be beneficial to call on Mrs. Blickson. I said I would pass along the suggestion to you, but her expression was...well, I can only describe it as *impatient*."

It took no effort for Jasper to picture that expression of hers. And knowing Leo, her impatience could have led to injudicious action. Like calling upon a woman he now suspected of kidnapping. Perhaps even murder.

He rushed to join␣Lewis and Warnock, praying Leo had not already found Paula Blickson and whatever danger came with her.

Leo slowed her gait as she strolled past the Epoch's main entrance on Whitfield Street. She'd been moving at a leisurely pace, hoping to appear casual, and now stopped to read the theatre bill pasted to the sooty limestone façade. A production of *The Pirates of Penzance* was set to debut in a week, though the derelict state of the theatre— its darkened, smudged windows, the limestone in dire need of a new coat of whitewash—left her doubting that the play would be of good quality.

It was barely noon, however, so the darkened windows weren't too out of the ordinary. She contemplated trying the handle on one of the front doors but refrained. Going inside the theatre alone would not be wise. On her short walk to the area around Fitzroy Square, she had thought plenty about the false beards the masked robbers had all worn the night of the dinner. A theatre could provide access to such stage props. And a trained actor would have a commanding, yet mellifluous voice—just as the brutal leader of the intruders had possessed.

Her pulse spluttered when she considered Paula's cousin, Felix Goodwin. She had only seen him in passing at the CID, but as Leo continued past the entrance to the theatre and across the street, she fetched the memory of that encounter effortlessly. The details of Paula's mourning gown and her stylish black hat with the tulle veil attached to its brim, fluttering as she passed Leo, were all crystalline in her mind. Though she'd paid him less attention at the time, the details of the man escorting Paula were etched in Leo's mind as well. His estimated height and weight, and his inflexible bearing were hers again to scrutinize. But more importantly, she recalled the small bob of his head, in acknowledgment, as he passed her, and his alert, dark, sapphire-blue eyes.

Held up in comparison to the pair she'd seen through the slits in the black cloth covering her abductor's head, Leo shivered. They were the same. Felix Goodwin had murdered his aunt, Martha Seabright, and he'd been the one to abduct Leo and later release her.

Across the street from the theatre, she paused at a news stall. The older man working the counter finished a transaction with another customer before turning his attention to her.

"*The Morning Chronicle*, please," she said, placing her coin on the counter. "And might you know when the Epoch opens today?"

The man handed her the newspaper and scoffed. "Won't be openin'. Closed down fer good."

"Closed?" Leo jolted with surprise. "The theatre bill says a play is opening next week. What happened?"

He gave an uninterested shrug. "One o' the actors wot come around me stall says the manager pulled the rug out from under everyone. He's movin' up ter Scotland."

Leo murmured her thanks as she rolled her newspaper and stepped aside. She glanced toward the theatre again, and its shuttered air made sense. With the production so close to its debut, everything at the theatre would have been arranged for weeks. The actors had practiced and memorized their lines, the stage design would be complete, the costumes nearly, if not already, finished. The funding for the play would have been in place too. For Felix Goodwin to have shut it down at the last moment like this was more than just suspicious. He was fleeing, and Leo had an excellent idea as to why.

Thwarted, she lingered by a lamppost while deciding what to do. She could not, under any circumstances, enter the theatre on her own. Jasper was endlessly complaining that she was too reckless, thoughtlessly putting herself in danger to follow some lead. Right now, however, she had no intention of risking her neck by chancing a meeting with Felix Goodwin.

There was a very good chance Felix and Paula had already left for Scotland, with George in tow. That image, however, did not sit right with her. A boy of thirteen could certainly have put up a fight if he didn't wish to go with them. And why would he choose to run away with people he did not know well, to a life that would be far less advantageous and comfortable than the one in which he had been raised by Mr. and Mrs. Hayes? Of course, at his age, George might not be thinking judiciously of the future, reacting out of anger and injury over having been lied to his entire life. But the possibility that Felix might do George harm if the boy put up a fight sat foremost in her mind.

There was no other choice now: The only thing Leo could do was to go directly to Scotland Yard and speak to Jasper. He would be furious that she'd gone to the Blicksons' home, but it didn't matter. She would endure his scolding if it meant that he and his fellow detectives were finally put on the right path toward finding George Hayes.

Leo tucked her issue of the *Morning Chronicle* under her arm and started toward the end of the street where she had seen an omnibus stand. She didn't have much money in her purse, but she could not walk the distance to Westminster again; the blisters from yesterday's trek still rubbed against the heels of her boots.

She was reaching into her purse for the sixpence it would cost when the driver of a dray shouted for someone to watch out. Leo looked up to see a woman in a dark purple skirt and short jacket crossing the street in a hurry. If not for her black hat, draped with a lace veil, Leo might not have looked twice at her.

Paula Blickson had her head down, her veil drawn aside, and she was walking quickly toward the Epoch. Leo stopped and stared as the woman passed the front door and continued toward the side of the theatre, where a narrow alley divided the Epoch from the neighboring building. In her gloved hands, she carried a small carpetbag, and in a blink, she disappeared into the alley.

Without stopping to think, Leo crossed the street again. She followed in Paula's steps to the edge of the theatre. Peering around the corner into the alley, she saw a tall gate made of weathered wooden slats a few yards ahead. It was most likely there to keep theatregoers from accessing the back doors of the Epoch. Paula was no longer in sight.

If she had not yet left the city, then neither had George. Had the theatre been shut down and the actors dismissed to conceal that he was being kept here?

Leo took a few cautious steps into the alley. At first, the gate appeared to be shut. But coming closer, she spied a brick on the ground, wedged to prop the gate open an inch. Enough to keep it from latching shut.

She should not go any farther, and truly, in her heart, she knew peeking past the propped gate would be deemed highly reckless by a certain Scotland Yard detective inspector. Still, she pulled on the gate, slowly and carefully, listening for the squealing of rusted hinges. It was silent, however, and when she peered into the gated half of the alley, it was empty.

No farther, Leo came Jasper's stern voice in her mind.

Leo pulled back, allowing the gate to rest against the brick again.

She'd been so focused on whether the gate's hinges would make noise and give her away that she had not considered any sounds might come from behind her.

Too late, her instinct sensed a presence at her back. As before, with Gavin Seabright, a hard object nudged her between her shoulder blades. This time, however, Leo knew it was not the harmless neck of a glass beer bottle.

"I do wish you would have ceased your investigating, Miss Spencer. This is going to be quite unpleasant for us both."

Chapter Twenty

"Open the gate," the smooth voice behind her commanded. The deluge of shock that coursed from the top of Leo's scalp down the back of her neck to her spine kept her from complying immediately. The gun's muzzle between her shoulder blades nudged harder.

"Do not think I am playing, Miss Spencer. The gate. Now."

Cursing herself for her heedless curiosity, Leo obeyed. She opened the gate, the newspaper she'd tucked under her arm coming free and fluttering to the ground. With another jab of the muzzle, Leo stepped through.

The gate closed and latched behind them without the weapon being removed from her back. Leo peered over her shoulder at her assailant.

In her first meeting with Esther Goodwin, the older woman had been seated on a settee, her choice of dress cumbersome enough to conceal that she was, in fact, quite tall. Taller than Leo, at any rate. Esther had exuded soft grace and elegance, and a slight degree of frailty. However now, her callous expression made it perfectly clear that she was, like her son, a proficient actor.

She urged Leo toward an open back door leading into the theatre. "Inside," she ordered, her tone no longer timorous as it had been at Gunnerson's Rest Home.

The darkened mouth of the open doorway swallowed them, and when the door shut, Leo could no longer see. At the soft hiss of gas igniting, a flare of light brightened where they stood in a narrow backstage corridor. Here, numerous shipping crates, folded swathes of painted backdrops, racks of costumes, and all manner of stage props such as chairs, a dining room table, and divan, were all shoved aside to create a thin passageway for the actors to traverse.

"Don't tarry, Miss Spencer," Esther commanded, giving another thrust of the revolver into her back to prompt Leo to move.

As she walked ahead, the danger of the situation pressed in on her from all sides. No one knew where she was. She had no weapon to defend herself. And she presumed she was about to meet again the man who'd abducted her a few days ago.

Defeatism and panic weren't going to help her, however. Leo had been in a few tight spots before, and she'd managed to use her wits to ease herself out of them. Then again, during those times, she had been with Jasper.

"Where are you taking me?" she asked Esther, if only to escape her own spiraling thoughts.

They'd reached the stage, where wine-red brocade curtains had been drawn together to hide a view of the house seats.

Esther didn't answer. Instead, once they'd crossed the

stage to another narrow back corridor, Leo was ordered to turn right. Straight ahead, the opening to a spiral stairwell led down to the pit under the stage, she presumed. To the left, a door was open to another room, already bright with lamplight.

Esther shepherded her into this room, which appeared to be an office. Inside, they joined Paula Blickson and George Hayes. The latter, Leo assessed quickly with a spring of her heart. The boy was seated on an old sofa, his eyes slightly unfocused as he peered at her. He did not flinch when Esther slammed the office door shut behind them.

"George? Are you all right?" Leo went toward him, but Paula, who'd been at the desk counting a stack of bank notes, darted forward.

"Stay away from him!" she shrieked.

Leo pulled back, and Paula sent an alarmed stare toward Esther. "Aunt, what are you doing? Who is this woman?"

"Did you dose the boy with laudanum?" Leo asked. To subdue him, perhaps? To keep him from running away.

"This is the nosy woman detective I told you about," Esther replied, remaining in front of the closed door. "I saw her through the lobby windows while I was waiting for you to return. She recognized you and followed you to the alley gate."

The little flutter of pride that Esther Goodwin had referred to her as a *detective* was poorly timed, but Leo felt it, nonetheless.

Paula's wide brown eyes looked pointedly at the revolver in her aunt's hand. "But why did you bring her in here? And what are you doing with that thing?"

"I couldn't allow her to leave, could I?" Esther hissed. "She found you. Followed you."

Paula had yet to remove her hat and gloves, and there were three large carpetbags in addition to the smaller one Leo had seen her carrying outside on the street. It was into this smaller bag that Paula stashed the thick pile of bank notes. They were leaving London, and very soon, it appeared.

On the sofa, George shifted forward, elbows coming to rest upon his knees. "Is that a gun?"

Esther lowered the weapon to her side, hiding it behind her skirt. She was holding it with her left hand. The masked leader of the robbers had been left-handed as well.

"Felix is left-handed too," Leo said, recalling his shooting hand from the benefit dinner. She met Esther's eyes. "Is that the weapon your son used to kill your sister?"

The older woman's hateful stare scalded Leo. She started to raise the revolver, no doubt to aim it at her. After flicking her gleaming eyes toward George on the sofa, however, Esther tucked it back behind her again. Her hesitation spurred on Leo. It wouldn't do to back down now. The few times Leo had been in treacherous situations, she'd had to be bold. She'd had to take chances. This time would be no different, even without Jasper close at hand.

"You don't know what you are talking about," Esther said tersely.

"I believe I know quite well." Leo looked toward Paula. She stood protectively next to the sofa, where George still sat, his interest in the situation visibly battling the administered laudanum dose.

"Mrs. Blickson, when did you learn that your mother had sold Edward to Stanley Hayes? I'm guessing it was shortly after you met George at the dinner Stanley and his wife hosted for your husband and you."

Paula's mouth opened, then closed again. Her stunned reaction quickly melted into tight-lipped fury.

"You went to see Martha," Leo went on. "And she what? Confessed?"

"Stop speaking this instant, Miss Spencer!" Esther ordered, but Leo had no intention of obeying. This woman planned to kill her. Being accommodating would get her nowhere. Besides, George's presence was a layer of protection. Esther did not want him to view her as a killer. She wanted him to like her. Trust her.

Leo believed she knew why.

"She laughed." Paula's voice trembled. "My mother laughed and said I was overreacting. She insisted that I'd known about the adoption all along, and if I hadn't, then I was stupid."

"You did suspect he was taken, though," Leo said.

"How do you know this?"

"Your brother, Gavin. I spoke to him."

Paula fluttered her lashes shut and shook her head. "Yes, I suspected it, but what could I do? Edward was gone. There was no proof of what had happened to him. But she had no right to give him away!"

"No, she didn't have the right, did she?" Leo said. "Because Edward wasn't her son to give away. He was yours."

Tears rushed to Paula's eyes, and her lips quivered.

Martha had not possessed a mole on her face like the one Paula and George shared, and siblings generally did not share matching birthmarks. That left only one possibility.

"Edward." George blinked slowly. "That was me. I was stolen."

These weren't questions, but rather they were statements. The boy knew the truth. Had he come here with them willingly, then?

"You were adopted, yes," Leo said. "And I am working with your father to find you and bring you home."

"That man is not his father!" Esther snapped, her teeth practically bared in a snarl. "Paula, take Edward into the alley. Wait for me there. I won't be long."

Indecisiveness swept the tearful anger from Paula's face. She didn't move to follow her aunt's order.

"Nurse Radcliff arranged for the adoption of Edward by the Hayeses," Leo continued, needing to keep Paula here. "Edward was only a few months old. You were still nursing him at the orphanage, I suspect, so the nurse knew the truth. And she and your mother decided that your baby would be better off with another family."

At just fourteen years old, Paula had certainly not been prepared to mother a child. But the cruelty of having her son taken away, of being told that he had died, must have been crippling, even for a girl of her young age.

"She didn't want him," Paula cried, her voice strident as she battled a sob. "She didn't even want me and Gavin. When she put us in that place, she promised I'd be able to take Edward with me when I left. I had two years. Just two years, and then, I could be his mum."

On the sofa, George buried his forehead in his hands

as though wanting to rub away an ache. They must have given him just enough laudanum to keep him compliant while they traveled from London to Scotland.

"When I discovered the truth and went to her, do you know what that hideous woman told me?" Paula demanded, voice trembling. "She said she'd done me a favor, and now that I'd married rich, I should *pay her back*."

Money seemed to have been Martha Seabright's prime obsession. She'd been blackmailing Stanley Hayes for years, after all. How bitter she must have felt when Paula married a man of high social standing and considerable wealth. Especially since, without Martha's decision all those years ago to sell her son, Archibald Blickson never would have considered Paula a suitable wife.

"There is no need to tell Miss Spencer any of this," Esther said, her pinched scowl deepening. "It is none of her business."

"It became my business when your son murdered a woman sitting next to me at the benefit dinner. He then threatened to do the same to me," Leo replied sharply.

"Murdered?" George tried to stand, but his legs wouldn't hold him. The boy fell back onto the cushions, Paula catching his arm to steady him.

"*Aunt*," she almost wailed, with a pleading look.

Esther would have known, of course, that Martha had not borne a child shortly before sending all three children away to the orphanage.

"You offered to take the children in rather than let your sister send them to the orphanage," Leo said to Esther. "But Martha denied you. Was it because she knew Felix was the boy's father?"

Leo wasn't as certain about this deduction as she had been about Paula being Edward's mother. However, it would answer why Esther and Felix had been willing to go to such dire lengths to get Edward back now.

The older woman's body, which was draped in a sensible ulster coat, an item usually only worn while traveling, went rigid. The barest flare of her nostrils indicated Leo had touched a nerve.

"Did Martha hold you responsible for her daughter's condition? Maybe she wanted to punish you, or Felix, by withholding Edward from you," Leo suggested.

Paula avoided Leo's eyes, giving a distinct impression of guilt. Seduced by her own, much older cousin.

"That is why you cut your sister from your life, isn't it?" Leo continued when neither of the other women spoke. "Because she denied you your own grandchild. A grandchild you were told died in the orphanage's care. And now, all these years later, you learned the truth just as Paula did. Felix too."

And here they were, preparing to set out with George in tow. Paula would leave her husband, and Felix his theatre, and they would be the family they ought to have been. Grandmother, included.

"Where is Felix now?" Leo asked, a small twinge of worry creeping in. Esther's reluctance to shoot her in front of Edward had buffered her from harm. From what Leo had experienced of Felix, however, he would not be so restrained.

"I'd like to get some air," George muttered, again trying to get to his feet. This time, he gripped the arm of the sofa and balanced himself with a helping hand from

Paula. She hushed him, telling him they would go outside soon.

Leo focused on her. "You warned Gavin not to go to the dinner. You said he'd be a traitor if he went, but it was really because you knew what Felix had planned, isn't that correct?"

Paula bit her bottom lip, still unable to look at Leo.

"You didn't want your brother to come to harm, just like you don't want George to come to harm. I can see you care about the boy. You *love* him."

"Of course she loves him," Esther hissed. "She is his mother. A mother will do anything for her child."

Esther had proven that to be true. She was just as complicit in the killing of Martha Seabright as her son. Not only had the three of them planned to take Edward back from the family he'd gone to, but they also wanted revenge. And not just on Martha.

"Nurse Radcliff arranged the adoption—"

"That woman *stole* our Edward. She knew Paula was the babe's mother, and yet she allowed my sister to accept that wretched man's money in exchange for a child she had no right to sell!"

In all truth, Esther wasn't wrong. Her fury was warranted, as was Paula's. Martha had done a horrible thing by taking her daughter's baby and giving him away. She'd profited for years off that adoption, blackmailing Stanley Hayes. And she had deprived her daughter the chance to be a mother to the boy, as she had promised when Paula entered the orphanage.

Martha Seabright had been a despicable sister and an even worse mother. But by murdering her, Esther, Paula, and Felix had lowered themselves to that same level of deplorability. Not to mention what they had planned for Nurse Radcliff.

"Felix went to Twickenham, didn't he?" Leo asked next. "Nurse Radcliff was found dead yesterday. Murdered, in fact. However, what Felix didn't know—couldn't have known—was that the woman he killed was not the Nurse Radcliff who had given Edward away to Stanley Hayes."

Paula's dark brows pulled taut in confusion.

"The woman he killed was Nurse Radcliff's elderly aunt, the former Matron Radcliff. Surely, you remember her, Paula?"

By the instant blanching of her skin, she did.

"The current matron at the orphanage, Caroline Westover, née Radcliff, handled the adoption. Imagine her shock when she found her aunt, an innocent old woman, murdered in cold blood."

Paula raised a tremulous hand to her lips. "*That* is where he went? To Twickenham? My God. I knew he'd gone somewhere, and I knew Felix was still so angry, but I never thought—"

Esther hissed between her teeth. "Quiet! Paula, take Edward—"

"I've told you, my name is George," the boy said, somewhat more lucid now. His pupils were larger, too. "I'm not sure about this any longer. You said I was stolen, and I guessed that I wasn't a Hayes by blood. I look nothing like my parents and sister. But… you didn't tell me anyone had been killed."

"Miss Spencer has upset you," Esther soothed, her tone changing to something more indulgent.

"I've merely told him the truth," Leo cut in. "George, do you wish to go back home to your mother and father?"

Paula made a soft wailing sound. George looked at her, his eyes swamped with doubt and guilt. It was obvious that he didn't want to hurt her feelings.

"He isn't going anywhere with you," Esther barked, her left hand beginning to shake as she visibly restrained herself from raising the gun. "*Paula*. Do as I say."

"You don't want to hurt him," Leo said swiftly to Paula, who'd hesitated again at her aunt's order.

"Of course, I don't," she said, tears brimming in her eyes.

"Taking the boy away from the only family he has ever known would be cruel," Leo said. "Your mother betrayed you, Paula. She broke your heart. But what you're doing isn't right. This isn't how you mend what has been done to you."

Having endured enough, Esther ripped open the office door. "Take the bags and the boy and wait in the alley for me."

But her niece had not yet complied with that order, and now, as tears rolled freely down her cheeks, Paula shook her head.

"Aunt, this has gone too far. Did you know Felix had traveled to the orphanage? And what he meant to do to Nurse Radcliff?"

Esther made no reply, her lips pursed tight with fury.

"I'm not sorry my mother is dead," Paula continued. "But an old woman who had nothing to do with Edward being taken away from us? And now you plan to be rid of this lady detective too? No. I cannot do it. This isn't what I wanted."

"Are you out of your mind?" Esther's voice rose. "You cannot take Edward back to that family. He is your son. My grandson!"

"You aren't thinking about what is best for George, Mrs. Goodwin," Leo said.

"My only thoughts have been for him!" Esther raised the gun at last, leveling it at her. George staggered forward, out of his mother's grip, and put himself in front of Leo.

"You cannot shoot her," he yelled, even as Leo and Paula pushed him back.

"Stay behind me, George," Leo urged him. "Paula, I will vouch for you with the detective inspector. He will listen to me when I tell him you've done what is best for your son. Come, help me bring George to safety."

Esther still blocked the door. "You are not going anywhere."

Though her insides quivered, Leo tucked her chin and walked directly toward the older woman. George stood close behind her, his hand clutching the back of her arm. Paula joined them.

"Aunt Esther, move aside," she said with more assertiveness than she'd yet shown. "You've lost control. So has Felix. It wasn't supposed to be like this. I…" Her confidence floundered. "I didn't think it would be like this."

Esther bared her teeth at her niece, as if in disgust. "Felix suspected you would be too weak to see this through. He thought you might go to your brother and confess our plan, or even to your heartless mother to warn her. He kept eyes on them both for weeks to make sure you didn't."

Paula gaped. "Felix didn't trust me?"

"No, and now I can see he was right not to!" Her aunt's hand shook, her throat working hard as she no doubt was panicking.

The distant sound of high-pitched whistling coming from another part of the theatre broke the stalemate.

"It's Felix," Paula said, gasping with fear.

Doubt only stilled Leo's legs for a second. She streamed forward, straight toward Esther. She couldn't shoot, not without the risk of striking George and Paula too. Leo shoved her aside, and the older woman growled with frustration as she staggered and fell.

"Felix!" she screamed from where she'd landed on the floor.

The whistling stopped, and Leo's heart lurched. She turned to Paula. "Is he coming from the alley or the front of the theatre?"

"The alley," she answered, her eyes like saucers.

That would bring him across the stage, directly here.

"Can we go out the front?" Leo asked, thinking of the curtains blocking the view of the house floor. But Paula shook her head.

"The front entrance is locked from the inside. I don't have the key."

The pounding of feet came across the hollow-bottomed stage.

"Hurry!" Paula said, then rushed forward to the spiral stairs leading below the stage. Leo moved George in front of her and followed them, as they descended the curling steps to the low-ceilinged space beneath the stage.

It was dark and musty there, with only the barest light filtering through grates set into the apron of the stage above their heads. Outlines of props, wooden backdrops, and some ropes and pulleys were visible, though not much else. As Leo tried to keep pace with the darkened shapes of Paula and George moving through the cavernous space, she tripped on objects in her path.

"Where does this lead?" she asked, her heart hammering in her chest. The memory of another dark, cluttered place barreled forward in her consciousness: the attic of her old home on Red Lion Street.

"To another set of steps leading up to a rear door," Paula replied.

Felix would know this, and he would double back and be there to meet them when they ascended from below the stage.

"Stop," Leo said. "Let me by, and you two return the way we came. Go out the alley door and find a police constable."

"No, miss!" George said, his voice pitched high with fright.

"I insist. Felix will go to the rear door of the theatre, thinking we'll emerge there. I'll make noise and let him believe we are doing just that. Paula, take George to safety. *Go.*"

Paula hesitated but must have seen the wisdom in separating, for she and George scooted past her. As Paula passed, she clutched Leo's arm.

"The staircase is to your left up ahead, past the sleigh. Be careful," she said, then she and George were quietly heading back the way they'd come.

Leo continued onward, her eyes peeled in the dim light for any sign of a sleigh. She pushed a wooden crate as she passed it, knocking it over and causing a ruckus, then did the same to a tall, wooden backdrop. Overhead, she heard the pounding of a pair of feet as someone crossed the stage. Felix had taken the bait.

The curved railing of a small sleigh came into view in the meager light, and then ahead, a muted gleam of iron—the set of cast iron spiral steps leading up to the rear door. Felix would be waiting there at the top. Leo paused at the base of the stairs. There was no chance Paula would have made it to the street yet to flag down a constable. Climbing the stairs would only guarantee Leo coming face-to-face with Felix Goodwin. She was trapped. The same way she had been trapped in the attic of her old home. Like then, she needed a place to hide. Leo hesitated on the bottom step, looking behind her for where she might conceal herself.

Then, light cascaded down the twisting iron steps as above, the rear door opened.

Chapter Twenty-One

Jasper sat on the edge of the bench seat inside the hired coach, every muscle in his body coiled. He'd been to the Blickson residence, where Paula's husband had confirmed that Leo had already come and gone that morning.

"A very odd young woman. She was quite forthright with her questions," he'd said, then shrugged. "However, as she is working with Scotland Yard, I suppose that is required."

At this, Lewis and Warnock had flicked Jasper questioning glances. He'd ignored them and asked if Mr. Blickson knew where Leo had gone after she'd left his residence.

"She was searching for my wife, as you are," he'd replied. Jasper had waited impatiently for him to continue. "But when I mentioned Mrs. Blickson's cousin, Felix Goodwin, she took a larger interest in him."

If Leo had taken an interest in Felix, there must have been good cause. And when the older gentleman had finally come around to telling them that Felix was the manager of a theatre, Jasper had understood exactly what Leo had deduced.

"The beards," he said to Lewis.

The detective sergeant had cursed. "The masked men that night…you don't suppose they were actors from this theatre?"

After another minute of struggling to wrangle the location of Felix's theatre from Mr. Blickson, they had departed with all haste. Stanley and Oliver Hayes had been waiting on the pavement outside.

"Well? Is George here?" Stanley asked as he craned his head toward the front door to see.

"No," Jasper reported, then, without pause, climbed back into the waiting coach. "Follow us," he commanded them.

Now, several minutes later, as they came upon the Epoch Theatre, Jasper's raw nerves jumped. If Leo had come here, entering the theatre by herself would have been asinine. She'd have recognized the danger of it, surely. She must have put together the possibility that Felix Goodwin was the leader of the masked men; she was far too perceptive not to have done.

He leapt down from the coach and went straight to the front door. It was locked.

Oliver and Stanley's carriage drew to a stop along the curb. "Why have you led us here?" Oliver asked as he descended to the pavement.

"I have reason to believe Paula Blickson is associated with this place," Jasper explained as he peered through one of the theatre's filthy windows. He couldn't see far inside but made out a ticket booth, queue posts, and ropes.

"Help! Somebody! Police!"

Jasper turned away from the window to see a woman running out of the alley next to the theatre—it was Paula Blickson. And with her was an adolescent boy.

"George!" Oliver shouted, breaking into a run toward them.

Paula's chin quivered. Reluctantly, she released George's arm so he could hurry to meet his cousin, and then, as Stanley shot like a bullet from the carriage, his father. As relieved as Jasper was to see the boy unharmed, the knot of dread in his stomach remained.

"Where is Miss Spencer?" he asked Paula as he took swift strides toward the corner of the building.

Paula's tear-filled eyes were wide with fear as she pointed toward an open alley gate. "In the theatre, under the stage. I'm supposed to be sending a constable. I'm so sorry. Felix, he's in there too, and my aunt has a gun, and—"

"Lewis, with me. Warnock, detain Mrs. Blickson in the carriage. Oliver, stay with George," Jasper ordered before darting through the alley gate.

"He'll have gone in through the rear door!" Paula called after him.

Jasper would sort out why the woman was helping him later, but clearly, it was Felix Goodwin and his mother who were the dangerous parties. Jasper sprinted down the alley, Lewis's footfalls directly behind him. They came first to an open door in the side of the building.

"Go in through here. Find your way to beneath the stage. We'll come at him from two sides," Jasper told the detective sergeant. "Have your Webley at the ready. And watch out for the old woman."

Lewis withdrew his police-issued revolver and disappeared into the building. Jasper kept moving to where the alley forked, his revolver already drawn. As Paula had advised, he found another door at the back leading into the theatre. It had been left wide open. Jasper approached, and an indiscernible voice emanated from within.

He crossed the threshold into a narrow corridor, his revolver raised; to his immediate right, a stairwell of curving steps led down into a darkened space.

"I shouldn't have been so generous the first time we met, Miss Spencer."

Felix Goodwin was down below. No reply came. Jasper deduced Leo was either incapacitated or hiding.

Light from the open rear door poured down the stairwell, but it wouldn't stretch far. Descending the steps would put Jasper directly into view, making him an easy target for Felix. But he could not stay up here when Leo was in danger down below.

"Imagine my surprise when I saw you at Scotland Yard," the man continued, his voice having drifted further away. Leo was hiding, Jasper was now certain.

He drew a deep breath and started down the spiral stairs. He kept his footfalls as light as possible to prevent the iron steps from announcing his presence.

"My mother warned me. Said you were meddlesome," Felix called out, masking an errant squeal of the iron steps.

"You may as well come out from wherever you're hiding," he went on. "I know I am close. I can trace your scent. Honeysuckle, is it?"

Jasper reached the bottom of the staircase, still bathed in light from the open door above. His eyes latched onto movement ahead—the back of a man's head and shoulders, the rest of his body blocked from view by a couple of stacked crates. As if sensing another person's presence in the space below stage, Felix whipped around to see Jasper, already aiming his weapon.

"Hands in the air, Goodwin!"

The man darted from his view. Jasper sprang forward in pursuit, though as he left the pool of light from above, he knew the dark would be dangerous. Felix was familiar with this space; he would know where to hide or how to escape.

"The theatre is surrounded, Goodwin," Jasper called loudly. "We have Paula and George in police custody."

He stepped carefully, slowly, toward what appeared to be a two-person sleigh. The stage grates above allowed in some light from the main house, but more light came from farther ahead. The guttering light of a gas lamp. Felix's figure darted from behind a large object and toward this source of light.

"Goodwin, stop!"

He didn't—not of his own volition, at least. Jasper heard a resounding crash, followed by a cry of anguish. Rushing forward, he found Felix trapped beneath what appeared to be a heavy, wooden hearth mantel. Repurposed as a stage prop, it had been tipped over. On the floor, a handful of yards away, was the gas lamp. The place where the mantel had been stored stood empty. It seemed unlikely the mantel had fallen over on its own, but Jasper didn't have a moment to spare thinking on it.

Beneath the stage prop, Felix Goodwin moaned and stirred.

"Guv, have you got him?" Lewis called from the top of the other circular staircase that led below stage too. Lewis tapped down the iron steps quickly, shaking the whole thing and making a ruckus.

Jasper holstered his Webley and removed the pair of handcuffs he always carried in his coat pocket. "Have you seen the old woman?"

"No one's up here. She must have done a runner. Where's Miss Spencer?"

That was the question still kinking Jasper's gut.

"Give me a hand," he said as he grasped the edge of the toppled mantel. Together, they hefted the heavy wooden prop off Felix. The man groaned and tried to shove up onto all fours, but Jasper jammed his knee into the middle of his back. He went down flat again.

He locked Felix's wrists into the cuffs. Before he could stand and yank the man to his feet, the telling click of a revolver's hammer being cocked sounded from behind him. Lewis reached for his holstered weapon, albeit too late.

"Don't, detective," came a calm female voice. "Raise your hands high."

Lewis did, though reluctantly and with a grimace of disgust—perhaps for himself, since he hadn't seen her sooner.

"And you, Inspector, remove those irons from my son's wrists."

Esther Goodwin. *Bloody hell.*

"I'm not going to do that, Mrs. Goodwin," he replied, his spine rigid and nerves skittering at knowing a gun was trained on him. "Your son is a murderer, and I am arresting him."

"Mother, shoot him," Felix grunted from where the side of his face was pressed to the floor. Jasper's knee still pinned him in place.

"She won't." Jasper twisted his knee, eliciting a squeal of pain from the man he'd pinned. "You're the killer here, not her."

Behind him, Esther rasped, "I will do what it takes to protect my son."

"Is that so? Why, then, didn't *you* lead the group of masked robbers into the benefit dinner and shoot your sister in the head?" Jasper queried. "And why didn't you travel to Twickenham to stab Nurse Radcliff in the back? By the way, Goodwin, you killed the wrong nurse."

Under Jasper's knee, the man went notably still.

"You could have spared your son the noose by doing it all yourself, Mrs. Goodwin, but you sent him instead," Jasper said.

"Loving mum that you are," Lewis tacked on, his hands still raised in the air.

"But what happened in Gavin Seabright's room, I wonder," Jasper mused. "That Harry fellow was pushed. Hit his head. That doesn't seem like your usual method, Goodwin. But in the end, what's another murder charge after two?"

"That wasn't him," Esther said, her voice no longer calm. It shook.

"Be quiet, Mother," Felix said, sawing out the words through the pain and humiliation of being pinned to the floor.

So, Esther had the altercation with Harry. Jasper

wanted to know more about the details, but this wasn't the time to press for them. She had come to the point where she either needed to follow through with her threat or give up. As she had yet to shoot him, Jasper was more apt to believe that if she were to pull the trigger, it would be due to a quiver of her finger. He needed her to lower the gun.

"Kill me or my sergeant, Mrs. Goodwin, and you will get the noose yourself," Jasper informed her. "Lay down your weapon. Sergeant Lewis will escort you from the theatre."

"Do as Inspector Reid says, Mrs. Goodwin."

Jasper's heart lurched. He twisted around at the new voice and saw Leo directly behind the older woman. She was holding something against Esther's back. A sword?

Christ. It was a sodding theatre prop.

"You didn't have a blade before," the woman said incredulously. And then, as if figuring it out, Esther grated out a bark of anger and whirled around. Leo's prop sword sliced downward against the woman's hand, and the report of a gun rang out.

Jasper pushed off Felix and rushed forward, like a battering ram, straight into Esther Goodwin. They slammed against the floor, the woman wriggling and wailing. He closed his hand around her left wrist, and a blink later, Leo's foot came down on top of her hand.

Esther's screams became sobs as Leo bent forward to pluck the weapon from the woman's weakened fingers.

Jasper pushed Esther onto her stomach, and Lewis was there in an instant, clapping his own pair of handcuffs around her wrists, one of which appeared to be bleeding.

Leo dropped the prop sword to the floor with a clatter.

"Gracious, I didn't think it was real," she said, breathing heavily.

Jasper got to his feet, his breath coming in short puffs as he took in the sight of her, searching for any sign of injury. Her dark hair had come loose from its combs and pins, but she appeared to be unharmed.

At last, the knot in his stomach unfurled. He didn't know if he wanted to throttle her or take her into his arms. He restrained himself from doing either, though just barely, as Lewis brought Esther to her feet.

"Bring her out," Jasper told the detective sergeant. "I have Felix."

The man was attempting to get onto his knees and then push himself to standing. Jasper took the gun Leo had recovered from Esther's hand. "Go with Lewis," he told her as he pocketed the weapon. "No arguments, please."

She glared at him. "I wasn't going to argue."

"Yes, you were."

With a defiant huff, Leo turned on her heel and followed Lewis.

Jasper hauled Felix to his feet. The man was tall and heavy, but all Jasper needed to do was remember how he so callously shot Martha Seabright, then took Leo from the dining room at gunpoint, and Jasper found he had all the strength necessary to push him forward and up the stairs. Felix chuckled darkly as they went.

"Now I understand why you looked as if you wanted to gut me at that dinner," he said.

"Be grateful I am a police officer," Jasper replied, giving him a hard push as they reached the top of the stairs.

The man guttered a laugh as they exited the building. "I can see that leaving Miss Spencer alive was a mistake. Had I killed her, I doubt the incompetent police would have ever found me."

Once they had moved into the alley, Jasper shoved Felix up against the exterior brick wall. He bent the man's hands upward at a painful angle.

"I would have hunted you down, Goodwin, no matter how long it took. And the moment I found you, I would have happily neglected my oath to preserve life."

He yanked Felix from the brick and pushed him forward, toward three approaching uniformed constables. They introduced themselves as officers of D Division, and Jasper handed Felix to them, with instructions to escort both him and Esther Goodwin to Scotland Yard.

Farther up the alley, Lewis was leading Esther toward the gate, where more constables had gathered to assist. Leo had stopped to wait for Jasper and now stepped aside, far out of the way of the D Division constables as they passed with Felix.

"A wooden stage sword? That was your weapon of choice? You could have been killed," Jasper said once they were alone. "What the hell were you thinking?"

"I was thinking that I didn't want Esther Goodwin shooting you in the back," she replied. "I saw the lantern when I was searching for a place to hide and suspected she was down there somewhere. After I pushed the mantel over onto Felix, I saw her sneaking up on you from behind. If I'd shouted to warn you, she might have fired off a shot before you could even turn around." Leo shrugged a shoulder. "I remembered the box of prop swords I'd knocked over earlier. It might not have been an entirely sound plan—"

"It wasn't a plan at all," he snapped. "You should have gone for help."

Her eyes flashed with defiance. "I wasn't leaving you, Jasper."

The rebuttal snuffed out the tension that had been stringing him tight. He released the breath he'd been holding and took Leo's shoulders in his hands. The desire to kiss her pounded through his veins. But he couldn't, not here.

"You've not been hurt?" he asked softly. She shook her head. Jasper allowed himself a quick sweep of his thumb against her cheek, then stepped away.

"Paula is Edward's—*George's*—mother, not his sister," Leo said. "I noticed the mole on her cheek—"

"There you are, Reid." Oliver came through the alley gate. Jasper glowered at the viscount for interrupting them. He was intrigued to hear more about what Leo had discovered. That Paula was, in fact, the boy's mother gave her motive for taking George more substance and reason.

Oliver slowed when he saw Leo. "Miss Spencer, I'm glad to see you're safe."

She cleared her throat as she turned to the viscount. "Is George well?"

"He's just fine, in no small part thanks to you. Reid, my uncle would like to take him home if that's all right. My aunt is waiting there for them."

Jasper had questions for the boy but nothing urgent enough to keep him from being brought home to his family. "That's fine. Tell Stanley I'll call at the house tomorrow."

Oliver nodded, then looked to Leo. "And you, Miss Spencer. May I escort you home?" He glanced at Jasper with a raised brow. "Unless the inspector plans to bring you into Scotland Yard for questioning?"

He did have questions for Leo—a lot of them, in fact. Including what had occurred inside the theatre and how she'd convinced Paula Blickson to reverse course and give up George. But for now, at least, he had his hands full with three suspects under arrest.

He nodded reluctantly, and Oliver extended his arm to Leo. She peered at it as if taken aback by the viscount's offer. Hesitantly, she linked her arm with Oliver's, and they started for the street.

Jasper followed behind them, slightly envious of his friend as he helped Leo into a cab, then climbed up to sit beside her.

"Guv," Lewis called as the cab rolled away into traffic.

The detective sergeant stood outside their waiting carriage. Warnock had seated himself next the driver on the bench to guard the ride back to the Yard. "Mrs. Blickson says she's ready to talk."

Chapter Twenty-Two

Leo lit the lamp on her desk in the morgue's office, illuminating the sheet of paper in the typewriter she'd been working on. It wasn't her account of her conversation with Esther Goodwin and Paula Blickson, as Jasper would no doubt have preferred, but a death certificate. At least a dozen had been backlogged while she'd been out the last handful of days, helping to solve Martha Seabright's murder. Connor, who'd been patient with her absences, would appreciate the certificates being finished when he arrived the next morning.

After leaving the Epoch, Leo had asked Viscount Hayes to bring her to the morgue instead of to Duke Street. Her limbs had still been trembling after the tumultuous events at the theatre, but the notion of going home to rest had made her even more jittery. The viscount, who successfully had pleaded with her to address him as Oliver rather than *my lord*, dropped her off at the Spring Street Morgue.

"I hope you'll forgive me, Miss Spencer," he'd said while handing her out of the hansom cab.

She'd been puzzled. "For what offense?" He'd been nothing but gracious since leaving the Epoch and had thanked her for her help in locating George. But a reticent expression had crossed his face just the same.

"I misjudged you," he said.

"How so?"

Oliver cringed in embarrassment, and Leo braced herself, suddenly uncomfortable. "I considered you to be…somewhat…odd."

"Oh." His blatant confession made her grin. "You weren't entirely wrong. I am a little odd. I must be, I suppose, to enjoy working here." She'd gestured toward the morgue's entrance.

But Oliver shook his head. "No, I now understand what Jasper meant when he said your temperament is different from that of other women. Your nature is quite admirable. "

"He said that?" She wanted to know when, and what more he'd had to say about her, but Oliver had only smiled and tipped his hat before returning to the cab.

Inside the morgue, the quiet stillness had been a balm to her senses. It was all over. Martha Seabright's killer, as well as Nurse Charlotte Radcliff's, had been caught. The mystery surrounding Edward Seabright's supposed death as an infant was solved. And George Hayes was home with his family—even if he was now aware of all the secrets Stanley and Melanie Hayes had kept from him. They had much to repair, and Leo didn't envy them the hardships that still lay ahead.

She felt a distinct dip in her spirits when she considered that the case was now closed. Of course, she was relieved. Jasper had made the necessary arrests, which would surely boost his standing at the CID. He had needed that victory, especially after the reprimands he'd received the last many months—mostly because of her.

That she'd played a role in solving this case but would not receive credit for her assistance didn't bother her. Leo didn't need it the way Jasper did. Even Oliver's praise, though kind and thoughtful, had not been necessary. It hadn't filled her with triumph—unlike how she felt when misaligned pieces of information finally came together and made sense. It was the act of answering a question, of solving a crime, or of bringing about justice that gave Leo a sense of contentedness. Not the acclaim that came afterward.

It was time to return her focus to the morgue. She fixed herself a pot of tea at the cottage range and got to work on the pile of folders and papers that Connor had left for her on her desk. If she was to be his assistant, she'd best not fall behind in her duties. She worked diligently, stopping only to let Tibia outside for a short caper. Rather than pausing to make a fresh pot of hot tea, she drank the cooled dregs of the first one.

She was pulling the final certificate from the platen when the grating chime of the front door's bell reached her in the office. As it was Sunday, the front door was locked, and the morgue closed to new corpses. But when the bell rang again, Leo set down the completed files, crossed the postmortem room to enter the lobby, and answered the door.

"Miss Hayes," she said after staring at the caller for a baffled moment.

Constance stood on the narrow portico, her fashionable Gainsborough hat angled in such a way that her face was partially blocked from passersby on the street. Visiting a morgue was not reputable, and by all appearances, she was alone.

Leo stepped aside to allow her in, and she entered with all haste.

"I didn't know to expect you," Leo said as she closed the door.

"I wasn't sure I would call." Constance held herself rigidly, as many people did when entering a morgue. Being near corpses unnerved many, and not just women.

"Oliver told me he brought you here," she went on. "I was on my way to see Jasper and thought I'd stop by and see if you were still in."

Leo couldn't imagine why Constance would wish to speak to her. They remained standing in the lobby, the next few seconds drawn and awkward.

"Has Jasper summoned you for an interview?" Leo asked, breaking the silence.

"No, I have some materials my mother believed Jasper should have. Letters."

To Martha Seabright from Caroline Radcliff, Leo imagined. Mrs. Hayes must have discovered them inside Martha's home and taken them.

Another few moments ticked by in which Leo remained uncertain why Constance had come. "Is everything all right with George?" she tried next.

"He's fine." She clasped her gloved hands together and tensed her arms. "George is exhausted but safe. Mother and Father are beside themselves with relief. It's an ugly business, of course. I'm sure once it all gets out, we'll be skewered in the gossip pages."

She referred to her brother's adoption. The police reports would not gloss over the motive for Martha's murder, nor George's kidnapping, and the information would make its way into more than just the gossip pages. The scrutiny would be severe. Leo doubted the Hayes family would stay in London to weather it.

"I don't wish to sound rude," Leo said after waiting for Constance to speak again. "But is there something I can do for you, Miss Hayes?"

"You can accept my gratitude," she answered swiftly. Though she was visibly uncomfortable, she held her chin proudly. "I know Oliver has already offered his thanks, and I want you to know I'm not so bitter that I cannot be grateful to you for your part in my brother's safe return. I have been made aware that you played a significant role in making that come to pass."

Stunned, Leo wasn't sure how to respond. Constance had come here just to say thank you?

"I…I'm glad I could help," she finally replied, though it seemed inadequate. "But I'm not sure I understand—why would I think you are bitter?"

She and Constance had never gotten on, but it had seemed like she disliked Leo more than usual yesterday when they'd met. Then again, Leo had been questioning Mr. Hayes and unearthing a painful secret that probably had changed the way Constance viewed her whole family. Perhaps that was what she was referring to. But then, with a scoff, the other woman's stare grew incisive again.

"Truly, Miss Spencer? You cannot imagine why, after

Jasper called off our courtship because of his feelings for you, I might dislike you?"

She stared at Constance, dumbstruck. Jasper had ended their courtship in May, but he'd never been explicit about the reason why other than he didn't want to marry her. It shouldn't have surprised Leo, not really. Deep down, she suspected that he must have cared for her for some time.

"He is in love with you." Constance stated it casually without an ounce of emotion. It gave Leo another unexpected jolt.

This time, however, she knew exactly how to respond. "Jasper isn't in love with me."

He had kissed her. Ardently, yes, and not just a chaste peck, but surely, that wasn't so out of the ordinary. He'd asked her to dinner, too. Neither of those things were declarations of love. *I care for you*. That was what he'd declared. Not love.

However, the burst of pleasure it gave Leo to consider he *might* feel that for her nearly lifted her feet from the floor.

Constance only shook her head and pressed her lips into a disheartened grin. "Do open your eyes, Miss Spencer. As I can no longer bring myself to hate you, I have no wish to see you trip and fall on your face."

She went to the door and let herself out, leaving Leo to stare after her, her mind spinning.

Jasper closed the door to the interview room, glad to be finished. He'd spent the last few hours questioning Felix

Goodwin, his mother, and Paula Blickson. At the close of each interview, he'd felt like punching a wall.

Felix had no remorse for what he'd done; he was an actor, and yet he hadn't even tried to make a show of it. When Jasper pressed him on the killing of Martha Seabright, a smug grin twitched the man's lips, as if the memory of her death amused him.

"She was a bitter old whore who deserved worse than she got," he'd said with simple finality.

After delivering Leo to the morgue, Oliver Hayes had come to the Yard. He'd explained the finer details of his uncle's underhanded adoption of Edward Seabright, including how Martha had continued to blackmail him over the years. Everything Jasper knew about Martha led him to believe that she was, indeed, a despicable woman. But Felix Goodwin was no better.

"And Nurse Radcliff?" Jasper had queried. "Did Paula send you to kill her?"

"Paula?" He'd sniffed dismissively. "All she cared about was getting Edward back. When her conniving mother told her everything, she came to us."

"You and Esther Goodwin," Sergeant Warnock clarified as he was taking notes at the table. Lewis would have usually sat in with Jasper during these interviews, but the young sergeant needed more training now that he'd earned a promotion.

"Yes," Felix answered with a sneer. In his arrogance, he appeared to hold himself up above all others; it was what had given him license to do as he pleased. "Paula told us it was Nurse Radcliff who sold my son. How was I to know the old lady wouldn't be the same one from back then?"

As Jasper was concluding the interview, he realized

how little it would have meant to Felix to kill the woman he'd abducted from the dinner. He could have pulled Leo from the coach in Battersea Park and shot her dead right there. It chilled Jasper to his bones, enraging him to the point of feeling ill.

"Why did you allow Miss Spencer to walk away?" he asked just as a pair of constables arrived to escort the prisoner to a Newgate Prison cell. There was ample evidence against him to secure a conviction and, undoubtedly, an execution.

The man had only smirked. Holding the detective inspector's stare, he seemed to know how Jasper felt for the woman in question and the power he'd held in his hands for that short amount of time.

"Luckily for Miss Spencer, I'd already shocked my mates enough for one evening. Had I done for her, more than just one of them would have turned on me."

The one who had, Harold Yardley, had been among the four actors at the Epoch who agreed to join their manager for the planned benefit dinner robbery in exchange for a cut of the profits. The sixth actor, Philip Green, had been picked up by constables at a pub he was known to haunt, and he'd cracked under the slightest pressure. The theatre had been struggling, he'd explained, their jobs at risk. When fenced, the jewels they stole would provide a nice payday. But the other actors, for whom Jasper now had names and addresses, hadn't known the job would involve a cold-blooded murder and an abduction by their leader. They'd been too nervous afterward to go out and fence any of the jewelry.

In the interview with Esther Goodwin, which Jasper had conducted while allowing Felix time to stew, she'd admitted to visiting a few pawnshops and posing as a wealthy widow who had fallen on hard times. The very same widow described by the pawnbroker at the jewelry shop Jasper had visited, it turned out.

Esther had also described Harold Yardley's agitation the night of the robbery when the troupe returned to the theatre. He'd made comments that, to Esther's ears, sounded as though he was considering turning traitor. She'd followed him the next morning, curious as to what he planned, and when, low and behold, he'd gone to her nephew Gavin Seabright's lodgings, she decided to have a word with him. She entered Mrs. Beardsley's home through the back, and when she confronted Harold, or Harry as he'd introduced himself to Gavin, their discussion turned into an altercation.

Esther's only regret appeared to be not leaving London the moment she and Paula rendezvoused with George at Holland Park, which abutted Hayes Manor. The boy had been willing, even eager, to leave, Esther claimed. This matched what Paula had told Jasper during her interview, on the carriage ride to Scotland Yard.

After meeting George at that auspicious dinner at the Hayes home, Paula confessed to hiring a private detective to dig into the circumstances surrounding the boy's birth. The detective, having bribed one of the family's more amenable servants, learned of the hushed-up adoption. Now certain that the boy was her lost child, Edward, Paula contacted George directly, sending a letter that was delivered by that same servant who'd been previously bribed. From there, mother and son struck up a correspondence.

George had always known he was different from his

parents and sister, and after overhearing whispered gossip from servants well before he first met Paula, he'd known that, biologically speaking, he was not a true Hayes. He was excited, Paula claimed, to meet his mother. Their matching moles, the striking similarities in their appearances, convinced him easily. Jasper also presumed the secrecy of their correspondence might have thrilled the thirteen-year-old boy too.

When Stanley set out for Hampshire abruptly the day after the benefit dinner, George sensed something was wrong. Paula received a message from him, posted from Hayes Manor, explaining that his father was taking him back to Hampshire. She'd replied with instructions to meet her in the southeast corner of Holland Park, just past midnight. George had complied.

Esther regretted that she and Paula hadn't disappeared with George right then. But Felix was still in Twickenham on his mission to kill Nurse Radcliff, and he'd also wanted to finish fencing the stolen jewels in order to have as much money in their pockets as possible when they left London. Pawning all the stolen goods at one shop would have been too suspicious. So, they had done it by piecemeal but not fast enough, it would seem. With the delay, Esther had resorted to giving George small doses of laudanum to keep him from changing his mind and trying to return home.

"You look done in, Reid," Chief Inspector Coughlan said in greeting as Jasper entered the DCI's office. It was getting late, and the chief was putting on his greatcoat to leave for the evening. News of the arrests had rumbled through the detective department, and Jasper had already been the recipient of a few pats on the back from passing officers. Now, for what might have been the first time since his appointment as detective inspector with the Met, Chief Coughlan leveled Jasper with a smile. Teeth and all. It was highly unnerving.

"Well done, lad, well done," he said, reaching for his hat. "I'm meeting the commissioner and Sir Eamon for dinner. They'll both be thoroughly pleased with how you've handled these cases. You will turn next to recovering the stolen jewelry from Sir Eamon's dinner guests, of course?"

"Yes, sir, constables will be sent out in the morning." In his boastful manner, Felix had revealed the names of the shops where he'd fenced a few of the items. Jasper was confident that Leo's pearls would be found, and he envisioned the pleasure on her face when he was able to return them to her.

"It's terrible about Stanley Hayes, of course," Coughlan continued. "The correspondence his daughter brought in proves the infant wasn't stolen, so while there is nothing wholly illegal in it, it is exceedingly immoral. I'll try to minimize how much gets into the official reports, but… well, you know how reporters are once they scent blood. Vultures."

Coughlan understood that no matter how scant or detailed the official report was, there were still plenty of officers who made a habit of selling whatever they knew to reporters to supplement their meager wages.

"Sir, I've charged Paula Blickson as an accomplice to murder, theft, and kidnapping," Jasper said. "But I want to note that she assisted the police in our apprehension of Mr. Goodwin and his mother. I believe some leniency is due her."

The chief inspector tucked his chin, the folds creasing as he considered Jasper's request. "Hmm. I suppose I can make a recommendation for leniency. But the woman will have to serve some time in prison. She should be grateful that she won't swing."

Jasper nodded and thanked him again; it was the best Paula could hope for now.

"Warnock is doing well, isn't he?" Coughlan went on in a more jovial tone as he started for the door.

"Yes, he's coming along," Jasper agreed. "Still green, but I'm sure he'll catch on quickly."

The chief inspector stopped at the door, sharing the threshold with Jasper. In a much lower voice, he said, "Don't think I am not aware that Miss Spencer was at the theatre during your arrests of the Goodwins and Mrs. Blickson. I also know you brought the young woman to a crime scene to identify a body."

Jasper tensed. *Sodding Warnock*. But then, Lewis had told him there were CID officers spying on him for Coughlan. Bringing her to Gavin's lodging room had been a risk. The gamble hadn't played out in his favor.

"I know you don't wish to hear it, sir, but Miss Spencer proved quite valuable in the closing of this case." He held his breath, prepared for Coughlan's good mood to evaporate. He kept his stare steady, unflinching.

"Are you telling me that Miss Spencer should be commended, instead of you, Inspector?"

The space between a rock and a hard place was a tight spot indeed. Jasper hesitated but then shook his head. "I only ask that you not view her as an enemy to this department, sir."

In the past, Coughlan had threatened to give Jasper a

demotion or send him to another division if he did not stop associating with Leo and allowing her to run roughshod through his investigations. Not associating with her wasn't an option, especially now that he'd made his feelings for her known and not just to Leo. He'd finally admitted them to himself as well. It seemed he was also inept at keeping her from any investigation that she took an interest in.

If Coughlan was going to sack him or toss him back to another division, he bloody well ought to do it now. Jasper stopped just short of telling him as much, but he thought his dueling glare might be making it clear.

The chief inspector backed down first. "I won't view her as an enemy of the CID so long as she doesn't make a nuisance of herself. Limit her involvement, Reid. I'm giving you an inch, not a mile. Is that understood?"

Jasper nodded, fighting to keep the surprise from his face as Coughlan continued toward the exit. Dazed, he walked toward his own small office. He honestly hadn't thought the chief inspector would relent. He also hadn't known how much he wanted to remain at the CID until the moment he'd been prepared to be tossed from it.

In his office, while collecting his coat and hat, Jasper pondered how to share Coughlan's decision with Leo. She might take it as an open invitation to insert herself into a future inquiry, when Jasper knew the chief inspector had not intended for that at all. They would have to be careful. Her assistance would need to be structured and well-controlled—the latter of which might prove difficult.

As he walked through the department, the desks were mostly empty. Lewis and Drake, as well as Warnock and Price, had peeled off once the Goodwins and Paula

Blickson were removed to their prison cells. There would be a mountain of paperwork tomorrow, but for now, a few pints were in order. Jasper left through the front of the building, planning to join the others at the Rising Sun for a short while. He'd then call on Leo. Knowing her, she would have asked Oliver to bring her to the morgue so she could type her statement of events. By now, she would be at home on Duke Street. Or perhaps she would have gone to his home on Charles Street to wait with Mrs. Zhao for his return.

The allure of her waiting for him at home shot through him, and he paused in the middle of the street to reconsider his plan to head to the pub first. That was when he felt the probing press of eyes on his back.

Jasper swiveled on his heel and found the orange-hatted man instantly. The stranger stood several yards away, leaning nonchalantly against a lamppost. Unlike before, the man didn't attempt to walk on, blend into a crowd, or vanish. He held Jasper's stare.

"Why are you following me?" He strode swiftly toward the man. He'd had enough with this game. "Who has sent you?"

The man didn't react. It should have alerted Jasper as odd, but he was intent on finally getting an answer. As such, the clatter of wheels and the approach of a coach and four did not faze him until the conveyance cut in between Jasper and the stranger and drew to an abrupt halt.

The door opened and a large, muscled man emerged. Jasper recognized him at once. *Bollocks*.

"Evening, Inspector," came a smooth greeting from

within the darkened coach. "Why don't you join me? We can have a talk."

Jasper's blood seemed to slow and turn to stone in his veins. He didn't need to see who it was to know the voice's identity.

Andrew Carter had come for him.

Chapter Twenty-Three

The lamp inside the coach flickered to life once Jasper took his seat. The hired muscle climbed in, followed closely by the man in the orange bowler. He had barely closed the door before the coach tore away from Scotland Yard.

Andrew was seated across from Jasper on the forward-facing seat. The single lantern's red glass globe cast his face and everything else in the coach in a devilish hue. Fitting, really.

"What do you want, Carter?" Jasper kept his voice firm and unaffected, though the absence of his Webley made him vulnerable; the hired muscle had taken it from its holster before ushering him into the coach. He hadn't been given a choice in the matter, what with the man in the bowler coming to stand with them and brandishing a snub-nosed revolver of his own.

"Don't sound so put out, Inspector," Andrew replied smoothly. "I thought we could have a friendly conversation. It's been a few months since we last spoke."

"To tell you the truth, I'd much rather be having a pint at the Rising Sun," Jasper replied.

Andrew chuckled lightly. "Not to worry, this won't take long."

"Good. Why don't you start by telling me why you've been having me followed."

Andrew crossed one leg over the other and clasped his hands over his flat stomach. In his mid-twenties, he was smooth-shaven, well-dressed, and handsome in a slick, predatory way. "You're not at Scotland Yard anymore, Inspector. You don't get to ask the questions." A sly grin curled his lips. "So, you tell me: Why did I stick a tail on you?"

Jasper had suspected the man in the orange bowler was associated with the Carters, though he'd hoped he was wrong.

"I can't read minds, Carter."

That sly grin spread wider. "Not even when it's family?"

Ice splintered through Jasper's chest and stabbed him low in his gut. *Shit.*

Andrew noted his reaction and laughed again. "I thought you looked familiar when you brought me in for that interview. There was something about your face, something that tugged right here." He tapped his temple as if to indicate his memories. "I couldn't place it. After I took care of Nelson, I let it go."

At nearly thirty years old, Jasper looked entirely different than he had as a boy of thirteen. When meeting Andrew for that first interview, he'd worried his cousin might recognize him. But beyond a momentary second glance and asking Jasper if they'd ever met before, the worry had seemed to be unfounded.

"I might never have thought about it again if I hadn't come across those articles on the tragic and strange Miss Leonora Spencer," Andrew continued. Jasper gritted his molars. He'd known those articles would cause trouble. "Do you know who else was mentioned in them?"

Jasper remained silent, though he knew the answer.

In a theatrical tone, Andrew recited, "*'Rescued from her family's slaughter by the late Detective Inspector Gregory Reid.'* Reid. Your father, I take it."

Jasper said nothing. Andrew didn't need him to.

"I asked my Aunt Myra—does her name sound familiar at all?—if she remembered the name of the officer who told her my cousin James had drowned. She did recall. Reid, it was. She also remembered that the boy was unrecognizable. Bloated. Split open and disfigured by water rot."

The coach slowed. Jasper glanced toward the windows, but the curtains were drawn, preventing him from seeing where they were. The stink of the river made itself known.

"I did some investigating of my own," Andrew said, his tone deceivingly friendly. "Gregory Reid's kiddies had died the previous year. Seems to me he wanted a son. Seems to me, he found one."

There was no use denying any of it. It would only make him look weak, and Andrew preyed on weakness. Jasper's cousins, the sons of Patrick Carter, had all been heartless bullies. They ranged widely in age, the oldest, Sean, ten years older than Jasper. Andrew, the youngest, had been the quiet one. Observant. Thoughtful. Not prone to temper. Somehow, it made him even more dangerous than his older brothers.

"Who else knows?" Jasper asked.

Andrew's friendly façade dropped, and Jasper was left staring into a pair of cold, calculating eyes. "You mean who else knows that you turned your back on your family, your blood, to become the son of a do-gooder policeman? And that you're now a copper yourself? For now, just me."

Jasper braced himself. Three against one, with no weapon, he wouldn't stand a chance. The slightest quiver of apprehension churned in his gut. His mind went straight to Leo and what she would do, how she would cope, if she were made to look upon him, laid out on one of the morgue's autopsy tables.

It gave him a jolt of determination not to let it happen. "What do you want, then?"

"Is that all you have to say for yourself?" Andrew let both feet touch the floor of the coach, then gave a jerk of his chin. Next to Jasper, the hired muscle pounded on the wall. The driver came to a full stop.

"What do you want me to say?" Jasper asked, aware he was about to shake a hive of angry bees. "How much I've missed you all?"

A silent moment passed. And then, Andrew barked with laughter. Genuine laughter, at that.

"You've grown a pair, haven't you? You ran off sniveling after that wallop from Uncle Robert—even I remember it—and here you sit, like a bloody king."

The beating Robert had levied for mucking up the job he'd been given, for not finding and killing the little girl hiding in the attic, was something Jasper still thought of regularly. Whenever he would enter the boxing ring at Oliver Hayes's club, he'd think of the humiliation of that thrashing, done in full view of his cousins and the other men who'd gone to the Spencer home that night. He'd think, too, of the pounding Robert had given Jasper's mother, Vera, which had resulted in her death and the death of his unborn sibling. In the boxing ring, he would fight every opponent he faced with Robert front of mind and with the secret hope that one day he would get his vengeance.

"I'm not sitting here like a king," Jasper began. "I'm sitting here like a detective inspector of Scotland Yard because that is exactly what I am. It is *who* I am. If you believe I regret one second of the last sixteen years or what I left behind, you are sorely mistaken."

If his response angered Andrew, the man didn't allow his face to show it. Instead, a callous grin formed.

"Have no fear, Jamey, you *will* come to regret every second. I'll see to that."

Jasper tensed. His mother had called him Jamey, and he'd only liked the nickname coming from her. Whenever his cousins used it, they'd sounded mocking, often coupling it with the word 'baby'.

He bristled, frustration pushing him toward recklessness. "Get to your point, Carter. You want something. Spit it out."

"I don't want a thing." Andrew shrugged. "Not right now, anyhow."

Jasper translated that easily: He would want something in the future. And when he approached Jasper for a favor, be it large or small, Andrew would dangle telling the rest of the family about him. Not only that James

Carter was alive, but that he had grown up to become a Scotland Yard detective inspector.

Jasper sat forward, hinging at the hip. It put the hired man next to him on alert, who then shifted, ready to spring. "I'm not a dirty copper."

"You won't be a copper at all if any of your colleagues find out who you really are," Andrew replied. "Hell, you might even land inside Newgate for deceiving your superiors. An ex-copper in one of Her Majesty's prisons? You won't last a full day before a shiv gets planted in your belly."

The deceit alone would not land him in prison, but there were plenty of Met officers who, feeling the sting of betrayal, might be just as dangerous as prisoners would be.

"As for Miss Spencer, well…" Andrew shook his head, again with fake concern, "I imagine she'll drop you like old mutton."

Jasper failed to cloak his reaction at the mention of Leo and Andrew's apparent understanding of their relationship. His cousin's mean grin stretched. "Muncie's seen enough to know that the lady is important to you. Of all people, Jamey, you should know how valuable a currency that is in negotiations."

The bloody, bloody bastard.

"Leave her out of this," Jasper said, though he well knew he'd been backed into a corner.

"I'll make every attempt," Andrew replied with more false affability. "But ultimately, her safety will be up to you, Jamey."

Just as he'd had no choice other than to hand over Terrence Nelson in March, he'd have no choice but to do

Andrew a favor when he came asking for one. So long as Leo was there to threaten, Andrew would get what he wanted.

Fury burned through him, from his head to his heart to his gut. Jasper clenched his hands into fists, thwarted. His wretched cousin knew it.

With another jerk of Andrew's chin, the man in the bowler, whom he'd called Muncie, opened the door.

"Until next time, Inspector."

Jasper rose from the bench and saw himself out of the coach. They had stopped on the south embankment, just off Westminster Bridge. Gas jets lit the bridge, and there were several passing conveyances, omnibuses, and cabs all around. The coach door shut, and the driver sped off.

Jasper stood on the pavement, his heart racing. The options the brief coach ride had left him with were intolerable. He could never accept becoming a corrupt police officer, doing Andrew's bidding, just to protect the identity he'd built for himself. Nor could he stand resolute and say no. He'd be exposed, everything he'd worked toward, destroyed. And the Carters, once aware that he still lived, would kill him for his betrayal, without a doubt. Not to mention the most significant risk of all, the one that weighed the heaviest on him: Leo's life.

He had vowed to protect her, and he would, no matter what price he wound up paying.

When a man passing by on the pavement bumped into his shoulder, Jasper blinked. He started walking across the bridge toward the north bank, half wishing Andrew had gutted him and thrown him into the Thames after all.

Chapter Twenty-Four

Leo glanced at the clock in her bedroom. It was nearly ten, hours after Jasper would have left Scotland Yard for the evening. She'd remained dressed for much longer than usual, believing he might still call on her.

But as the clock's hands came together at the top of the hour, she sighed and started to undo the collar buttons on her shirtwaist. He was likely at the Rising Sun with the other officers, celebrating the arrests. She couldn't begrudge him that, even though she'd hoped to see him. And not just to give him her typed witness statement.

Leo had finished it after Constance Hayes had departed the morgue. She'd been baffled by her visit, and the more Leo parsed through their awkward conversation in the morgue lobby, the more she'd started to doubt Constance had truly come to thank her for helping George. Rather, she'd seemed to want a confrontation regarding Jasper. *He is in love with you.* Who was she to make such a statement? And to do so while her eyes were filled with disbelief, as if questioning how it could possibly be so.

Or perhaps Leo was overthinking it all.

She'd just released the clasps on her skirt's waist when there came a knocking at her bedroom door: Claude's signature two quick raps.

"You've a visitor," he called through the thin wood.

With a leap of her pulse, she refastened the clasps, then started on the shirtwaist buttons. When she'd made it to her collar, she opened the door. Still standing in the upstairs hallway, Claude had one snow-white eyebrow raised.

"Jasper is here. He came to the kitchen door and is waiting for you in the front room. He looks to be in a terrible mood."

The detective inspector's caution in going to the back door was certainly meant to protect Leo's reputation; even though she lived with her aunt and uncle, a man calling so late at night might be noted by nosy neighbors. She didn't care about such things—she was already a woman of questionable reputation, considering her work at the morgue—but Jasper's care touched her.

Claude didn't follow her downstairs. He bid her a goodnight and reminded her to lock up once the inspector left. It had been a long afternoon and evening for her uncle. Flora's sobs earlier that morning when muttering about a baby boy had left her in a morose state for the rest of the day; it had similarly affected Claude as well. When Leo brought it up a little bit ago, he'd sighed and brushed it off, but she could tell her aunt's deterioration was truly weighing on him. Soon, they'd need to have a frank conversation about what was to be done on the matter. But not tonight.

Leo reached the bottom of the stairs and turned into the front sitting room.

Flora had done the small room in dove gray and rose ages ago. The floral paper on the walls had faded somewhat, and the fabric on the chairs and sofa was a bit threadbare, but the room was tidy and not overly cluttered. Usually, Leo's attention went directly to the hearth mantel, where four framed photographs were positioned. One was of her parents; another showed a young Leo holding her baby sister, Agnes, with Jacob standing next to them; a tintype of a much younger Claude and Flora; and finally, a portrait of Leo, taken the year she turned eighteen.

It was this portrait she found Jasper looking at as he stood in front of the hearth, waiting for her.

"I've never liked that photograph," Leo commented. He turned to her, his hat in his hand. "I look far too grim."

"You look determined," he replied, coming away from the line of photographs. "Maybe a little angry."

She hadn't liked sitting for the photographer, but Flora had insisted. Her aunt had hoped that, at eighteen, Leo would begin to take an interest in finding a husband, as most young women did. But she had been a disappointment in that area. Her only interest had been in joining Claude at the Spring Street Morgue.

In the corner of the room, her uncle kept a decanter of brandy for guests. Leo went to the small table and wiped the dust from the glasses with her sleeve before pouring them each a drink. Jasper preferred whisky, but as Claude did not keep other spirits in the house, this would have to do.

"How did everything proceed at the Yard?" she asked as she extended a glass to him. "I have my statement. I can get it, if you like."

"No," he said, sipping the brandy as soon as he had it in hand. "Not right now. I don't really want to talk about the case."

He lowered himself onto the sofa. It wasn't nearly as wide or as long as the Chesterfield in his study on Charles Street, so when Leo joined him on it, she was within arm's reach of him.

"At least tell me if Paula Blickson is going to be charged." The woman could not be entirely absolved of wrongdoing—she had played a role in every crime that Felix and Esther Goodwin had committed. But Leo hoped her cooperation at the theatre and, ultimately, her choice to put George's best interests above her own would reduce the charges brought against her.

"She will likely be shown some leniency," Jasper replied. "It will help that Stanley isn't going to bring charges against her. Miss Hayes said as much when she came to the Yard earlier. She brought letters from Nurse Radcliff to Martha Seabright, detailing the adoption."

Constance had mentioned she was on her way to see Jasper, though Leo kept quiet about her earlier visit to the morgue.

"These were the letters Martha used to blackmail Mr. Hayes over the years," Leo presumed. "And they were what Mrs. Hayes found in Martha's home?"

Jasper lifted his glass as if to toast her for being correct.

"Apparently, Mrs. Hayes was mortified to learn what her husband had done. She feels strongly that Paula has the right to know George and deserves empathy not punishment."

Leo found she agreed. She hoped that Melanie Hayes might go so far as to allow Paula into George's life in the future. Perhaps even his uncle, Gavin.

"Is there any word on Gavin Seabright?" she asked. "He should be informed that he is no longer suspected of murder."

"Nothing yet that I know of," Jasper said. "Though once the arrests are reported in the newspapers, he will deduce that for himself."

Leo hoped that would be the case.

"Moles," Jasper said, peeling back his drink just as he was about to sip it. He squinted at her. "That is how you knew they were mother and son instead of sister and brother?"

Leo had explained to Oliver on their carriage ride, and she could see the viscount had relayed the information to Jasper.

"It's what convinced me. I'd already suspected, what with her longstanding obsession with Edward's supposed death. Gavin said she never really recovered." Leo looked to the mantel, to one of the photographs there. "My siblings were taken from me, and eventually, I was able to move on. I'm not sure I would have been able to if it had been a child I'd borne."

Then again, she could not speak from a place of knowing. She had not yet borne a child, after all. With a furtive glimpse at Jasper, she sipped her drink.

"It's much sweeter than whisky, I'm afraid," she said.

He grunted. "It's drinkable."

Leo shifted on the sofa and braced an arm on the curved wooden backing. "My uncle was right; you're in a wretched mood."

"I'm sorry." He didn't offer anything more for an excuse.

"It's all right. I think I understand."

Jasper shifted on his cushion to face her. "Do you?"

"This case. It's unsettling to feel some sympathy for Esther and Felix Goodwin. He killed in cold blood, and she threatened to as well, and yet…they were both severely wronged by their victims with the exception of Harold Yardley. I can see how they became furious enough to blindly go after revenge once they discovered what Martha had done."

"You would not have done what they did," Jasper said, secure in his belief.

"No, I wouldn't have," she agreed.

There were just some things a person knew they could not do. Lines they would not cross. Not too long ago, Jasper had confessed the reason why he could not go back to his family after running away: Had he returned, they would have made him into a killer. A cold-hearted criminal. And that was something Jasper had known, even at a young age, he could never be.

"What did Matron Westover have to say on the matter?" Leo asked.

"By the time I got to the orphanage after reading your telegram, she was gone." Leo nearly spilled her brandy as she sat forward in surprise. Jasper held up a palm. "I've had word from the sergeant in Twickenham that she was tracked down in Putney. The adoption was strictly legal, so I doubt any charges will be levied against her. But she'll most definitely lose her position at the orphanage as matron."

Leo thought she deserved markedly more than a stripping of her title and livelihood for the anguish she'd put Paula through. But she was learning to accept that justice was often delivered via meandering routes.

Caroline Westover would come to rue the day she facilitated the adoption of Edward Seabright. And who knew how many more children she had placed with other families without their parents' permission?

Jasper was staring into the fireless hearth, the only sound the steady ticking of the tall standing clock behind them. He looked done in. The lamplight caught on the shadow of a honey-gold beard on his cheeks, chin, and upper lip. He hadn't taken a razor to it that morning.

"I'm sorry. You didn't want to talk about the case," she said. Though, she wondered what he might like to talk about instead. His work was such a large part of his life. He didn't leave his role as detective inspector at the door whenever he returned home each day. Like the Inspector had, Jasper lived and breathed detective work.

She knew him well, and yet, she also wondered if there was a side to him that he'd never shown her. What did he do with his time off from the Yard? Did he even take a day for himself during the week like he was entitled to do?

When he grinned half-heartedly, Leo suspected it was more than just a bad mood plaguing him.

"What is wrong?" she asked.

He was wrestling with something. He'd swallowed the rest of his brandy and was now staring intently into his empty glass. At last, he said softly, "We cannot go out to dine."

Leo's pulse fluttered. "It is a little late in the evening for that, I admit," she said lightly, though she suspected that wasn't what he'd meant.

Jasper met her gaze but held his tongue. He had something difficult to say, and she thought she knew what it was.

"You regret kissing me, is that it?" Leo whispered, an invisible spear sinking into her heart.

He winced. "No. In fact, there is little else I've been able to think about. Even while working."

His work was everything to him. And she had made that difficult at the Yard, among his fellow officers and superiors. He'd told her a few times now that he needed to keep her out of CID inquiries, or else.

"Is it Chief Inspector Coughlan? Or Superintendent Monroe? Have they reprimanded you because I was involved with the case?" For the slimmest second, she felt regret and guilt. But then, Jasper had been the one to invite her to Gavin Seabright's room to view a dead body and interview the woman who would ultimately be the nefarious mastermind behind the whole murder plot.

"No. Actually, Coughlan wasn't as upset about your involvement this time."

That did surprise her.

"Then, I don't understand. Why have you changed your mind?" After the kiss they'd shared in the morgue's office, Leo had been certain his feelings for her were sincere.

Jasper got up from the sofa with a groan, as if his bones ached. He went to the decanter and poured himself another brandy. With his back to her, he said, "There is going to be trouble soon. I'm afraid there is no avoiding it."

He faced her, and at his severe mien, Leo rose to her feet, bracing herself for whatever he had to say.

"Andrew Carter picked me up as I was leaving the Yard this evening."

She hadn't known what to expect, but it wasn't that. "Why? What did he want?"

Belatedly, she assessed Jasper for any injuries that he might have been concealing. But his tie was neat; his clothing, if rumpled, wasn't damaged. He didn't sport so much as a bruise.

"He knows who I am."

The words shoved at her. She didn't—couldn't—draw breath.

"He knows what the Inspector did, presenting the drowned boy wearing my clothes and in possession of my grandmother's rosary beads as me to my aunt."

That day, the Inspector had bent the letter of the law, though Leo didn't believe it was for personal gain. He'd wanted to protect Jasper from what would happen to him if he were sent back to his aunt and uncle. So, he'd gotten creative and taken a risk, and for sixteen years, it had worked. Until now.

"Do they all know?"

Jasper shook his head. "Not yet."

She crossed the room to where he continued to stand. "What does he want?" But then, she considered Jasper's job, his position with the Metropolitan Police, and answered her own question: "He plans to blackmail you."

It was the only reason Andrew Carter would keep

such knowledge to himself rather than share it with the rest of his family.

Jasper looked down into his glass, unable to meet her gaze. "He knows what I stand to lose if anyone at the Yard learns the truth. And if he informs the others…well, I don't need to articulate what they will do."

A swirl of cold nausea struck her. No, he needn't articulate that. The Carters would see what Jasper had done as a betrayal. They would punish him the same way they had her father. The bilious spin of her stomach intensified when she thought of how Jasper would answer any demands Andrew made.

"You won't bend to his will."

Jasper would rather give up his career, his very life, than become corrupted.

"I won't," he agreed. At last, he looked up at her. "Unless he threatens you. That is why it would be best if we don't change how things stand between us."

Leo shook her head, confused. The two points failed to connect in her mind. "Why would you say that?"

Jasper set his still full glass of brandy on the drinks table. "He's had a man watching me for some time. He's seen you. Us."

That word—*us*—brought her back to the morgue office when they'd kissed in the open doorway. Sergeant Lewis had come upon them, but perhaps someone else had been watching too.

"Andrew doesn't seem to know that you're already aware of the truth. He believes the threat to expose to you who I am and what I did on the night of your family's murders will sway me to fall in line."

"But that will fail to work in his favor," Leo said, catching on.

"And then he will find another way to use you." Jasper's eyes filled with torment. "I will give up my job, my reputation, if pressed. But I will not risk you or your safety."

Leo knew how strongly he felt about protecting her. He'd made a vow to keep her safe, no matter what. But he wasn't thinking clearly. "Ending things between us now will do nothing to stop Andrew. He already knows you care for me and that I care for you."

Saying it aloud brought a rush of blood to her cheeks. But she wasn't sorry. It was the truth. She no longer wished to confine her feelings for him or guard them.

"Besides, you said it yourself," she went on. "There can be no going back to the way things were."

The ripple of a muscle along Jasper's jaw displayed his deep frustration. With discernable misery, he reached for her hand. "I never meant to put you in danger."

Though he'd only taken her hand, the gesture made her unpredictably bold. Leo stepped closer, and lifting to her toes, she pressed her lips to his. He stood rigid, and her daring faltered. As she began to lower her heels to the floor and pull away, Jasper's arm hooked her waist and dragged her mouth firmly back to his. The heated pressure of his lips only lasted another few moments though. He broke the kiss, but rather than step away, he kept her tight against him.

"A part of me wishes you were appropriately afraid and that you'd tell me to leave," he said softly, the tip of his nose brushing against hers. "But a much larger, more selfish part of me is deliriously happy you're so bloody stubborn."

Leo laughed and, though she longed to kiss him again, restrained herself. She did, however, allow herself to enjoy how he was holding her. Especially the feel of his palms as they slid along her back, warming her through her shirtwaist.

"Does this mean you'll take me to dinner after all?"

"I will," he replied, though he still sounded reluctant. "But, Leo, we cannot ignore the danger the Carters now pose." His palms reached the waist of her skirt. There, they held still.

"We'll find a solution," she said, and for the moment, she did not mind so much that any notion of what that might be felt miles away. "You must agree that we will find it better together than we will apart."

He made a sound in the back of his throat, something between a grunt of doubt and a sigh of surrender.

Reluctantly, he released her and stepped away. "I need to go."

Leo nodded, knowing he must. It was late, and though Claude had said he was turning in, he was surely listening for the kitchen door to shut and lock after Jasper's departure.

Leo led him to the kitchen. He picked up his hat from where he'd left it on the table as she opened the door. As he passed her, he paused. Then, Jasper leaned over and kissed her cheek.

"I'll pick you up for dinner tomorrow at seven o'clock," he said, putting on his hat and stepping outside.

"With any luck, you won't need to postpone."

"Then, let's hope for a boring day," he replied.

She shot him a teasing frown. "When has that ever happened?"

Jasper only grinned, then tipped the brim of his hat and set off into the dark.

Leo watched him for a few moments, worry tripping through her that Andrew Carter might be out there, waiting. But no. First, he would want to extort Jasper to the fullest potential.

As she shut and locked the kitchen door, some of the delight that had filled her to the point of giddiness—a state she did not often reach—diminished. Jasper had been right: They could not ignore the truth. Andrew was a danger to them both, and he had every intention of pressing Jasper to a breaking point. But as Leo made her way to the sitting room to douse the lamps, she decided that for tonight, at least, she would go to sleep thinking only of Jasper.

She would not give the East Rip or his threats another thought.

Those were worries for tomorrow.

Thank you for reading Cloaked in Deception, the fourth book in the Spencer & Reid Mysteries!
Please leave a rating and review on Amazon to help other readers discover the series.

Leo and Jasper's next book, Tears for the Forsaken releases in January 2026.

Also by Cara Devlin

The Spencer & Reid Mysteries
SHADOW AT THE MORGUE
METHOD OF REVENGE
COURIER OF DEATH
CLOAKED IN DECEPTION
TEARS FOR THE FORSAKEN

The Bow Street Duchess Mysteries
MURDER AT THE SEVEN DIALS
DEATH AT FOURNIER DOWNS
SILENCE OF DECEIT
PENANCE FOR THE DEAD
FATAL BY DESIGN
NATURE OF THE CRIME
TAKEN TO THE GRAVE
THE LADY'S LAST MISTAKE (A Bow Street Duchess Romance)

The Sage Canyon Series
A HEART WORTH HEALING
A CURE IN THE WILD

A LAND OF FIERCE MERCY

THE DARING TIMES OF FERN ADAIR

A Romantic Historical Fiction Novel

THE TROUBLE WE KEEP

A Second Chance Western Romance

About the Author

Cara is the author of the bestselling Bow Street Duchess Mystery series. She loves to write romantic historical fiction and mystery, especially when the romance is a slow burn and the mystery is multi-layered and twisty. She lives in rural New England with her husband and their three daughters. Cara is currently at work on the rest of the Spencer & Reid Mysteries. The fifth book, TEARS FOR THE FORSAKEN, releases January 2026.

Printed in Dunstable, United Kingdom

67929893R00180